THE KING OF EVERYTHING

JACK MOODY

TIMBER GHOST PRESS

The King of Everything

Copyright © 2025

Published by Timber Ghost Press

Printed in the United States of America

Edited by: Beverly Bernard

Cover Art and Design by: Don Noble

Interior Design: Timber Ghost Press

Print ISBN: 979-8-9925767-0-2

www.TimberGhostPress.com

For Percy and Theo.
And for Hemingway. The cat, not the man.
I'll see you again in another life.

PART ONE

Hastur

Upon opening his eyes to the morning light, the man again finds that last night he did not die.

He awakens in an empty bed in a small ground floor apartment behind a double-locked door. Yesterday, he woke up in an empty house. The day before, he awoke atop a makeshift nest of sweatshirts and sweatpants and wedding dresses gently arranged beneath a cherry blossom tree enclosed by four high, red walls. Beside the tree was a koi pond and a trickling waterfall that bubbled across its surface. The koi fish were of many colors and many sizes. They would bob in the water with their gaping mouths as he leaned over to watch them swim, and he would tear off pieces of bread for them to eat until his own reflection became too much to bear. This was his favorite place he'd yet found, but no more could he return. That place is no longer safe. And this is fine. He always finds another beautiful speck within the vast city to rest and breathe. He can never stay in one place for too long. This nomadic routine is second nature to the man now. Nothing is permanent, and he finds attachment in nothing but the familiar sensation of movement.

He feels safe when confined within walls and a roof while he sleeps, and especially behind a locked door. A room is its own world, easy to fathom and understand. Here are its parameters. This is where the world ends, here at this wall, and here at that wall. The space in between is empty and free to use as one sees fit. Nothing can get in. But while safer, it's a matter of time before claustrophobia gets the better of him, the walls shift, and the ceiling shrinks, and the heart beating inside his chest pumps blood into his ears until it's as if he's underwater. His body loses the ability to breathe, choked by invisible liquid rising like flood water inside his lungs. And again, the man must brave the massive, empty city that awaits his arrival as it does each morning.

He unlatches the first lock and the next, the door swings open, and the great white light of the larger world erupts inside the dark apartment. The man hoists his satchel bag over his shoulder and steps out beneath the towering skyscrapers, out into the street lined with empty cars that will never move again. He is no longer afraid, not like he is at night. While the sun still hangs in the sky, there's nothing to fear but his own illogical neuroses. Nothing to fear but fear itself. He read that in a book once; a quote ascribed to a vaguely familiar man who no longer exists. He knows that man no longer exists because he is dead, because he lived a long time ago. Not because he once walked the earth when it happened. The man can differentiate the two events. People once lived, and then they died, and they were buried in graveyards or burned and placed in ceramic urns. What happened to the rest of humanity was not death but something else. The man once spent many agonizing hours contemplating what it really was that happened and why it was that he was spared, but no longer. It is now nothing but another question without an answer. To continue to dwell on what really occurred all those months or years or decades ago would only be a certain fast track towards utter insanity. To ask why he is still here would be no different than asking if there is a God. It's not for him to know. He has made peace with that. And besides, isolation suits him. It always has. Little changed when it happened. Where before he lived a life in a box, now he has an entire city of boxes to call his own. He is the King of Everything.

The man strolls across the center of the road, listening to the chirping birds as they flitter in mass clouds overhead, watching for the brief glimpse of a deer or dog as it darts between trees and cars on its way towards another meal. The dogs approach him often, and he holds out his hand for them to sniff. Some have collars, and he bends down to read the words etched into this relic. He forms the word in his head, a name once given by an owner, and he says it aloud to the dog. Sometimes the animal's ears will perk up as if they are hearing lovely music, and sometimes the word will create no reaction at all. The man will then remove the collar. The dog does not need it anymore. The one who placed it around its neck is never coming back. It's best to shed the evidence of a life that will never return.

He loves each and every dog. He loves every bird in the sky. He loves the deer that vanish so quickly behind buildings like blurry hallucinations. It has always been this way. People once horrified the man in a manner that he still can't articulate. As time has gone by, he can only view those of his species through a faded lens, a fractured memory. Where once there was surely a plethora of interactions, good and bad, what now remains are only the ghosts of the very worst of them. Those who harmed him and broke his spirit, and those who made the world a darker place. They are the only ones his mind can still conjure from that evaporating well of recollection. During those many contemplative days and nights, the man had long wondered if it were the Rapture. If on that morning he awoke in a home whose location he has since forgotten, the billions and billions of his ilk had all been spirited away to a heaven in which he did not believe, and only he had been left to fester in the hell humanity had left behind. But the man now knows that it cannot be true. This new world is much better than it ever was. It is alight with the sounds of a forest that each day seeps farther and farther into the once impenetrable metropolis of steel and concrete. The animals have returned in great numbers, wandering wide open roads and alleys, making nests in empty stadiums and cathedrals. The city is now quiet in the way it never was and erupts with sound in the way it could have never before. No, there was no Rapture. It's Eden in which the man now walks. Every day is Paradise until the sun sets again and the world becomes something else. But the man doesn't think about that until he has to. The sun is out, the sky is clear, and he has the whole of an abandoned city to himself. When the darkness comes, it comes. And like every night, he will do what he must to see the sun again. He no longer dreams when he sleeps. It is only a deep black chasm, perforated by the horrid cries of those who come alive in those abysmal hours, as if they can reach their shadowy claws inside his head. But that is the most they can have—his hollowed dreams and nothing more. What they are is not man or animal. He knows this much. But what they are doesn't matter. He is safe when the door is locked. When the entrance is barricaded. When the walls are firm and thick. That is the furthest his mind allows him to dwell on their existence. For as long as the sun burns in the sky, the city is his. For as long as the light touches the earth, he is the King of Everything.

He first decides to get food. This is no longer an issue. Food is everywhere. In convenience stores and grocery stores and stockpiled in the walk-in freezers of restaurants that once catered to the highest of the upper class. His species' insistence on creating foods that can never spoil, that will go on surviving the elements from within their vacuum sealed packaging and beneath piles and piles of salt, has ensured that the man will never go hungry again. Too, curiously, most of the great city still remains humming with electricity. Walking down the wide-open avenues, the man looks up at the hundreds of glass windows adorning each steel behemoth and sees the yellow lights reflecting off the glass from within.

It had never occurred to him that if their creators were to suddenly disappear, the many inventions and contraptions and systems that had been emplaced would go on humming and whirring almost indefinitely even without maintenance. Logically he knows, despite his rudimentary understanding of electricity and power plants, the fact this city still has power at all is impossible. Entirely impossible. There are no people left to take care of the hydroelectric plants; the turbines must have flooded a long time ago. There are no men left to shovel coal. While the city had, in a previous age, made great and desperate attempts to convert to wind and solar power, there could be no way that this miles-long buzzing patchwork of glass and steel and cables could be upheld solely by the natural elements. Logically he knows this, but it is one more question that needs no answer. The lights remain on, the freezers stay cold, and the water still runs. There is no purpose in questioning a miracle—this or any other. A generator, the man thought one night as he sat huddled in the corner of a hotel lobby, watching the lit chandelier flicker and sway, desperate to distract himself from the terrible cacophony occurring outside the walls. A massive perpetual generator forever pumping like the heart of a god. That's as good an answer as any. Upon recognizing the ridiculousness of the idea, the man quickly banished the thought and swore never to think on it again.

To be sure, there are sections of the city that had been sundered and returned to a time before the industrial revolution, but this was only as a result of the odd lightning storm or heavy rain that happened to topple a tree across some powerlines. The man now simply avoids these areas, as he's learned that nothing good occurs in places hidden from the light, miraculously artificial or otherwise. There is no reason to go venturing into these places for supplies. The city once stood like a great tribe of sedentary metal giants, surrounded by forest, and it was built to support a population in the millions. The man will want for nothing for the rest of his life. Even if he lives for hundreds and hundreds of years, he has been gifted with the bounty and splendor of an emperor. Even the animals here have grown fat and lazy, poisoned by the residual effects of man's modern lifestyle. They don't need to hunt or kill to protect themselves. Every squirrel and fox and dog and deer and lynx and sparrow can eat and drink their fill in perpetuity, happy to live out the remainder of their varying lives as scavengers, picking meat off the skeleton of a species that had once caused them so much fear. It is only fair, the man thinks. We owe them this now. Let them too get fat and lazy and learn what it is to live upon the earth at the apex. The food chain has crumbled into dust, and as the man walks through the center of a lush and green park, he stops to sit at a bench beside a small pond. He looks out upon the reflective blue water at the ducks paddling aimlessly, at two hawks circling each other in the sky overhead, and at a collarless dog hesitantly sniffing at a young deer that has never known the concept of a predator. The man leans back and sighs and again thinks to himself that this is Eden that's risen from the ashes of a once terrible organism. It must be.

He doesn't miss conversation, nor any of the aspects of life that living amongst a large community of his own kind had brought. He was never a talkative man, content with silence or rudimentary self-talk that was never vocalized. Though the longer he lives in this new setting, the more stoic and calm he has become. The idea of spoken language now feels like an archaic form of communication. He watches the animals each day, and their vocalizations do pierce the veil of quiet often, but so much more than these cries or howls, he sees how they communicate so clearly, so effortlessly, with only their bodies. So much can be gleaned from a skittering step or a tail high in the air, even more from a tail tucked between the legs, and the more time he spends around these creatures as nothing but a passive observer, the more he comes to understand the intelligence of animals. It's an intelligence that isn't performative or boastful, but an intuitive intellect that serves no purpose towards any kind of hierarchy. It is a simple and economic intelligence that blooms into many forms depending on the animal's place in the world. He watches how each species interacts with those of their ilk and those separated by genus, and through this the man sees a diverse field of many-colored flowers, each growing into their own, making true use of the abilities that their unique body and adaptations have created. It is one great, shifting puzzle where each piece, regardless of how the puzzle contorts based on differing days and circumstances, still perfectly fits into one another. There is no energy wasted and no superfluous splintering aspects of their evolution. Everything is as it should be. The man observes this seamless living tapestry from the comfort of the bench, and without forming the actual words in his mind, he understands why man believed that this paradise couldn't have been achieved by anything but some divine omnipotent architect. It is perfect. It is only when a light and cool breeze causes him to turn away and he again catches a glimpse of the looming metal structures that tower over the trees that he witnesses something out of place and alien. The city doesn't fit. Not like the other puzzle pieces. It feels like something beamed in from another planet, thrust atop the natural world like an invasive species. It's all wrong. This city will exist far beyond the creatures that built it, but even now the vines crawl across structural beams, and flowers sprout from beneath cracks in the sidewalks. The Earth knows naught but to continue its cyclical march, and like the human body reacting to a bullet lodged deep in the flesh, slowly it will simply heal around the foreign object, enveloping it within the caress of the natural order. One day, the gray alien metropolis will be just another landscape overtaken by a quilt of green and brown. Moss and dirt and leaves and stone and trickling water. The great buildings will collapse and be buried beneath the earth like the bones of any other extinct species. Billboards and signposts and plastic and crumbled asphalt will rest in a deep grave alongside dinosaur skeletons, and the Earth will continue to spin through the cosmos, blissfully unaware.

Feeling his stomach rumble, the man regretfully stands to leave and steps out from beneath the safety of the trees' canopy, back onto the empty road towards food and other earthly delights. Some cars he passes still sport a yellow parking ticket stuffed beneath the windshield wiper, and the man finds gallows humor in the fact that this person will never have to pay another bill again. The traffic lights still blink red and yellow and green, and sometimes just for fun the man will stand at the white line and wait for the green before continuing forward. He soon comes to a familiar strip of buildings he's visited much before and enters one whose door has remained closed. It's a simple corner store, and its aisles have steadily become bare from his many repeating visits. The man reaches the refrigerated drinks and retrieves a single tall plastic water bottle, untwists the cap, and drinks until the cold water dribbles across his long and scraggly beard. He then saunters up and down the food aisles, deciding on whether or not to make a marginally healthier decision this morning. He decides on a bag of potato chips and beef jerky, telling himself that this afternoon he will dine in a fine restaurant, raiding the walk-in freezer to cook up a meal of filet mignon and baked potatoes with grilled asparagus. Maybe a glass of red wine. This feels healthy enough, and so this morning he can eat what he wants. The man never hovers above an average weight and build, as he walks everywhere, often twenty miles on any given day, and also visits park playgrounds to exercise using his own body weight. He is not particularly athletic, but he is fit enough to live under the circumstances. Only during great times of stress or terror does he resort to smoking a single cigarette hidden deep in the bag that bounces against his ribs as he walks. His mental wellbeing is important to him, and overreliance on habit-forming substances will only put him at a disadvantage if some extreme event should occur. But that won't happen. He will decide on a place to sleep long before the sun sets, and so nothing will happen. Not tonight and not any night. Survival is a simple thing when you tear away the unnecessary requirements deemed by a human society. Before leaving, the man climbs behind the counter and reaches into the small electric cooler that the clerk must have once used for personal effects. Inside the cooler is a small wad of bleeding beef wrapped in plastic. He places the beef into his bag and continues on towards his next destination. Maybe Mable will talk to him today if he finds her when she's still hungry.

The man eats as he walks. Though he tries to take in each moment as it happens, he is acutely aware of the passage of time. Safety is a finite resource that is exhausted by the end of each day. He has a difficult relationship with the city. It is where he was born. It is where he has lived his entire life. There are times he wants to escape, to run into the woods and be surrounded by the natural world that makes sense, but this, this city, is all he knows. He is frightened to leave. Frightened by the unknown.

It always felt large because it is large, but now without the constant sound of civilization, the crowded sidewalks and packed roads, the city feels larger still. Far too large. The man does his best not to look up often, for at times when he does, the skyscrapers appear as living and breathing monstrosities, looming over him and watching. An irrational fear blossoms from the nucleus of his mammalian instincts that structures of this size aren't meant to exist, and at any moment they may come toppling down upon him. There is too much empty space out here. The buildings rise and rise until his neck is craned straight towards the sky, just able to see the edges of the flat rooftops, and a curious, overwhelming sensation of vertigo assaults his mind at the very base of his brain. He sometimes passes it off as a survival instinct; that to be alone so out in the open is allowing predators that no longer exist a clean shot at ending his life, as if he were an injured prey animal left behind by the herd. Man is a social animal by evolution. To be alone for so long is unnatural, whether or not he consciously feels this way. There is safety in numbers. The other animals know this. Though the need to hunt has long since been extinguished, the instinct to hunt and to avoid being hunted still exists, and the animals adhere to the vague structures of the societies they had long ago created. There is some assimilation between species, but it is an unnatural thing, and only certain animals have adopted this behavior for a purpose both they and the man can't quite grasp.

It wasn't until the people disappeared that the man realized just how many domesticated dogs there really were in the world. Almost overnight, the city became a massive system of stray animals that soon formed packs. Already well adjusted, both through shared evolution and millennia of domestication, the packs of dogs often approach the man excitedly as they would any other human being. He takes the time to pet them and talk to them, but despite his deep affection for these poor creatures and his own desire for an animal's companionship, the man has never entertained the idea of adopting one of the many dogs that over time have slowly begun resorting back to a wild or feral mentality. It is too much of a risk, he tells himself. Dogs are loud and impatient and perhaps less aware of the night's dangers than he. If he were to bring one along and that night the unknown entities again began to stalk the streets, who is to say the animal wouldn't begin to bark and whine upon recognizing a threat lurking beyond the locked door? It could attract their attention. Though he doesn't know what they look like, he knows what they are capable of. The evidence of their nocturnal existence appears every morning. It's not a matter of if but when the man will eventually stumble upon the horrible results of the previous night.

No, he only yearns for Mable, the one who wants nothing to do with him. It's to protect her, he tells himself. Each morning, he walks great lengths—for leisure and exercise, yes, but mostly in the desperate hope that he will find her. Still breathing. Still miraculously alive. For as much as the man can pretend that the food chain has dissolved with its former apex predator rendered obsolete—try as he might to banish the reality that comes when the moon arrives behind the clouds—he understands that nothing is safe when the sun descends. Everything from a great bear to a skittish mouse is at the mercy of those shadowy things. He wants only to save Mable, for he cannot save them all.

His next stop is a large department store a few blocks away. By now, his mind can conjure a grid map of the city without consciously thinking about it. He always knows where he is and where to go. The few places he hasn't yet explored never will be, for they are far too unsafe or without power, or they are places that require a dedicated day with a solid plan set out for navigation. The man cannot go into uncharted territory without the proper provisions and an emergency plan if he finds himself lost as the sun begins to set. So, he doesn't explore those places at all; the risk is far too great. Besides, he has everything he needs already. But things do happen. He can almost never sleep in the same place for more than a single night. He must remain on the move. They can never get a bead on him, on his typical whereabouts. The things are smart. At least smart enough. He has seen too much to believe otherwise.

The man stopped keeping count of the days and months quite

soon after it happened. He realized time, at least on a longer scale, was irrelevant. Only the position of the sun in the sky matters. But the day before he noticed a chill in the air, and the leaves on the deciduous trees have begun to change colors. The parks have erupted into fiery displays of warm gradients. Autumn must be approaching, or it's simply a late start. Either way, the man decides to find new clothes that will better suit the frigid weather to come.

He never cared much for clothes beyond the necessary value they provided. He was never a flashy dresser. But in hindsight the man now sees that this was born from embarrassment. He was afraid as to how he would appear to others. Now that this no longer applies, the man finds great joy in trying on every manner of clothing he can find, just for the sake of it. He collects clothing to wear, and when he is done with a particular shirt or pair of pants, he will repurpose them for reasons that never quite matter. If he wants to sleep somewhere at least partly outdoors with a view of the sky, somewhere still with walls of course, he will stockpile a good amount of the warmest and fluffiest articles he can find and use them that night as bedding like any other animal. He enjoys the routine of this: building a nest. It's comforting, and it makes him feel less human. Which is to say, it makes him feel more like everything else that lives and breathes in this new world. It breeds a distant sense of community and belonging. Kinship.

Sometimes, the man will try on dresses and makeup just to see how it feels. It's largely uncomfortable, not innately but physically, and besides in the summer months when the temperatures explode and the heat is nearly unbearable, a flowy dress isn't a good choice for the strenuous exercise undertaken each day. He enjoys the game of it, pretending that he isn't who he is or what he is—like a child playing doctor. But beyond this, he sticks to clothing that will provide the most protection from the elements: a good pair of boots, pants with many pockets, multiple layers that he can shed and utilize for whatever task comes up. He feels no need to shave until the heat grows too much, and so perhaps once a year he will plug batteries into an electric razor and shear his face and head like one would a sheep. In the rare moments that he catches a glimpse of himself in a mirror or in a pond's reflection, he is struck with the horror of having witnessed something alien, something that is not him. Something so very out of place. The man does not like being reminded of his nature. He wishes for nothing more than to tear away from his previous identity. He knows that as long as he lives in the city—and lives off the city—he can never truly shed his humanity. But he can pretend. He can pretend he is just another animal in the world. The last of his kind. The last of some obscure species of hairless ape and nothing more.

As he exits the store with many new layers adorning his frame and stuffed inside his satchel, the man crosses through the small produce section. It is, as it has always been, untouched. There are rows and rows of lettuce, cabbages, potatoes, and carrots, apples and grapes, oranges and bananas. The man hates this place more than any other in the city. It terrifies him. It represents something that cannot be explained and cannot be ignored, and whenever he enters a grocery store, he makes certain to avoid these areas. It has been many seasons, for this is how he vaguely keeps track of time, and for all these seasons, cold and warm and hot and temperate, rainy and snowy and terribly dry, the fruits and vegetables—all the fruits and vegetables in this entire city—have never gone bad. They do not rot, and they remain uneaten. This fact is what frightens him most. Even the animals don't dare attempt to consume the immortal things. There are many odd aspects of this place, many unexplainable secrets, but for reasons beyond his comprehension, this is the one that the man can't bear to confront. He sees the humor in it, that this, of all things, is what frightens him so much. But it's not the fruits themselves, it's precisely what they are indicative of that causes the hair on his arms to stand when he walks through the misted aisles. Like something out of an ancient myth, this bounty of tropical fruits accumulated from all over the world, ripe and unblemished forever, is enticing him to take a bite. His mind resorts to base fear and reacts as if he's witnessed some terrible witchcraft. It just doesn't make sense.

Sometimes, he will stop and stare at a banana—if the morning is still early and there is little on his docket to complete for the day. The man will kneel before the fruit and contemplate its impossible existence. There are no bruises. No marks where an animal may have tentatively nibbled at the skin before realizing what the man intuitively knows. It has remained the same as it was all those seasons ago. He can ignore the lights. They are a necessity, a saving grace, and the man can rest in ignorance knowing that for whatever magical reason, they work. But there's something about the scene, how they are all laid out in perfect rows, shiny and brightly colored like a colony of poisonous frogs. Like a still life. And it's exactly that: still life. He hates it. He fucking hates it.

Today, there is too much to do, and the man has no time to ponder the cosmic mystery of immortal produce, so he shuffles as quickly as one can through the aisles, his eyes glued to his boots, until the crisp air of the outdoors tousles his hair, and finally, he breathes in something that can be explained. And besides, if there is time, he knows a place where those forbidden delicacies can be found in a natural setting. It's no temptation to eat the fruit or vegetables. It is only a terrible, terrible misstep in reality that cannot be accounted for. Something that the mind will never understand, though he does not want to. The implication is too much to analyze without descending into madness. Madness is another luxury in which he can no longer partake. So, once he steps far enough away from the enormous building's doors, the thought is banished. Smoke in the wind. That's all it can be.

The most important way to stave off insanity is to engage in recreation. It's as vital as eating and finding shelter each night. The man sees it not as leisure but as any other necessity for each day. For this, there are three places, and the first is the downtown library. He makes a great effort to sleep within a brisk walking distance from the library so he can be assured that a day won't be missed without its addition to the schedule. He doesn't read in the hope that in one of the many thousands of books he will find answers to his predicament. It is strictly for pleasure. He is so strict that others may have found his methodology one that defeats the purpose entirely. But this is his way. And of course, almost all of what the man now knows of survival, of lighting fires and preparing foods and basic medical procedures, he has learned from those dense and boring nonfiction tomes on the subjects. But more crucial than that is the simple act of finding a good work of fiction and allowing oneself to be transported to a different world. As much as the man tells himself that this is a beautiful new paradise in which he lives, it is too a harsh and lonely existence. Loneliness, even to the most introverted man, can breed illness of the mind and body, and nothing has worked so well to combat this loneliness than to read about the many adventures of Sherlock Holmes, Huckleberry Finn, Beowulf, and Hercule Poirot.

The man gravitates most often towards pulp mystery and detective stories, as if by following the mind of a great unraveller of secrets, by the narrative's end he too will gain the satisfaction of having finally solved something. In his waking life there are too many mysteries that he knows will go unsolved, and so these novels are the closest thing to closure he will find. But when he feels like changing the scenery in his mind, the man is happy to sit in one of the library's many dusty corners, curl into an upholstered armchair, and devour any genre of book as long as it is fiction—as long as it takes place as far away from his reality as possible. With Isaac Asimov, he has travelled through time and space, witnessed the birth of stars and galaxies, and conversed with extraterrestrial beings who possess celestial knowledge that he could only dream of obtaining. With Homer and Dante Alighieri, he has ventured into the worlds of gods and demons, heroes and villains, great battles for the soul of mankind, and for a love he has never known. The older the book, the more time he takes to understand the archaic language, but after so long, there are entire Shakespearean plays that the man can recite to himself from memory, and each word sings in the way it must have to its creator's ear centuries ago.

His mind now swells with stories, and in those long, dark hours where the screams pierce the veil of silence, hordes of heavy footsteps stampede through the streets, and talons like knives tear at the outer walls in some desperate attempt to kill the living thing they must know dwells within, the man closes his eyes, focusing deeply on his breathing, and conjures the images those lovely words evoked. He conducts plays inside his head, scene for scene, word for word, until slowly, painfully slowly, the darkness evaporates into the dim red light of early dawn, and the shadowy things again retreat from whence they came. The books have saved his life, and so the man takes great precedent in arriving to the library every day. It is a matter of survival.

It was just a matter of time before he came upon something. It always happens. He can do nothing but stare and compartmentalize if he can, stuffing the image deep down into the abyss of his subconscious. As he rounds the corner onto the street where the great library waits, the stench first strikes before the scene registers. It's as if his mind only has the resources to protect one sense or the other. His eyes adjust, and the large pyre comes into focus. The man stops. In one of his sparsely read nonfiction books, a 21st century American psychologist detailed the phenomenon known as fight or flight. This psychologist argued for an amendment to this binary system of terror response: freeze. And yes, the man thought, that makes much more sense. Freeze. For that is what he does each time he stumbles across one.

Arranged in the very center of the four-way intersection, standing directly before the library as if some deliberate affront to the man's main source of comfort, is an enormous pile of bodies. They are dogs and they are deer and rats and birds and squirrels and raccoons and foxes and cats, doused in gasoline and lit on fire. The black smoke rises into the air like a smoke signal telling of the apocalypse to come, and the stench is sweet and decadent in such a way that the man believes he may never desire to taste food again. Fur melts together with bone and sinew, and jaws hang agape, sharp teeth dripping with the essence of their own liquified tongues. The pile of bodies reaches higher than the previous; it towers close to the sapling treetops that line the opposite sidewalk. The flames lick the air like the spirit of a basilisk, and they flicker red and orange and black. They slither across the layers of corpses as if trying to touch the clouds overhead. It's clear that the pyre has been burning for hours now, as many of the bodies on the bottom layer have turned to ash and bones with only gleaming coats of fat bubbling atop what remains. They know he goes here. They know he loves this place. And they know the anguish this causes him. His only solace, as it is each time he comes upon one of the many sacrificial pyres, is that it's abundantly clear the poor animals were slaughtered quickly before being set ablaze. They don't do this for food, or for the thrill of murder, but to cause the man pain. He has escaped the beings' grasp for too long now, and they are growing angry.

The man's body reacts intuitively before his mind can comprehend the horror. Tears well up in his eyes, and a pain like a knife twisted into his gut erupts and spreads throughout his torso until reaching his knees. He collapses to the asphalt, and there the tears come in great torrents, and guttural, animalistic howls emit from his throat without conscious effort. And still, his mind remains silent. There are no thoughts, only a physical reaction to incomprehensible violence. An act like this can't be understood, and so as a protective measure, his mind simply shuts off until the body's innate response subsides. His entire being convulses, emotion passing across him like waves in a storm, and the stench wafts with each new breeze that stings his reddened face until all that can be felt is the miasma of burnt death. Finally, the man leans forward and retches until the meager amount of food ejects from his stomach. He remains on his hands and knees, spitting up bile that hangs in yellow strings from his nostrils and teeth. When it is done, he straightens and approaches.

Mable would stand out immediately. She is so unlike the others. He needs only to look as long as he can bear before accepting that no, she is not a part of this horrible mass. He knows she can't be. Whether it's true or not doesn't matter. This lie will keep him from committing suicide. And so it is one he clings to like the promise of salvation.

When the pyres first started appearing, he believed they were some kind of ritualistic altar. Some dark religious ceremony performed after nightfall. Maybe these beings were creatures of beliefs and habits, not unlike him. But any similarity between him and the shadowy things was something he could not abide. Still, he learned they were organized. Capable of thought. And it couldn't be ignored that these sites were so very reminiscent of something man might do. Might have once done. Humanity resorts to terrible extremes when faced with insurmountable events, things that cannot be explained. He sometimes believes that these creatures are as trapped here as he is and that these pyres are a barbaric attempt to communicate with their higher power. Begging for help. For answers. It would only make sense that such evil things like them would worship a god as equally evil. But the man can no longer surmise as to their purpose. He does not wish to understand them, nor does he find any qualities in them that he may find in himself. They are not of this earth any more than the fantastical creatures detailed in his novels. They are something no man or god even could fathom to create. Long ago, he stopped searching for answers about the foul things. It is better this way. He wishes to never learn a single thing about them, much less to meet them.

The scene has ripped any bright mood from his future, and the man now has no desire to read. It would be impossible to be transported to any place but back to this very moment. He walks away slowly at first, but his pace soon devolves into a jog. Then a sprint. A mad sprint. Where doesn't matter, just as long as he arrives some place far from there.

These are the moments when the man's childlike ignorance can no longer fog the world. Of course, this place is no Eden. He dares not say the actual word that comes to mind.

The movie theater lies far enough away that he can remain content with the distance put between himself and the smoldering pyre. This is, and has always been, his second refuge. In times of duress, it's easier for the man to stare at the thirty-foot screen and disassociate than it would be when reading a book. The mind must still work like a muscle when reading, however lighthearted the novel, and there are moments like these where he simply can't muster the strength.

He enters the lobby and smells the familiar scent of burnt popcorn, and sometimes, very seldom, he can almost hear the vague sounds of people chatting and shuffling about as they had so long ago. Today, it is silent. There are no ghosts to keep him company. As his own ritual, the man climbs behind the counter and sifts through the cabinet where various candy and snacks still remain. The theater's original stock had long ago been exhausted after his many visits, but now the man takes trips once a week to different stores to refill the shelves. It gives him a sense of purpose, and the childlike excitement he still feels when picking out a candy bar and watching the machine create the popcorn from so many kernels is a tiny miracle that will never grow old. He reaches in with his hands to fill up the bag, douses it with butter, and chooses two different candy bars—one for the duration of the film and one for now to make up for the food previously ejected.

The purple carpets are stained brown and black with dirt and dried animal blood, but in the precious darkness of the theater they appear as nothing more than decoration. He walks down the wide hallway, candy in one hand and bag of popcorn tucked against his chest, and finally the brief glimmer of a smile appears on his face. Today he decides on Screen Number Two. It doesn't matter which, because the man is the one to choose which film plays, but even the illusion of variety can be a comfort.

The longer the man spends alone in this vast empty place, the more he has recognized that routine and minute rituals make up every single day. That is all each day really is: a series of familiar patterns. These patterns keep the mind afloat, and he knows this only because when they are broken by extenuating circumstances, his mood sinks. When all is said and done, this is his reason to live. He once imagined that if the world were to plummet into disrepair, whether by some nuclear war or pandemic or natural disaster, then quickly people would abandon their routines and run wild, resorting back to animalistic chaos. But he now knows this wouldn't be the case. Many would do exactly as he does, go about their day as they always had with even more certainty, merely to keep sane. People would continue showing up to their office jobs at nine a.m. on the dot, clacking away at TPS reports, smiling with the face of a braindead mute as they glanced out the window now and then to admire the apocalypse crawling ever nearer. He would never look down on these people, not now. In fact, he would admire them. To become feral under such events would be far too easy, but to remain dedicated to the patterns of their humanity despite the inevitable, that is something of beauty. It's laughing in the face of death simply by the stubborn continuance of mundanity.

He finds a seat near the back, cloaked in the cool, damp darkness, and leans back. The screen remains black. Somewhere in front a sudden rustling comes, and a small shadow emerges in the center aisle. Before he can react, the shadow comes closer and reveals itself as a rabbit, trembling with nerves and energy, scraps of food adhered to its whiskers and face. The man holds up his hand to wave, and the rabbit cocks its head, staring, before reaching its back paw behind its ear to scratch. It then wanders off into another row of seats, combing the floor like a metal detector on the beach, indifferent to the man's presence.

Many, if not most, animals that now live in this city, whether born here or born elsewhere before migrating in, were by now born much after humanity disappeared. This rabbit doesn't know to fear the man. It has no need to. Wild animals have in a sense become domesticated by the absence of mankind. Regardless of species or temperament, they all regard the man as any other creature. If he remains at a distance and makes no sudden movements that may indicate aggression, the behavior of every being from a rat to a mountain lion is unchanged. The city is one great melting pot of coexisting animals. From this is where the man developed his naïve delusion of it being some modern Eden. He must only feign ignorance to the bear mauling the deer in the middle of the street on his late afternoon walks, but this too is natural. It's not malice. As much as he wants to believe the animals can somehow survive purely off the food scraps left behind by his fellow man, of course the tiger hasn't shed its instinct to kill. The snake hasn't shed its instinct to strike at any larger being that comes too close. It's just that it's easier for him to pretend it no longer exists. The animals live in harmony with him because he doesn't hunt them and so they must act the same with one another. It's one more story he tells himself to find peace. But then what does this say about the man? Has he shed his instincts? He wishes never to hurt another creature, though an argument could be made that this is engrained deeply within the brain of every human being. He has then decided that this instinct only applies to other people. We wish to harm one another, and any animals that are then harmed in the process are simply unfortunate collateral. With no other people left, perhaps the man has evolved beyond the instinct that no longer serves a purpose, like those lucky enough never to be born with their wisdom teeth still lodged inside the jaw. The man doesn't wish to believe that he is some saintlike anomaly of his species, instead deciding that any human being would develop the same way if faced with identical circumstances.

Beyond all this, however, from his many docile interactions with his cohabitants, the man has learned this: the beings, whatever they are, who wreak destruction and terror and violence each night, cannot be similar to *Homo sapiens*. They are something altogether apart from man or animal. This is but one more thing that he and the other fauna have in common. There exists in this new world an apex predator, and it is not them.

He sits in silence for a long while, absentmindedly stuffing popcorn in his mouth, watching the blank screen, before he decides. Then the images come. A classic, black and white adaptation of *Macbeth*, Cary Grant playing the titular role, Audrey Hepburn donning the desirable persona of Lady Macbeth. Just for fun, something to add a small dose of levity to such a tragic drama, the man decides on The Three Stooges to play The Three Witches. They look fantastic in their feminine yet bedraggled garb, and they take their roles quite seriously, performing with an uncanny air of elegance and depth. How they never won an Oscar for their portrayal is beyond him. As for the score, the man decides on Beethoven's Piano Concertos, all five, to play throughout the runtime's duration. The music then erupts forth, and out of the simmering gray fog comes Macbeth and his ever-faithful friend Banquo, played with subtle humility by Humphrey Bogart in the performance of a lifetime.

The man laughs and cries and remains dutifully silent during the iconic monologues, gasps throughout the final act, and when the images from his mind finally reach their conclusion and the screen returns to a blank, black canvas, he stands to applaud. Bravo. Bravo. What a breathtaking achievement. His empty popcorn bag sits at his feet, the candy wrappers nestled safely in his new coat pocket, and the rabbit hops between his legs to tear at the paper and eat whatever morsels still remain, licking the solidified butter containing enough salt to shut down its kidneys if the animal's body hadn't already acclimated to this diet.

It's different than it was the last time he saw it, and therein lies its beauty. No two films are identical, even if they're the same. Sometimes Macbeth even survives. Sometimes he becomes a good and just king of Scotland. Sometimes, the great tragedy still has a happy ending.

The man will at times wonder if he's gone insane. There's certainly the possibility. And ample evidence. It would explain many phenomena. But from where he now stands, the man long ago decided that it does not matter. Insanity only carries weight when there are sane people who live alongside you. If there's no comparative way of being then what difference does it make? It's only when one is declared insane by those of sound mind that danger and repercussions truly follow. And so while his mind does wander towards these thoughts, he gives them little time to fester and bloom. If this is insanity then so be it. He has no temptation to test it out. This way of life suits him just fine, even if perhaps once there was an era where it didn't. He would much prefer to be comfortably insane and unaware of it than spiraling down a path of overthinking and self-doubt. How overwhelming it must feel to be in a constant state of analysis. Things are much simpler when you don't question reality but instead take strides to assimilate yourself into this new existence. This, the man believes, is an important factor as to why he still survives. Most people will never have to contend with this inner conflict. But of course, the man is not most people. Most people are gone. Everyone is gone. And yet he remains. Thus, there is no reason to change a single thing. The efficacy of his mindset is self-evident.

Upon stepping back outside, the man sees the white sun still hanging high in the cloudless air. Time passes slowly here. He both loves and hates this experience. It gives him plenty of beautiful moments, blissful moments to traverse his kingdom, but too it prolongs the agony of night. But he would prefer this to the alternative. With shorter days and shorter nights, his inevitable death would only come that much sooner, and despite the horrors that persist, he still yearns for more of this life. As much as he can have. The precious hours of seclusion and the heights to which they raise his mood are worth what comes after. He feels this wholeheartedly, with the entirety of his soul. The irony being that in those distant, murky memories of the past, of what he now considers a different life altogether as if having been reincarnated, what he remembers more than anything is the constant pain of living and the persistent desire to die. Now, like a baptism, he has come into this fresh world a new man. He has many desires, but death is no longer one of them. He wishes now to live more than anything.

It didn't take him much time to recognize the antidote to this malady of self-annihilation: solitude. It was people who sickened him. People who gouged his spirit and hollowed his mind. The presence of his fellow man was a taxing experience like none other because it was impossible to avoid. A storm of threats and screams and pointless infighting over culture and politics and differing stances on this or that. It was meaningless to him. And the vitriol that would occur; it was terrifying to bear such constant witness. Inescapable witness.

A vast network of communication, miracles invented and reinvented every day like a species of earthly gods, and yet his fellow man had no eyes for anything but conflict. As if they were addicted to that anger, that incessant desire for power, even on the smallest scale. No argument was unnecessary, no opinion too stupid to warrant a second thought. Everyone believed themselves to be right—and not only right but intelligent—when obviously and statistically this couldn't be further from the truth. It was a world-conquering tribe of idiots with megaphones hurling insults for the sake of trivial things that would never again matter once they all were gone. A part of the man hated people, but mostly it was a terrible fear of mankind. The species of which he was a part was so foreign to him that he couldn't wrap his head around the simple fact that he and they were brothers and sisters, however distantly. It bred within him a pervasive sense of self-hatred too. For there was nothing he could ever do but be human. Painfully, pointlessly human. Born with the same brain, the same anatomy, hands, arms, legs, cock, and balls, instincts, and inherent desires. He knew he was no better than anyone else. He too harbored these same ill intents. It couldn't be avoided. It had been long baked into the very fabric of his genetics, after centuries and centuries of offspring bearing offspring. And so the man could not live with himself, not without absconding from his species as much as one could, locking himself away in the delusional hope that with time alone he could slowly develop across a different path. Like self-imposed imprisonment, forced meditation upon the nature of man. And to no avail.

From where he now stands, the only true release from this prison of self is the total abandonment of all humanity. With them gone, despite the trials that continue and the horrors that often prevail, he has found peace. Only now can he shout knowing there is no one to hear it, and so he has no desire anymore to shout at all. He is the last living *Homo sapiens*. The King of Everything. Now and forever until that regretful, inevitable death. All hail the King of Everything.

The man takes side roads and alleyways to his next destination, his third refuge. The sight of those plasticene fruits and vegetables bred the desire for the real thing, and in all of the city there is but one place where he knows it can be found.

Sometime before, no doubt as another impotent conservation effort imposed by the city alongside their various solar panel projects, an empty lot beside a 17th century pioneer cemetery was donated by the local government for use as a local community garden. Rumors had long plagued this graveyard, since it remained an archaic reminder of an older age as the land around it was modernized and used as fertile soil upon which to erect apartment complexes and condos to satisfy the growing population. The cemetery's upkeep had ceased decades prior, and the weeds were allowed to overtake the once elegant resting place of those original founders. And so the land then took on the ominous appearance that lent itself to the whispers that followed, ghosts and the like, the prime location for midnight satanic rituals or black cat sacrifices beneath a bloodred moon. Especially in those cool and morbid late-autumn evenings when the fog and mist would rise from the earth like restless spirits themselves. No one wished to enter the graveyard any longer except drunken teenagers looking to test each other's mettle or take one another's virginity atop the bones of a man buried centuries ago. And so with this folklore firmly established, the open plot of land reserved for further burials was forgone by all families of the deceased, opting instead for the crematorium or donation to the body farm the next town over.

Though once the city granted this empty plot for public use, those intrepid pillars of the community got to work planting vegetables and flowers to encourage growth of the honeybee population which was, like every other creature save the human being, in rapid decline. But the garden's crowning achievement, its centerpiece that helped to dispel the fear and superstition, was an apple tree sapling donated by a family-owned orchard just outside of the city and replanted to serve as some attempt at poetic analogy. The tree was well tended and oft visited, and after many years it grew to a healthy adult size. Its branches and leaves bloomed with vivid shades of earthen brown and sea green, and finally, one summer, the first pink lady appeared like a precious jewel. Citizens from all corners of the industrialized metropolis flocked to view this vague testament to the indomitable perseverance of nature despite our best efforts.

The following year, the tree was in full bloom, heavy with apples like a decorated Christmas tree, and those same community pillars who first oversaw the achievement enacted a rule that no apple could be picked but only taken off the ground once one had fallen onto the soil. This, they said, was in somber remembrance of our instinctive gluttony as a species, and while there were those intrepid few who ripped the odd fruit from its mother, these people were quickly reprimanded and barred from the garden. Christian organizations, upon hearing of this rule, saw great merit in the biblical analogy and took it upon themselves to lend members as volunteer guardians of the garden to ensure that unlike that traitorous Eve, no man, woman, or child would ever again break our sullied oath to God.

The man approaches the gate, reaches over the top to unlock the latch, and walks inside, careful to relock the entrance behind him. And there it stands: a tall, healthy apple tree, surrounded by rows of lilies and violet foxgloves and red roses. The grass has grown long, just up to his shins, but it remains bright green, and upon kneeling down to feel the soft earth on his palms, he sees an ecosystem of ladybugs and grasshoppers and praying mantises leaping from one blade to another. Patrols of black ants wind through the uneven ground like a pilgrims' procession across a vast unknown paradise. He slides beneath the tree's shade, and yes, it must be autumn, as the fallen leaves ignite the soil around him in every shade of yellow and orange, and when the brisk wind passes through, more leaves float across the air like things in a dream.

He picks up one of the many apples that litter the ground and finds it to be hollowed through the center by all manner of insects and inchworms. But this doesn't bother him. Not at all. Because with each next apple retrieved, he sees bruises upon their skin, black and brown, and he can feel the squelching fruit that's grown overripe and molded, and through this he is reminded of the true nature of things. Here in the garden, the lifecycle persists. Leaves fall and die for the mother tree to be reborn, the apples decompose upon the soil, becoming food and shelter for those tiny creatures, and while the man remains in this place he too exists as nothing more than another living creature, as much a part of this ecosystem as everything else. Here, he is not separate. Here, his mind that so constantly churns and worries finally melts into the steady rhythm of symbiotic biology.

When the man does die, he wishes it to be somewhere like this. He wishes his body's remains to dissolve into the earth and feed the soil. When he is gone, after that regrettable final day of his life, he needs no tombstone, no marker denoting the day of his birth, nor an epitaph proclaiming his accomplishments in a single sentence. For even if there were still those left to read the words, it would do him no good. It would make no difference. He wishes only for the apple tree to remain and grow old in the garden. If the nutrients his corpse leaves behind help to prolong its life by even a brief moment, then that is all the legacy he desires.

The man stands and reaches up until a single perfect fruit brushes against his fingers. He plucks it from its stem then sits, leaning against the great tree's trunk, and eats. It is his favorite meal.

Before leaving, the man cuts a few roses and places them carefully in his satchel bag, keeping open the flap so the sun still touches their petals. Now he has but one final stop to make before finding shelter for the long night to come. The man exits the garden, taking a moment to gaze at the tree through the gate. Always, he locks the gate. If it were to be left open, deer and any other animal would come in, and they would eat the flowers, they would scratch the tree's bark, and they would topple the apples from their branches. It's not his right to make this decision and he knows this, but still he persists with his stewardship of the garden. Maybe one day he will be ready to let go. But not today. The garden is his. Only his. Of all the city, overtaken in the day and under siege at night, this place is the only remaining sanctuary of mankind. He knows this is wrong. He knows this is selfish. But some things can't be helped. It is, after all, in his nature. The man is only human.

The bar is no refuge, though within its sullied walls lies an artifact of great importance to the man. *The Cursed Sailor* was once a bustling dive in an undesirable area of the city, a haunt for the downtrodden and addicted and violent and criminally ill. Nestled in a back alley between a sex shop and a Chinese restaurant infamous for the many drug-related murders that once took place in front of its doors, *The Cursed Sailor*'s neon red lights were a beacon for poor souls to drink away their gambling winnings and would-be child support payments before securing a place on the sidewalk to keel over and find some fitful rest or the merciful peace of an overdose. The cracks in the weathered concrete have since sprouted weeds, and mushrooms now grow in large white patches up and down the alleyway, having discovered a perfect home amongst the moisture and perpetual darkness, though humanity's specter remains in the disposed needles and liquor bottles that still litter the surrounding area like offerings to some debauched goddess.

Animals rarely venture out to this area of the city, as if intuitively aware of its history. The man doesn't particularly enjoy coming here either, as it exists on the far edge of the mapped territory, but what this neighborhood promises are two things that cannot—as he has searched high and low for alternatives to no avail—be found anywhere else.

The sun is bleached a deep crimson, beginning its slow descent towards the western horizon as the man steps through the door left ajar. He doesn't think much of it, but there is a brief flicker of worry while he attempts to recall whether or not this was his doing. Perhaps on a previous day he'd had a bit too much to drink and forgot to shut the door after leaving. It's unlikely, but as long as the daylight remains, he has no reason to fear anything that could be lurking inside.

The Cursed Sailor is in a state of disrepair with mugs shattered into glinting pieces across the floor, beer bottles lying sideways dripping amber liquid atop the tables, and barstools flipped over, their cheap wooden legs splintered. The bar top is slick with weeks of unattended spills, and only a single light hangs from the ceiling in the very center of the dark room. The few windows that once allowed in precious slivers of sunlight have since been covered with overlapping posters and graffiti. It remains exactly how it was on the last day of humanity. The bar is a perfect snapshot of a human experience, frozen in time like some romantic oil painting.

The man treads carefully around broken glass and stagnant beer puddles towards the only real thing of use in this place: Sitting against the corner wall is a jukebox—a beautiful, worn jukebox. Something that came with the bar decades ago and was never replaced, never updated. It is the heart and soul of this establishment and its unofficial mascot. This jukebox makes a statement, and the statement was and still is this: *Here, we do not change. We do not shift with the tides of societal progression.* This bar is a product of its time, once a haven for seamen on leave and prostitutes on the shift, and it will remain this way until the Earth crumbles into dust. As the man looks over the many record sleeves contained within the jukebox's cracked glass wall, all bathed in its immortal red glow, he knows now that *The Cursed Sailor* has succeeded. It is the stone in the riverbed. He respects the bar as he would a man-eating tiger—with macabre curiosity, caution, and preferably from a distance.

Given the nature of the bar, most of its musical library is comprised of artists whose contributions date back to a time before the man's birth. This is the best way he can now ascertain his own age. In those brief and unpleasant moments where he catches a glimpse of his own reflection, the man can never quite tell if he looks his age. It's easiest to determine in the summer months when his head and face are shorn, but even then what he most recognizes is that he appears as some timeless amalgamation of youthful and elderly features. His skin is tanned and taut, his eyes rest in deep pockets, and they bulge like a frightened animal's against his high cheekbones and skeletal facial structure. His entire body is a mass of lean and sinewy muscle accrued by the nature of his lifestyle, and his face is no different, sharp and angular and seemingly in a perpetual state of expressive exhaustion. He appears to himself as a man who has never known rest.

The longer he has spent in this empty world, the fewer memories he retains of his previous life. There exist no images of a childhood, nor a mother or father, siblings, or friends. He doesn't know where, if at all, he received an education. Nor does he recall what his profession may have once been. He doesn't believe he has children and has no recollection of a wife or partner, and though he does understand the intricate puzzle of physical intimacy, any urge towards this instinct no longer plagues his mind as he assumes it once did. There's simply too much to do. Other things that demand attention. Love, though—love remains a staple of his existence. He knows this not by any logical means but through the abstract. Love manifests in the silent moments of observation as the sun rises over the skyscrapers and when a stray dog comes stumbling towards him to sniff his hand and beg for food. Love blooms from simple things, and it arrives without thought but as a subtle warmth that fills his being in much the same way food and water does. It is another necessity the body requires. And like any other resource, man had long waged wars over its control, though the man finds this humorous. It is not finite. Love is as renewable as wind and solar. Fighting over love would be no different than battling for the ability to breathe oxygen.

He absentmindedly flips through the records until deciding on something familiar. The machine chugs and hums, and the record is placed. The needle descends, and like a light in an abyss, Frank Sinatra's voice erupts across the room. The man regains some lightness in his step, bounding towards the bar, and climbing over to peruse the shelves of so many bottles. He picks out a decent scotch—the best this bar would ever supply—and reaches beside the well for a glass. It's chipped at the top and stained with the ghostly outline of a woman's red lipstick. He pours a healthy amount into the glass and leaves it atop the counter while he heads for the back to find ice and something edible.

Layering the narrow hallway that leads to the walk-in and kitchen is a patchwork of dozens and dozens of polaroid photos tacked to the wall. In each photo, eyes squinted both from drunkenness and the abrasive flash, are women of all ages, ethnicities, body types and temperaments. Each woman grins, and each woman is posed shirtless. The wall is a tapestry of breasts. The man doesn't know why this exists, whether it was some kind of humiliation ritual for free drinks or something done of their own volition, but here, like everything else in *The Cursed Sailor*, it remains. Sometimes the man will stop to gaze at the women, and in these moments he's reminded of his innate desires, but then the sobering realization comes that these women no longer exist, and the desire evaporates.

He wonders if it was painful, this mass death or perhaps transmutation into another plane. But it does no good to dwell. What's done is done. The dead don't require pity. They've played their part with grace or without, but regardless, their role is finished. They now require nothing at all. Remembrance and sorrow are a burden reserved only for the living. The torch of agony is passed down between generations, and the moment the flame's light glows upon the next of kin, and its previous bearer slips into darkness, their agony is no more. The man believes this because he has to. Pain cannot last forever. For even the worst anguish dissolves into numbness if never relented. This is why the concept of Hell never much bothered the man. If there is a realm of the Devil and a frozen lake for the damned, as Dante so poetically envisioned, then it would not echo with screams and cries. It would curate a silence as never before heard. If Hell exists, it harbors only an infinite legion of the profoundly bored.

When the man turns the corner, he finds the door to the walk-in freezer left open just a crack in much the same way as the bar entrance. In the dim lighting, cold air escapes as thick, white wisps that twirl and evaporate across the ceiling. He opens the ice machine and takes a handful of its contents, pops one cube in his mouth to suck on, and upon shutting it closed, a harsh whine emits from inside the walk-in. Now acutely aware of each other, the man and whatever this creature may be both stop. It becomes a tense standoff, a show of guile. Neither being wants to make another sound. His heartbeat begins thumping inside his chest, and his ears fill with the echoes of shifting blood. This isn't a formerly domesticated animal; it's far too skittish. Any dog would have come bounding out from the walk-in and into his arms. It's frightened—he knows this without thinking—but this does little to comfort him. A frightened animal is a dangerous one. It's best to step slowly away, never turning one's back to the noise. Defuse the tension. He tries to calculate the yelp in his head, running through a list of animals it could be, whether predator or something more benign, but comes to no conclusion. His curiosity desperately wants him to come closer, to check on this creature. The noise was something born from fear—or worse, pain—and always his thoughts drift towards Mable. Beautiful Mable. The pyre reignites inside his mind, the acrid scent still lingers like residue inside his nose, and a terrible worry overcomes him. The animal couldn't have come here for food; everything in the freezer is inedible until cooked or at the very least thawed. It must have come here to hide.

Deciding that leaving is the most respectful option, the man hurries his pace, but without seeing where he's going, he crashes hard into the corner and lets out a yelp of his own, and the creature reacts as any frightened thing would. It howls. Not a dog or a wolf, but irrefutably canine. This frigid, cowering animal wants nothing more than to be left alone. To die? To soothe its wounds with the cold air? No animal creates such fear in another anymore. This standoff is the result of some unspeakable interaction last night. The man must at least let the poor thing know the sun has returned. Are his footsteps so similar to those shadowy beings?

Finally, before disappearing around the corner, he allows himself to speak a single soft word, if only to let it know what he is—or more pertinently, what he is not. The word escapes his throat like an involuntary act, and where in his mind it formed without thought, upon echoing across the thick walls it sounds alien and impossible. Once his brain catches up to the sound, he realizes it wasn't any word at all. Language is now a useless tool, and the man will go weeks or months without exercising the ability that was once so important. And to little surprise, this presentation of his own mind's descent from humanness elicits only more fear. The animal howls again and slams into a shelf or something else, and at once a great pile of frozen goods comes crashing down. The man can hear the frantic skittering of nails across the floor, and before he can provide ample space, it launches from out of the walk-in, a blur of orange and black fur, narrow and long and alive. Mable tears past the man, down the hallway, and out of sight, where at last the noise and chaos ceases.

The man stands in silence for a long time, only pulled from this state of shock when a terrible burning sensation erupts across his palm, and he sees the melted ice dripping from within his closed fist. But it doesn't matter. He's forgotten why he needed it at all. Mable is alive.

He creeps back down the hallway, too distracted to glance at the wall of breasts, and enters the barroom. Sinatra's voice crescendos, filling up the static air with a sound far too jovial, but it masks any noise the man makes as he returns to the stool and sees the glass of tepid scotch. His nerves are shot, his heart still racing, his fingers numb and pinpricked, and he shoots down the foul, warm liquor just as the song thankfully ends. He sits down and inhales until his chest balloons, and he traces the scotch as it runs through his body, warming his center and bringing color back to his face. And there in that brief silence between songs, he hears her, panicked and heavy panting that again disappears as the brass section to *New York, New York* bursts forth from the ancient artifact.

He would recognize her anywhere, from any distance. It's what first drew him to that gorgeous creature and what causes him to worry about her wellbeing so much more than any other. Her coat is exceptionally rare, and it no doubt causes her great difficulty in camouflaging as her kin would. She stands out always. How she's lived this long the man has no clue. She refuses help, refuses close contact. He has watched her grow up from a distance since a small kit. Like the ghost of some celestial being, she appears on an empty road or behind an oak tree before noticing his penetrating stare and taking off into the shadows. It's for this reason too he desires her company like no other animal, though he would never admit that to himself. She wants nothing to do with him. Even black bears will come lumbering by, close enough that if he were stupid he could reach out and stroke their thick coat. Deer approach in great herds to sniff his odd and furless form, accepting food from his palm. Even those of Mable's own species have grown accustomed to his presence, allowing him to come close enough to witness the streaks of amber in their irises, but not her. She is alone and seems to have made this decision consciously. He never finds her alongside the other foxes. It is as if they had abandoned her in a fit of jealousy, and instead of begging for forgiveness in the interest of safety, she stubbornly decided to go her own way despite the obvious risk. The man holds a deep respect for her, whether this is true or not. He has many stories to tell himself about her personality, her habits, her interests. He has decided that she is abnormally intelligent or otherwise fiercely adept at the act of living. Because like him, Mable has forsaken her own kind and yet survived.

He leans over the counter very slowly and sees there on the other side a trembling animal, eyes already staring back at him. She does not run. This is the closest the man has ever gotten to Mable, and he must stifle the overwhelming urge to leap across the counter and wrap her in his arms. Her eyes are sunstones placed lovingly atop a bed of soil and autumn leaves. Her muzzle is long and streaked with those same multi-colored shades of orange and black like paint strokes. She is the most beautiful thing he has ever seen, and he loves her as much as he did after first laying eyes on her. He imagines it is what a father feels when he first holds his newborn infant daughter against his chest.

The man extends his hand to let her watch it reaching into his bag, where he rifles through layers of clothing, careful not to damage the roses, and clutches the wad of bleeding beef wrapped in plastic. He then places it atop the counter, peels away the plastic, and the scent of cooked flesh rises, and so too does Mable's snout. They then remain like that, quietly eyeing each other from across the counter, her gaze flickering upon the flesh for only a moment at a time until he nudges the food forward, knocking it onto the floor beside Mable's paw. She jolts up onto all fours, rigid and cautious, and sniffs the beef before leaping back, ears pinned to her head, and snarling. She bares her long, yellow fangs, saliva dripping from her black gums, and the man understands this as a warning to back away. He then does so, lifting off the barstool and stepping across the open floor. Those few minutes of close proximity were enough, more than enough. He wanted only to watch her, to study the details that he'd never before been allowed to witness, and to make sure she wasn't injured. And she is not. Mable is a specimen of perfect health: glowing coat, full body, bright-eyed. She is, as the man would later learn, a melanistic red fox. Blessed and cursed with a peculiar genetic mutation, she is the result of a red fox breeding with a silver fox, which produces an animal that he could only describe as an aesthetic masterpiece of evolution.

She prods the beef with her nose and yelps, growling as if it may reanimate and attack. The man understands. It is precisely this fear and this level of hypervigilance that has kept her alive. He and Mable have this in common. They are survivors.

The song ends, and as though this silence gives her the courage to act, Mable takes the food in her jaws, looks this way and that, and sprints around the bar counter, across the empty, dark room, and out the front door.

This is, as far as the man can remember, the greatest day of his life.

The man stays for another drink, if only to sit in silence and allow Mable to fully form in his mind's eye. He wants to remember every detail of her and each patch of fur, how the red blends into orange and then to silver and black like a living sunset. The colors seem to shift and meld, and the man is frustrated by his imperfect memory. Things often slip from his grasp. Only those experiences that may serve to prolong his life ever remain. Simple moments of beauty never stay. They can only be replaced by another. He has vague recollections of the koi fish in the pond and their many colors and their curiosity, but where he once recalled a particular white and gold fish he'd taken a liking to, he now can't for the life of him remember whether it ever existed at all. For that matter, the man isn't sure whether that garden with its red walls and cherry blossom tree was but a fraction of some distant dream he'd once had.

The only things that remain concrete are those pivotal lessons learned in times of great danger. Things he'd just as soon forget. He wants only to remember the serenity that comes in short bursts, but these perforations in the abyss fade away as if the abyss itself swallows them whole. As if his own mind is scolding him like a daydreaming schoolboy, demanding he let go of frivolous things, as this world is a harsh and unforgiving place and there is no time to dwell on illusory fancies. But that's no way to live. There is more to living than survival. There must be.

Why else does he live? Why else would these blissful moments present themselves? To taunt him? Or is it the carrot on a stick—tempting him towards the delusion that life is actually worth the effort? Otherwise, then he would never reproduce, never fulfill his genetic obligation. So, it's simply a matter of reminding his instinctual urges that there is nothing to be done about that. He is alone. But despite how often he tells himself this fact he never quite believes it. There is always a spark of hope—hope? terror?—that there are others. There must be. Both his conscious and subconscious still refuse to accept what has time and time again proven itself to be true: He is the last living human being. But allowing this realization to take hold, to breed, could risk extinguishing something of utmost importance. If one day he were to acknowledge with absolute certainty that, yes, he is the last of his kind, then something terrible may awaken—a self-destruct mechanism or the like. If his mind and body truly understood, perhaps they would just shut off. Like a machine without maintenance. Outdated and unnecessary.

It's like the concept of death, he imagines. Of course, we understand that it comes for us all, and yet we believe in some deep, unreachable well of self that somehow, through some miracle that needs no examination, we—the individuals that we are—cannot and will never die. It's an impossible thing to accept until there is no way around its inevitability. The man presumes that not until those final gasping breaths will he realize, like the sudden failure of a vital lightbulb: *Oh. I'm going to die now. Aren't I?* As obvious as it is, as much time as we spend dwelling on it as nothing but an abstract thought exercise, our own death will always be a horrific revelation saved for that last stubborn second.

He hates it when his mind takes him to these places. It's a pointless use of time. The man climbs off the barstool and stumbles. Drunk. He's drunk. Two drinks are all it takes. What a pity. With the metabolism that comes from constant exercise and the meager amount of food he's consumed today, the scotch strikes the center of his head, and his thoughts scatter into warm, pretty things. He returns to the wall of breasts. He wonders if in that previous, distant life he once knew any of them. If they knew him. It's funny how the mind works when reduced to its base needs. Just before, he was hungry. Now he is not. Something else can just as easily satiate need. He imagines that if a man were to maintain a constant revolving state of sex and orgasm, that man could go without food and water indefinitely.

He's already in the area. Before, he wasn't sure if it was worth the trip. The sun must be coming down soon, but she's right there, just across the street. He's sure she wants to see him. He wants to see her too. There's no shame in that. In wanting company. He brought roses for a reason. There's no need to be coy now. Yes, then, it's settled.

The man steps back out into the street, and my god, it's beautiful. Isn't it? That sunset? Mable's coat bristles across the darkening sky, glittering with the veil of stars that pierce through the deep colors like burning gemstones. He wants to dance. He wishes he could remember a song, a particular song he used to love. But he can't, and so he twirls and stomps across the wide road in silence, humming notes in different octaves inside his head as if composing a ballad. He could be a great artist. A lovely soul. If only someone were here to confirm it.

He collapses against a car overgrown with moss and vines to find the cigarette pack and lighter inside his bag, leans back with his eyes to the stars, and inhales smoke. He watches it float until the wind takes it away. Behind him lies *The Adult Shop*. That's its name. Sometimes there is no room for nuance. He rarely ventures inside, even if he's already in this part of town to raid *The Cursed Sailor*'s liquor shelves and walk-in. She likes her space, as does he. That's why he likes her. She rarely complains. Almost never. Most of the time, she's happy to see him and never asks where he's been. What he's been doing. Why it's taken him so long to visit. She requires little of him and he of her. They have an understanding.

The man enters the shop and closes the door behind him. The room is lit up with strings of fairy lights and Christmas lights of every color that stretch across the walls, and plastic glow-in-the-dark stars emanate a dim green in uneven patches on the ceiling. He loves this room. Whatever stench of human fluids may have once permeated this place has long since faded away, and to sit down in the very center on the cold floor is like watching the universe being born. It is a kaleidoscope of greens and blues and yellows and purples, and they all twinkle and burst as if each individual light is vying for his attention. In his half-drunken state, the colors blur and swirl together like forming galaxies emerging from black matter, and it is a wonderful, wonderful thing.

Along each wall are shelves of VHS tapes of porn films, and sometimes when the man is bored, he'll pick one at random to play on the old television situated behind the counter. His favorites are those that are parodies of more famous movies, and when he watches the actors recite their wooden dialogue between orgy scenes and anal penetration he believes that he too could have been an actor. The wonderful thing about the massive amount of pornography is that inevitably an adult film was made to parody every great work of art ever created, and because of this the man has watched classics from *Citizen Cock* to *Indiana Bones and the Masturbators of the Cock Art*. Sometimes the titles are a stretch, but he appreciates the attempt at homage. He particularly enjoys when it's clear the director was a fan of the film parodied and so went to great lengths to stay true to the original's finer plot points. Simply switch out a golden idol statue for a dildo and you still have the makings of a fantastically tense opening scene if placed in the right creative hands.

In the back corner of the room is an open doorway only covered by a mesh of hanging beads, and through here is where she waits, as she always does. He once thought about asking her to live with him but didn't want to ruin a good thing. They have their own lives, and his solitude is important to him. She has explained at length that this is her home, and he is a man without roots, always traveling from one place to another. She could never settle down with a man like that anyway.

He steps through the beaded veil and enters a long, dark hallway with many stalls lined up on either side. And at the end of the hall, propped up on a stained loveseat, surrounded by tangled Christmas lights like an altar to her deification, she watches the man. He approaches and smiles and sits down cross-legged at her feet. For a while, they don't talk, only staring at one another as those intimately knowledgeable oft are comfortable to do.

Are you drunk? she asks.

No, of course not.

The man reaches out in silence to caress her rubber arm. She doesn't react.

I missed you.

Did you? she says.

Yes.

Then why has it been so long? You leave me here alone for days at a time. What do you expect me to do with myself? Pine for you like some star-crossed lover awaiting her husband's return from war?

You're in a mood today. Since when has this bothered you?

She doesn't respond. The man fixes the kimono draped across her body, covers the parts that can be covered. When he met her, she was naked. Cold, surely. Left alone in this empty shop. Eyes open and blank. Mouth agape, lips parted as if just waiting for someone to arrive so she could finally speak what she needed to say. The man clothed her and doted on her as a friend. Brought her food and water and gifts. She would never leave this place, as if she were shackled here by some unseen force. Fear of the unknown, perhaps.

I saw Mable today, he says finally.

Did you? Her expression doesn't change—always locked in that perpetual state of surprise—but he can see she's interested in hearing what he has to tell.

I did. She let me feed her.

Did she really? That must be—

The first time, he says, grinning. Yes.

That's lovely.

Do you think she'll come back?

I'm sure she will. She knows you're a good man. That you mean no harm. Some just need more time than others to feel safe.

The man hesitates but opens the flap of his satchel and holds up the bouquet of roses. I brought you these.

Oh, how kind! How kind! Are they—

From the garden, says the man. Yes.

He places the flowers in her lap, careful to arrange them so a thorn doesn't pierce her skin. This has happened only once before. He patched the hole quickly, but even so, she's never looked quite the same. More aged. She was once firm-bodied, unblemished. Now she looks as any older woman does: a bit flabbier around the arms and neck, wrinkled in the face. Less supple to the touch. Though he would never tell her this to her face. It's only natural. He knows he too doesn't look how he once did. There's nothing wrong with it—carrying one's age like scars. It reminds us what we've been through. How much we've learned in our time on Earth.

The man begins caressing her leg, sliding his hand beneath the kimono.

What do you think you're doing? she says.

He flinches. I thought—

You thought what? That because you brought me a gift you're entitled to it?

No, no. Of course not. I just—

You go gallivanting around, living your life while I just—what? Wait with legs spread for you to stop by on a whim? And you think that's fine? You think that's romantic?

I just thought it might be nice. I missed you.

No, you didn't, she hisses. You're incapable.

That's not true. I went to the garden just for you. To get you those roses. I knew you'd like them. I've been looking forward to seeing you all day.

Fine, she says. Then talk to me first. Keep me company.

Talk to you? About what?

About what? she growls. Is it that much of a chore? A simple conversation?

He removes his hand from her leg. Okay. What would you have me say then?

Forget it.

Forget it? What do you mean forget it?

I mean forget it if talking to me is such a burden. I don't know what kind of girls you're used to, but I'm not just some floozy to pop in on for a roll in the hay before disappearing for weeks at a time. I have a mind, and I have my own needs. I get lonely, you know.

Lonely? says the man. You like your space. You said it yourself. I thought we had an understanding.

No, no, no. YOU had an understanding. Which you then forced upon me. There was never a discussion. You never ask me what *I* want. What *I* would like out of this. Sometimes, I swear, I think you're incapable of—

Incapable of what?

Let me finish. This is exactly what I mean. Incapable of love. Intimacy. Communication. You care for those mangy animals more than a living, breathing woman.

That's just not true, he lies.

It is. It absolutely is. And you know why? Would you like to know?

Yes, more than anything. Though you'll no doubt tell me whether I want to hear it or not.

It's because, she says, they don't require work. You hate that I'm dependent on you—even if only in the smallest ways. A simple *Hello, how are you, dear?* But even that's a strain. You can't fathom that I actually require something in this relationship. You're lazy. And selfish. People are too much work for you. It's always been like that. A dog will love you unconditionally. You can only love if it doesn't necessitate sacrifice. But then that's not love. That's ownership.

The man stands and points an accusatory finger. Don't make me say it.

Say what, *dear*? What else could you say to break my heart more than you already have?

You are entitled! he shouts. I owe you nothing! And those *mangy animals* understand that better than you ever will. They understand a man's need for solitude. Privacy. Personal space. Silence... *Silence*, you understand? They ask nothing of me and I nothing of them. And that breeds respect—something you obviously don't have for me.

THEN GO FUCK THE DOGS, she screams.

Maybe I will! It'd probably be better than the lifeless performance YOU put on!

HOW *DARE* YOU!

The man picks up the bouquet of roses and hurls them against the wall. Flower petals come loose and float down around his head like suspended blood droplets. *YOU... You have no idea what love is. I* know. *I* know what love is. Because I feel its absence whenever you're near.

She begins to cry, her face still paralyzed in that gaping state of shock that now finally suits her demeanor. You don't mean that.

I do, says the man. I hate people. I'm glad you're all gone.

Take it back! Take it back right now!

No. It's the best thing that's ever happened to me. I can finally be alone.

She remains silent for a very long time. The delusion fades as her final words slip from his mind, translated through the doll's parted cheap rubber lips: What about at night?

The man snaps out of his trance and whips around, staring down the long, dark hallway.

It's time to go.

He hesitates and thinks to speak to her, but the doll is lifeless and soulless, and there is nothing here to save. It's all the same. This was the truest conversation they'd yet had, and it would be foolish to leave on a false sentiment expressed only to assuage guilt.

As he heads for the door, unaware of the time and terrified of what shades the sky may present, the man is nonetheless filled with a sense of peace. He has broken one of the last remaining chains that once tethered him to his own waning humanity. This was for the best.

If it weren't the harbinger of terrible things to come, the man would stand out in the middle of the street and stare. He lifts into a trot, then a jog, and then a full sprint, down the road, back towards anywhere more familiar as the bloodred sky bathes the trees and buildings in long shadows. The blackness overhead encompasses the Earth, and only a sliver of warm colors brims just on the horizon like a blanketing fire. The stars are alight, and the moon is a glowing yellow crescent. And all these things are an awful misfortune for the man, for if under any other circumstances, in another life, they would be truly beautiful things to behold. But this new world no longer allows for the cool evening air and the brilliant hues to be anything but omens.

There lies deep within the man's memory a fading recollection of the peace and the awe he once felt when looking up at the cosmos. He holds the faintest image of a night long ago, somewhere far away from the city, any city, and that image is one so powerful that despite the passage of time and hallucinatory nature of his existence it can still be conjured like the spirit of a dead loved one. And in those precious moments when it can be called upon, it is as real and true as the air inside his lungs. Somewhere in the woods the man was once alone, but not in any way like he is now. He sat upon the silted shore of a lake, and all around him trees stood, cloaking him in their shade like great silent guardians. A small campfire flickered and spat beside him. This was a place far removed from people, from civilization, but he felt less isolated than he'd ever been. Owls hooted in the branches, frogs croaked from the shallow waters, and crickets, thousands of crickets, chirped and sang like some masterful choir that echoed across the lake's surface. The man craned his neck up to the midnight sky and there he saw the infinite: a million stars glittering across the vast tapestry of purple and black, and like an open wound seeping the very life essence of the universe the Milky Way stretched across the night's center. One perfect cloud of magenta and pink, giving even more brilliance to each star just as the wind powers a turbine. The man made a game of focusing on each star, one at a time, and guessing as to whether it still lived. For some stars, regardless of the vibrant beauty that still imbued them, had been dead for years and years and years. But still they burned. Still their light illuminated the sky. Still the imponderable energy they once emitted had traveled across millions of light-years, unimpeded by time or distance or illusion, to reach this very place for the man's eyes and the man's eyes alone. And the greatest beauty of this game was that no matter how long he stared, and no matter how hard he tried, it was impossible to know which were alive and which were merely the ever-traveling specters of a once great celestial being.

In that moment, the man discovered a better answer to the un-known than he'd ever found in a church or a book or the words of a wise man. All he had to do was look up, and the answer to the question of life beyond death presented itself in vivid light. Those alive and those deceased both burned equally bright despite the insurmountable black void of Everything. A lifetime of fear evaporated from the man's soul that night, and he finally understood exactly why no answer had ever arrived through these other means. It simply had to be witnessed. This was an answer that human language was unfit to provide. Stories and words can only take us so far.

The man then stood at the edge of the lake and witnessed a miracle. Its water was so calm that no ripples occurred, not one blemish on that flat and pristine surface, and so staring upon the lake was to look into a perfect reflection of the infinite above. The whole of the cosmos, all glittering and black and magenta, every star alive and dead and dying, were contained across the water from one shore to the next. The man descended into that lake with no fear of drowning, no fear of death at all, and as his lungs filled with the universe's watery twin, he could feel the warmth of the stars on his skin until all that existed was the lights in the dark, and the man floated there, suspended in space, one being fully assimilated into the cosmic soup of Everything.

Now, this memory is the furthest thing from his mind. Night is a terrifying thing, and there is no time to lament this change. The man races against the setting sun itself, against the growing shadows crawling across the concrete and asphalt like living creatures. His own skin is doused red from the dwindling light, seeping beneath his arms and fingers as though attempting to slow him down, begging him through force to submit to the inevitable darkness. But this is no new sensation. His only mistake was visiting her in some flaccid attempt at retaining his humanity, a mistake he now will never repeat. It's a rare thing that the man is still outside this close to the hourglass's end, but nothing he hasn't experienced before. He has emergency protocols to enact for this very scenario. He will be fine. He will live. Those words circle his mind in a desperate effort to banish anxiety.

As he runs, it takes immense effort not to dwell on the silence. All living things are subject to the horrors of night, and much more so than the man, and those animals' instincts command them to abscond and hide long before these final safe moments. So there is nothing. No rustling in the bushes and no snapping of twigs beneath hooves or paws. No chirping birds or chittering bats. Even the breeze seems to halt, and the air becomes damp and stagnant, a chore to breathe. A profound vibration rises from the soil, as if the Earth itself is trembling at the thought of what's to come. And that is the true fear: nothing knows what they are. Perhaps those that once knew were granted knowledge only in that final second before annihilation.

His sprint devolves to a jog, and a sudden pinch strikes the base of his stomach. The man bends over in the middle of the road to vomit water and bile before forcing himself to continue on. The drunk pours out of his skin with pungent sweat, the cigarette's lingering ache pulsates inside his lungs, and there is a brief panic-inducing terror that blooms from out his chest upon the thought that perhaps this is the final day of his life. The artificial lights bursting forth from streetlamps and neon signs, and the many windows of each looming building blot out the stars, barring that distant recollection of the lake and its lesson, and so the man is overtaken by the full brunt of mortality and its finite nature. He does not want to die.

The urban area slowly transforms into narrower streets and quaint neighborhoods, overgrown grass lawns and white fences, and though this area is unfamiliar to the man, it is nonetheless a sure haven as long as one of these house's doors remain unlocked. In any other circumstance, the man would be content to break a window or shatter the lock and then search the house for materials to bar the new entrance from the inside, but this luxury is no longer an option. The sun has fully descended, and only the finest sliver of dim pink still undulates around the tree trunks like a bleeding mist.

The man comes to a halt in the street, staring down two perpendicular rows of identical houses. Like toy houses. Fake houses. Any remnant of the civilization that once existed feels like an illusory thing now. They don't make sense here. He approaches the front yard of the first house on the right and tries the doorknob: locked. Next, he circles around the back, climbing over a short fence where the glass door presents that tantalizing safety of the indoors. But that door too is locked. The glass is thick but nothing he couldn't shatter with a swift elbow. As much as the man wishes to risk the action and search through the home for plywood and nails, doing this would be suicide. It is that simple. So with much hesitation he leaps back over the fence and returns. The streetlamps now burn bright—a sickening artificial yellow—and whatever remained of that precious sunset has disappeared. It's too late. Night has fallen.

The man takes a deep breath and closes his eyes, relishing the final moment of silence. Knowing what is to come. But then, in that silence, a sound echoes through the trees. A familiar sound. Not the inhuman noises that are sure to erupt any second, but familiar—and not in the way that may provide comfort, a reminder of the living things that still persist in this night-borne hellscape, but familiar in such a way that cannot be.

Footsteps.

Surely, he must be hallucinating.

The fear has seeped too far into his nervous system.

But again, the sound.

Solid, echoing footsteps. Heavy. Unmistakable. A gait similar to his own, frantic and afraid. Slamming across the asphalt road.

The man's survival instinct is completely overridden. He can do nothing but stare. Paralyzed in place, out in the open. But there it is. A shadow emerges. Cast beneath a lamppost not half a block away, long, and black and lanky. Human.

Impossible.

But human.

Cloaked by darkness and shadow, and blurred by distance but—

There.

Standing.

Like a mirror placed before the man.

The black visage of a human being.

Seconds pass. Or minutes. Time stops.

They watch one another through the night's veil, unable or unwilling to speak, two emissaries from uncontacted tribes. The stranger flinches, and like a mirror, the man reacts the same. Far too much distance between them to read expressions. To see the color in each other's eyes. To decipher reality from hallucination. Only body language, emanating shock more than fear but fear all the same. Their elongated shadows serving as imaginary bodyguards, ten times in size, looming over one another, having their own standoff, silent.

God, the silence. A quiet impossible to comprehend, forcing the ears to ring, if only to give this nauseating tension a buffer, to ease their fluttering hearts.

Then, it's over.

The war cry erupts, as if ripped from out the shadows themselves—a horde of screeches, or a many-tongued beast, an impossible army of infinite sound. It is shrill and violent, both far and close, in all directions, on top of one another, an apocalyptic bomb in turn detonating a series of its kin. Like a wildfire sparked across the Earth in a single instant, burrowing deep inside his ears, carried by the wind, and collapsing upon him as if careening down from the black sky. If the planet could speak, this would be the sound it created. Agony and rage. At once ear-piercing and bone-trembling frequencies, swallowing the very hum of the universe. The man could ponder this sound for decades and still fail to describe its utter magnitude.

They're awake.

He turns instinctively to the stranger, as if for comfort, but the unknowable thing has already fled, launching into a sprint and evaporating back into the shadows from where it arrived. His mind shuts off, and instinct takes hold of his movement as the reins to a horse, and he too sprints, smashing into the front door of another house, banging on the solid wood as though someone will be there to open it before realizing deep beneath his mammalian response that there is no one. No one but that which is now coming.

He goes for the knob: locked.

There's no time to submit to horror. The man wheels around the side of the house, jumping over the fence and crashing down atop soft earth and grass, and there at the identical glass sliding door is another, smaller entrance. A metal square with a rubber flap: A dog door. The man collapses onto his hands and knees, and without the thought to first examine its dimensions, he hurls forth his satchel and springs headfirst through the flap. He emerges on the inside, his body down to the waist now presented with the safety of a warm home. A locked home. Four walls. Salvation. Still, the great tumult echoes, shaking the very bones of the earth, but the sound has split into many directions like a multiplying virus, spreading its armada of individual cells across the blackened world. The cries and howls are now many-fold, piercing the air not as one great beast but thousands, and the gnashing of limbs or claws tears across the ground as an invading force, ever closer. And they know he's here. They always know. They're coming.

The man shifts his weight to no avail. His hips are caught, his legs dangling in the darkness, ready to be sundered from himself, and a morbid curiosity, for only a brief moment, overcomes the man: *I want to see what they look like.* But just as quickly as this fascination washes over him, it leaves like the blood rushing from a wound, and his need to survive overrides all else. With one violent and swift motion, he propels his body forward, crying out as the sharp metal edges tear his clothes and slice open the flesh underneath, but it's enough. He lurches across the hardwood floor, his whole body encompassed by the safety of a vanished stranger's home.

The man immediately gets to his feet, closes the shutters, and finds—this miracle of all miracles—the tin sheet that blocks the dog door, leaning just beside its metal frame now dripping with his own blood.

He is alive.

Still more blood pools on the floor around his boot; the left pant leg flayed, revealing the long and deep, crimson gash running the length of his hip down to the thigh, weeping fluids and pulsating to the rapid beat of his heart. And outside the sounds do not cease but grow louder still, enraged but solemn, mourning this failure to kill or contort or corrupt, or whatever foul act it is that these beings commit, but he is alive.

Night has fallen again, and the man is alive.

Here is Golgotha perverted, ever repeating. Each night, a piece of the man dies, and each morning, he will be reborn as something a little less human. This thing, this city, strips everything of what they once were, leaving them bare. The city is alive. The shadowy beings, these entities beyond the comprehensible, they are its children. This is what the man believes. He too believes that with each passing day the city swallows him, bit by bit, regurgitating only enough to grant him the peaceful illusion of retaining his identity: Man. Human. *Homo sapiens*. He clutches to this identity because it is all he knows, and as much as he wishes to rid himself of what he sees as human traits, these very things are also what keep him sane. They are what keep him alive. People are industrious creatures, but the city does not like this. The city wants to revert him back to something less than a beast. The city wants him to step outside beneath the moon with open arms and greet its children as brothers and sisters. Slowly, it eats away at his mind, his memory, and so perhaps in defiance he maintains his grasp on those frivolous activities that are quintessentially human. He will not go willingly into the horrors. He will fight tooth and nail, staking his own claim in this corpse of a civilization like a stubborn parasite.

Truer than anything, though—something far too true for the man to accept—is that at any time, he could leave. There is a great forest surrounding this city. He watches it creep in farther and farther with each season. The forest wants to swallow the city alive, and so the man and the woods have a common enemy. He knows that some new kind of safety exists out there. But it is unknown. Utterly unknown. And herein lies his predicament. The city, regardless that it is now a twisted phantom of its former self, is all the man has ever known. Even more so as his memory wanes. Soon this violent, living entity of empty buildings and concrete will be all that has ever existed. He will forget the woods as what they are and begin to see them only as a forbidden and perilous dystopia teeming with whatever horrors his mind creates. A great wall will be erected by his thoughts alone, and the man will have trapped himself in a slaughterhouse, believing it to be Eden. He knows he will have to leave but cannot bring himself to do so and would rather condemn himself to die in a familiar prison than risk the chance of death in a foreign place.

Sometimes as he attempts to sleep, the awful screeching and cries seep into the walls, and he can feel their vibrations inside his skin. Like insects crawling through his veins, excavating the human elements as fuel, hollowing out the bones to contort his anatomy into those which claw at the windows. The city is becoming more attuned to its existence as a sentient thing, prying open its own skeleton to learn about itself. Soon, there will be nowhere to hide. Soon, the walls too will be its skin, black blood pumping underneath, and there are times at night when the man can even hear it. Pulsing. Deep beneath the floorboards and behind the cracks in the ceiling. Its blood rushing through the body like a river through the Earth's crust.

Time is growing short here. Soon, he will submit unwillingly, as a viral cell is destroyed by the immune system and assimilated into the body. He sees it happening already. He knows, somewhere within, that this is no city in which he dwells. It is the stomach of a world-eater, feeding him the scraps of its previous meals, those beautiful and familiar things, exactly what he needs to see and feel to find peace in the process. Just enough. Just enough that the illusion of a life once lived, even if terribly warped, still appears real. And slowly, as it lures him back into docility with the trees and the animals it has allowed to survive, or perhaps conjured as the god of a damned realm, the city's juices will digest the man.

One day, he will wake up and the city will appear before him as it truly is, and the man will look upon himself and see a shadow. Then, he will finally understand his new siblings' wails and screams. For what else would there be left to do? It is during these terrible moments of self-reflection after nightfall that he realizes how his species disappeared. But that's just a story. Like Eden. Like *Macbeth* and *Beowulf*. Just stories to make sense of the world. Surely. Surely that.

It does no good to dwell, the man thinks, and he gets up from the corner of the living room. No matter how many nights he's spent in the city, it always takes a few hours before he can adjust to the tumult outside. Until then, he spends that time as a frightened puppy, cowering against a wall as far from any windows as possible, his hands over his ears. Only once his nervous system acclimates can he explore his temporary home. Find food. Water. Peace.

He creeps towards the glass door and glimpses through the blinds. There is nothing. But that's what terrifies him. Those things are out there in great numbers. Just on the other side of the glass. Stalking back and forth, so very aware of his presence. The man is looking right at them; he knows this. They are not invisible or hidden in the shadows, for there's nothing to hide. They are, by their very nature, their atomic makeup, something the human senses are incapable of relaying to the brain. Like trying to taste infrared light. No body to inhabit, no physical form. And yet undeniable in their existence. For those incessant screams perforate the abyss beyond the walls. They ring from every direction, near and far, above and below, like hallucinations more than something tangible. But that's only because the man cannot grasp the concept of a creature without mass, without shape. It's as if the darkness itself howls in agony. This is not madness. He is far *too* sane, in fact. Madness, in the midst of this, would be a great mercy. Then the man could find refuge in his psychosis and remain blissfully crazed, content in believing it's not real. Life could become one vivid lucid dream, and opening a door to see the moon one last time would only mean waking up.

Against every instinct, the man presses his hand against the glass. Without a second's pause, a violent force smashes against the barrier, again and again and again, the glass bending like a frightful trick, and from somewhere far away but still close—so close it's as if phantom lips kiss his inner ear—a rattling scream ignites, and the man falls backward. Talons or claws or many knives strike at the glass in a flurry, like a rabid dog desperate to break through its kennel.

That's enough, he decides. Morbid curiosity will kill you yet.

He doesn't worry about the glass breaking. It never does and it never will. This isn't a matter of physical strength; time and time again, the shadowy things have proven they possess that in excess. No, it's something else. The man would have died his first night in the new city if they were permitted to enter. And that's the key. Permittance. Something greater than them, or maybe the greater aspect *of* them, will not allow the destruction of its own body. Buildings stay intact. Walls remain forever upright. Only breathing, organic beings are fair game. This is why the man knows it hates the forest. It hates the woods like a child afraid of the dark. The forest is alive, and it too breathes, but the city has no power over its encroachment. The man can only hope the natural world will overtake the city like a jungle to ancient ruins.

Sometimes, this is why he believes they erect their pyres, in some vulgar profane ceremony to appease themselves atop the corpses of those which only nature can birth. To appease the city. The only visible, hideous aspect of their unfathomable god.

There's a war being fought, a war of attrition, with those resembling manmade creations swallowed whole by the ever-marching Green, and so in turn its children are slaughtered and thrown to the flames. On some days, the man will climb to the top floor of a tall building, and he will look down upon the city and see dozens of smoke columns rising into the air, across all corners of the gray and black grid. A hundred corpses. More. By the afternoon he will forget. Amnesia in this place is a double-edged blade; some things are best left buried, if only for sanity's sake.

Somewhere out there, a stifled yelp can be heard, and another lurch of movement arises from the other side of the glass. The horde is shifting towards the promise of blood. Another victim, some poor thing unable to stay concealed. He can't help but feel it's retribution for his cowardice. Every new pyre this next morning will be deaths on his hands. The man feels no need to repress this guilt, though. That empathy for the animals is what centers him. It is the core of his diminishing self, something that can never be taken away. What he could never see in his fellow man he sees tenfold in those innocent creatures, and that worrying truth makes it all the more important to protect. The day he comes upon a pyre and feels nothing is the day he will give himself gladly to the night. Empathy and survival are intimately linked. It takes no philosophizing to understand this.

He can't begin to think about Mable. Where she is. If it was her cry he heard. Somewhere she is safe, he must tell himself. Nestled in a bed of ferns and soil. Sleeping beneath guardian oaks alongside her kin, blissfully unaware of the horrid screams. There are times when he wants to escape and follow her out into the woods, into a night that promises quiet. Long evenings of crackling leaves, harvest winds carrying hoots and chirps through reddened branches, birdsongs and babbling water. Stars reflected across a lake. Nothing more.

He could only undergo the pilgrimage with another's company. He hasn't the courage otherwise. As much as he values his solitude, his self-sufficiency, in reality, the man's idea of rugged isolationism is one that only exists by virtue of the city's endless bounty. He has no reason to believe he can truly survive in hermitage, far away from the luxuries this city provides like square meals to a prisoner. This isn't real living, what the man has engaged in. It is feeding off the teat of his captor, ensuring his dependency on that which saps him of the very reasons for being alive at all.

The man gets up and enters the kitchen and begins rummaging through the cupboards and freezer for something to cook. He has decided at this moment, as the howls of living darkness spread like echoes across the city, that he will escape. He must. After the winter passes. Yes. That's it. When the weather warms and the fruits emerge, he will venture out. This place will not take him like it took the rest of his kind.

The rest of his kind.

In all the chaos, he had forgotten entirely.

There is another.

Is there?

After so long.

Such a very long time alone...

Another?

Only one thing now comes to mind. The man is not ashamed nor confused by it:

If it is true, may they be dead come morning.

And this is the last thought he has on the matter.

In the freezer he finds a microwaveable meal and a can of beans in the cupboard. He heats up the food and begins wandering around the home while he waits. It's large, with an open floor plan. Spacious and warmly lit. A fake chandelier hangs from the living room ceiling, and its glow flickers white and yellow across the floor. The furniture is upholstered and clean. This family liked warm colors. Orange rugs and red couches. All the windows are narrow and high up on the walls, providing no real use but to let in natural light. The man couldn't imagine living in a place like this, so guarded and sterile—like a castle. Or a dungeon. But for the circumstances, it is perfect. The sliding glass door, too, is thick and flexible. Bulletproof, even. Were they paranoiacs? Or simply unsocial? Either way, they are gone.

The man finds an old record player sitting atop a coffee table. Beneath the table is a stack of vinyl. Music! Lovely music. He sits down cross-legged before this treasure like a child on Christmas and rifles through the albums as the microwave dings. Still, the cacophony outside persists, and he couldn't ask for a better solution. Nights are so long now. He never really grasped how long the darkness remains until he began sleeping just three or four hours at most. So much time was spent sleeping, and in this world he understands that need more than ever. To sleep is to escape. When waking life is unfathomably terrifying, even nightmares are a mercy.

The family were white, upper-class, and rich. The man needed not to even glance at the various family photos decorating the home. One can learn everything they need about a person by perusing their choice of music: Van Morrison, Billy Joel, Elton John, Bruce Springsteen. Fine artists but undeniable as to their target audience. After making it through the more contemporary hits the man finds the real gems—and the evidence towards their socioeconomic status: Classical. But not just that delicate background noise for nobility to entertain guests with an air of importance. Masterpieces! True masterpieces. Beethoven's 9th symphony, his *Piano Concerto No. 5*. Brahms' four symphonies in their entirety, Chopin's *Nocturnes*, Vivaldi's *The Four Seasons*; Satie's *Gymnopédies* and *Gnossiennes*, those fraternal twins. Brilliant pieces, all of them.

It's been so long since the man has been allowed to hear anything but the same thirty songs on *The Cursed Sailor*'s jukebox that the din outside, if only for a moment, blurs and dissolves beneath his own excitement. He gently pulls the record from its sleeve, places it onto the player, lowers the needle, and presses play. *1. Allegro* lilts and settles across the room like laughing gas. Speakers are arranged in each corner of the living room, and the sound undulates and warbles. The man turns up the volume, and the music sings until the static air is doused in color. The man stands and begins to stomp and twirl like a mad, delighted creature without worry or thought.

He glides across the room towards the microwave and takes his meal, forgoing silverware and eating the lukewarm mush with his hands, head nodding, body swaying, eyes closed in rapture. The night explodes with fury and howls as this empty home brims over in delectable and ethereal peace. It is a beautiful thing. There are times when the man is genuinely thankful for these circumstances, for this reality and all its horrors, because without the depths of fear and depression this city so unrelentingly hurls his way, he would never realize the magnitude of these heavenly moments when they arrive. It's a tenuous balance of extremes, and perhaps if the man had the choice he would prefer the simple life of a monotone baseline. But this is not his life, and so this hypothetical scenario is meaningless. That is where the pondering ends.

You are given what you are given, and there is beauty to be found in Hell, certainly just as there would be ugliness within the cracks of Heaven. Otherwise, it wouldn't be Heaven at all. To be in constant peace, constant contentment, would be to never understand what peace really is. It would just *be*. Heaven, in that archaic and traditional sense, would be no different than the Church's perception of Hell—a vast and inescapable prison built to house those poor, raptured souls who would never feel anything at all. He can see the merits in this, of course. He can see the allure, but only in the sense that he could see the same allure in a freshly lobotomized maniac. And that's no way to live. Not to the man. It's a complicated dance—being alive. At once bliss and terror. Madness and elation. But therein lies its perfection: The act of living means the opportunity and understanding of both.

Beyond the kitchen lies a long hallway with three doors. The man opens the first door to find a bathroom. He immediately goes to relieve himself, relishing his ability to leave the door open, to hear Beethoven's concerto still oscillating throughout the hall like cathedral bells. When he's finished he washes his hands and face and takes off his clothes to briefly scrub beneath his arms and around his crotch with soap and water before redressing. The next door opens to a dark study. A desk and computer sit on one side of the room, facing a bookshelf. The man peruses the tomes but finds only nonfiction—self-help books and hardcovers about the economy and stock trade. Useless things as they were before. More fit for kindling than anything else. Through the walls, he can hear the shadowy things sprinting back and forth, digging in circles as if excavating for underground tunnels, screeching and ululating and slamming against the glass door. But the man is safe, and so these terrible noises slowly become nothing but a bad storm. He stops before leaving to stare at a framed photograph on the desk. A man and a woman look into each other's eyes, smiles creating wrinkles along their cheeks, one dressed in a black tuxedo, the other adorned in a long, white dress with a veil to match. They stand beneath an arch gilded with red roses, and blue and yellow lilies rest in decorative piles around their feet. The bride and groom are young, probably younger than the man, but he can never tell. A pinch of guilt blossoms, and he's struck with the genuine wish that their end was sudden and unexpected. They are strangers and they are dead or displaced, and dwelling on their fates will achieve nothing but vague remorse for an act he never committed, and so the man exits the room, closing the door behind him.

He then comes to the last entrance at the end of the hall, which he can only assume leads to the bedroom. Upon opening the door, he is greeted by an altogether different place, alien to the rest of the tailored, polished home. The lights are off, the room bathed in darkness, but even through the shadows he can see the room is in complete disrepair. The armoire has been thrown to the floor, its ornate wood chipped and splintered, piles of ripped clothing strewn in all directions. The large bed sits sunken atop a fractured leg, and framed paintings once adorning the walls now lie shattered. Broken glass twinkles in the sparse light pouring in at his back. The whole room is thick with the overpowering miasma of piss and excrement, so much so the man pulls his shirt collar over his nose to keep from gagging. He reaches blindly along the wall for a light switch and sees the inside of the door. The wood has been slashed hundreds of times. Hundreds of long, thin slits decorate its surface as if something was trying to get out. To call for help. A sickening chill runs down his spine, and the man becomes dizzy. A fine layer of splinters and wood dust carpets the floor around his feet. This was an act of total desperation. Hours and hours of scratching at the door to no avail. The man then feels the switch and pauses for a long time before flicking it on, preparing himself for whatever will appear in the new light.

A single domed bulb flickers and then burns, the room is revealed, and the man bears witness. He then immediately switches it off and closes the door, steps back into the hallway, slides down against the wall and onto his haunches, and hugs his knees. Beethoven's concerto vibrates inside his ears, and he wishes for the wherewithal to get up and turn off the record so the brief image he saw won't be now forever connected to such a beautiful sound. But it is too late, and now the man must look. There is no escaping it. Best to look now and accept.

It's probably been dead for a long time. Long enough that decomposition has set in, but recent enough that the man knows what it once was. The crumpled, coagulating remains of a small dog lie in a pile of fur and liquids and bones at the foot of the bed. Something ill-fitted for survival without a master. Pomeranian or chihuahua. Whenever the great displacement occurred, its owners must have left it locked inside their bedroom, never knowing the horrible fate that would befall the poor creature. The carpet is stained with trails of piss, and dried excrement dots the floor like mole hills. The man now looks at the state of the room and the destruction wrought upon the inside of the door, and whether he wishes to or not, he can picture the animal's last days in vivid detail. This was a torture like nothing else. A man could fathom his own looming death, make peace with his doom, but this dog knew nothing. Only that its owners wouldn't come to its aid. No matter how hard it cried nor how vigorously it attempted escape.

This is one matter in which the man is glad to be human. Man possesses the ever-present awareness of his coming demise, and so he has ample time to prepare for it, to ponder its many tendrils and agonies. While we may never truly accept death and even scream and cower upon its approach, we are intimately familiar with its work and all the terrible possibilities of its aftermath. This dog knew only that it was alone and in pain. Until the pain grew too great.

The man closes the door and begins to cry. For reasons unknown to him, he attempts to stifle the sobs. Every day in some sense or another he dwells on the reality that perhaps every single human on Earth is dead. And yet he feels nothing. Not even shame for that glaring absence of empathy. Sometimes, he tries very hard to conjure a feeling of remorse. He pictures the faces of small children, stiff and pale, dying, orphaned. But nothing comes. No tears, no tightness in the chest. There is nothing within himself that's bothered by the mass extinction of mankind, even children. Children are the innocent among us, only malleable things to be contorted to the wills of whomever raises them. If a child grows to be a bigot, the blame can't be placed anywhere but on the adult guardian who instilled those beliefs. It's not the child's fault. But still, the man can't separate the innocence of a child from the monstrosity of the species into which it was born. He at times worries that there's something wrong with him for thinking this way, but that worry quickly dissipates.

Animals are vicious in nature, as they must be. They are products of the world, which too is vicious. But this is the contrast; an animal's violence is committed without malice. It is merely a reflection of the greater indifference of the universe itself. Only man commits atrocities for the exact purpose of causing harm, of filling some empty well within himself by spreading his own fear and hatred on to others in some futile attempt to self-soothe. An animal's violence is a blameless act, no more worthy of disdain than a blackhole swallowing up a star cluster. To hate the lion for killing the antelope is to hate the universe for remaining in balance. This is foolish, and too, this is the heart of the man's philosophy. Humanity's violence is inherently imbalanced. Our innate nature goes against every other working mechanism of life. And so for this, the man can easily blame human beings. He feels about children how he feels about all of his ilk. They are evil in nature. It's only a matter of when that evil will rear its head.

Animals too lack the capacity to ponder the implication of their violence. The cat doesn't sit and wonder whether the mouse it killed wanted very much to live for its children. The mouse is food or otherwise prey. In either case, there is no reason for self-analysis. Sin is a phenomenon unique to human beings because we are able to fathom the ramifications of our actions. With our greater understanding of ourselves and our role in the universe we have been granted the binary reality of right and wrong. We assign negative and positive labels to our actions, and through this we have created a terrible systematic failure. Whether we want it or not, right and wrong now exist. The crown of our making lies heavy on our heads, and time and time again we choose to wear this crown not as a benevolent ruler but a tyrant. For this, the man feels no sympathy like he does for the little dog rotting atop its masters' bed. It is a victim like every animal at the mercy of our negligence.

Those shadowy things remind him very much of man. He wishes

not to dwell on it. Instead, he wants only to give the dog in death what it couldn't receive in life—come morning. For now, he wishes to sleep. Obviously, the bedroom is no longer an option, so he shuffles back into the living room, turns off the record player, and sits down on the couch. Without reasonable cause, he blames that mysterious, shadow-cloaked humanoid for the dog's death, and he wishes now with even more fervor that tonight is their last. We turned wild things into living plushie toys, forced them to depend on us, and now there is one less innocent creature in the world.

Outside, the freed dogs wander the woods without collars or masters, scrounging for food and mating with the offspring of their shared ancestors, and the man takes a breath, content with the fantasy that one day soon there will be no dachshunds or labradoodles or bull terriers but only a hundred thousand packs of feral wolves. If they even can be killed, he hopes that tonight the dogs he's met are slaughtering those intangible horrors. He hopes the many screams and cries are of anguish as dagger-sharp canines sink into the flesh that cannot be seen.

As the evening progresses, the man becomes more and more aware of time—or the lack of its presence. Time stops at night, as though some elaborate psychological torture employed by the cosmos. He believes in brief, panicked moments that if he were to go without sleep, the sun would simply never rise again. That blank, static respite found in the place beneath consciousness becomes a miraculous act, capable of forcing the universe to recall its linear nature and return to its duty of expansion. The man knows time so intimately now that the concept feels like an enemy. It toys with him, slowing and speeding and warping like some amorphous being. He cannot control it, and it seems to relish in that fact.

The only signifier that the Earth continues to spin comes once his eyelids are at their heaviest. In the very darkest hours of night, the city's omnipresent screeches begin to dull, and what once were great eruptions of deafening wails soon dissolve into a noise far more unsettling. It is a mournful sound, low and deep like the vibrations before an earthquake. The shadowy things speak. Not words—barely discernible as an utterance emitted from anything resembling vocal cords—but the baritone chittering of ghastly things beyond the concept of speech. Nothing in the man's life has ever created a sonic imprint such as this phenomenon, but it is undeniable that those creatures are the ones making it. He less so hears it than he feels its reverberations. His bones begin to tremble at the impossible weight of its frequency, and his heart struggles to maintain its rhythm. Chanting is what the man would call it, if only the demonic gibbering came from an organic being's mouth. It blooms from specific pockets, as if the things are congregating together in various points across the city and then spreads like a toxic mist until reaching his ears from each direction at once. This is a solemn chant akin to what one may hear through the stained-glass windows of a midnight mass. The frequency builds and builds until there is so much pressure in his ears that the man fears his eardrums may burst, the hairs stand on his arms and neck, the air feels thick and magnetized inside his lungs, and finally it takes on some vague form of musicality. There are notes that can be followed, and perhaps if he were musically inclined, the man could even transcribe on paper this haunting melody. All guttural babbling, wet like an ancient recording trapped at the bottom of a vat of mucous and phlegm. This lasts for a length of time unknown, but when it ends, it ends without warning. The chant ceases, and for the remainder of the dark hours there is absolute silence. Only now does the man allow his eyes to shut. For only now will his body allow him the brief mercy of sleep, too exhausted to do anything else. When death isn't an option, this is the best compromise it will accept.

In the morning, the man finds a shovel in a shed behind the house and digs a shallow grave in the front yard. He picks up the remains of the dead animal, wraps the bones and fur and pooled liquids in a blanket, and lays it gently in the hole. The birds sing in a nearby tree, the air is cool, and the wind is calm. The leaves fall in piles of bright colors up and down the empty road, and the man tamps down the earth until it appears as any other patch of dirt.

He doesn't know why he was compelled to do this. It's a uniquely human act—burial of the dead. But still he knows he must. If at least now the little dog is shown compassion, albeit far too late, then it is one less regret that will weigh upon his mind. The last living man on Earth cared for the animals, no one will say. Of course, the man realizes that this act was for nobody but himself. The dog doesn't care, but heavy lies the crown. Heavy lies the crown atop the head of the King of Everything. He is a good and just king, and this is a good and just thing to do. That's the end of it, and the man thinks no more.

He plucks a bright yellow flower from a bush growing through a neighbor's fence and sticks it into the soil. So, here lies a good dog. A good and innocent creature. The flower too will wilt and die, and now neither beautiful little thing will disappear from this Earth alone.

It's a comforting and naïve sentiment, and it makes the man happy for a while. At this moment, the man makes a promise to himself to never let go of naivety. It will save him. From what, he doesn't know. And that's entirely the point. Some things don't have to be known. Some things shouldn't be.

It's another morning, and the man is alive. What a beautiful thing that is.

Autumn sets in like a gorgeous blazing fire across the city. The man spends his time away from *The Cursed Sailor* and *The Adult Shop*. He has no wish to see her ever again, and if the urge for music comes to him, the man will revisit the home and listen to records whenever he so wants. He will put on Vivaldi or Satie—musicians so perfectly suited for the vivid, natural transformation occurring all around—and he will turn up the volume as high as it will go, opening all windows and doors, and sit outside on the front lawn next to the little dog's grave.

There they listen to the music together, and at times he will speak softly under his breath. The man talks to the animal as a friend, and he regales it with the stories of its adventurous, short life: The little dog was once ushered into army ranks, fitted with its own bulletproof vest, and tasked with the important job of sniffing out bombs hidden beneath piles of trash and other inconspicuous articles. The little dog saved many lives in its short military career and was awarded two bronze stars for its acts of valor under distress.

After the little dog's honorable discharge, it was swept up in a grand exploit. Finding itself in an Alaskan port, the dog was quickly regarded as a brave and strong animal and was invited to join a team of Malamute sled dogs on a journey across the tundra to return a crate of rare and valuable artifacts to an Inuit tribe living in the Aleutian Islands. The journey was long and arduous and colder than the harshest winter the little dog had ever experienced, but it was outfitted with the finest booties and fur-lined coat, and under the little dog's leadership at the helm of the team, the sled arrived without a hitch. While traveling those great distances in the snow and ice, the little dog witnessed things of such beauty they were beyond comprehension to all who saw. Many nights, the aurora borealis burned across the sky like a great celestial snake, all alight in greens and reds and purples, and the little dog would stare up in awe at this fantastic event and wonder at the utter radiance and grandiosity of this big, wide world on which it lived.

Upon returning to port, the little dog was again offered a job of the highest esteem, for by now its name was well known and revered all across the continent. It was a party of treasure hunters, headed by an illustrious, fine man of reputable status. He wished for nothing more than the little dog to accompany him to the heart of the Amazon jungle, in search of El Dorado. Yes, that El Dorado, the man whispered, patting the little dog's head. The City of Gold! They stowed away on a cargo plane and touched down directly upon the mighty river, and alongside a party numbering six experts in different fields, the little dog set out through the thicket of a green and alien world with nothing but its instincts and attuned nose to lead the brave men to riches the likes of which the world had never seen. The days were humid and treacherous, and many times the dog fought off all manner of beasts, including one particularly nasty altercation with a black jaguar, but time and time again, the little dog's bravery proved to be too great. The men were saved from the wilds on too many occasions to count, all by the wit and quick reflexes of the little dog. At night, the jungle was a concert of chirps and coos and screams, and the rain came down in great sheets of water like the sky itself had split open, but the little dog was unafraid. The illustrious man too remained calm, for he knew as long as their party had the little dog by their side that no harm would come to them. Soon, the day arrived when the little dog caught the scent of riches so strong that it knew they were close, and side by side, the illustrious man and the little dog cut through the thick jungle until boot and paw found footing atop a gilded road. They followed the road into the very darkest heart of the Amazon until massive gold pyramids appeared from behind the trees, and the men rejoiced—for they had found it! They had found the lost El Dorado! The City of Gold! The explorers received a hero's welcome upon their return to the States, and the illustrious man—after ensuring that his team would be more than properly compensated—insisted that the lion's share of the wealth would be donated to the distant kin of this once prosperous civilization. For he was a good and just man.

But by now, the little dog had seen so much of the world and had spent so much of its short life in the most dangerous of circumstances that it wished only to retire in peace. The little dog only wanted a home of its own to dawdle away its final years as a happy animal, content with the beautiful adventure that had been its life. And too the illustrious man could see this wish in the little dog's eyes. So, one day he made a proposition. He asked the little dog if it wouldn't come home to live with him and his lovely wife. It was a wonderful and guarded home in a pretty neighborhood. Just wait until autumn arrives! he told the little dog. There will be nothing but colorful leaves as far as the eye can see, all just for you to frolic and play whenever you wish. Naturally, the little dog accepted, for the illustrious man was a kind and good person, and they were bonded as the very best of friends. The little dog could think of no better way to spend its twilight years.

After all the adventure, this final period of the little dog's life was by far its greatest and most fulfilling. Days were spent on long walks around the neighborhood with the illustrious man and his lovely wife—and she was lovely, a caring, doting woman who loved the little dog more than it ever thought possible. Nights were spent in the living room atop his great friend's lap, resting beside the fireplace as the most gorgeous music swooned across the home.

Now an old and fulfilled animal, the little dog was ready to part with its friend and the wonderful world that it had seen so very much of. It had been such an adventure, and as it lay down on the bed, nestled in its old friend's arms, the little dog closed its eyes, and there in the darkness came all the memories. The little dog saw the faces of the many soldiers it had saved with instinct and tenacity, it gazed once more at the ethereal beauty of the aurora borealis from a desolate and white tundra at the top of the globe, and it watched the colorful tree frogs hopping from leaves and lily pads in the South American jungle. And the last thing the little dog saw from behind its closed eyelids was the face of the illustrious man—its greatest and oldest friend. A good and just man. And then there, wrapped in the warm embrace of its friend's arms, the little dog passed away peacefully in its sleep. What a wonderful life I've had, the little dog thought. What a wonderful life to have lived.

The man sits beside the grave almost every day as autumn grows colder and darker, and every time he tells the little dog the story of its life. He tells the little dog this story because he knows that somewhere, somehow, the dog can hear his words. If he tells the story enough times, the little dog will begin to recall. *That's right*, the little dog will think—from whatever ephemeral realm it may reside. *I just misremembered. It was a truly wonderful life. Wasn't it?*

Yes, the man whispers. It was.

The man sees more and more of Mable each day. While on his routine walks, sauntering between the library and theater and the little dog's grave, he catches glimpses of her walking at the same pace on the other side of the roads. She makes great effort to match his speed, though she stops every once in a while to sniff plants and other passing animals or to stare up in wonder at the colonies of brightly colored birds as they fly overhead between trees and power lines. Every time she does this, the man halts, allowing her to take in whatever sights and sounds have captured her fancy before continuing forward once she's ready. They glance at one another, a silent recognition of each other's presence, but never approach closer than a dozen paces. The man makes no attempt at shortening this gap. He is overjoyed that she is alive each morning. Beyond that first sight of her, anything else is a series of little miracles.

As the days go on and the trees produce ever more brilliant autumnal shades, Mable grows more comfortable with letting her presence be known to the man. She begins to trot ahead, unbothered that the man is at her flank where he could so easily ambush her if this were his intention, and she whines and whimpers when the man falls too far behind. When once they are again beside each other, Mable hops and runs in circles, chasing her tail in some fit of excitement or play, and returns to an even pace.

While at the library, the man forgoes his escapist fiction for a time, opting instead to skim through encyclopedic tomes on ethology and anthrozoology, wanting to learn all he can on the nature of foxes. He discovers their dietary habits and various temperaments and how to spot those temperaments by observing body language, though he quickly finds that merely by coexisting alongside this pretty creature he learns far more about her than what's available in any book. He learns that she is a cautious animal, more so than the others of her species, and the subtle flicker of a tail or a snout in the air could be the sign of something amiss miles away. She prefers to mirror him from a distance, and he does not know how she would react if he chose to come closer, as this is beyond the question. Their burgeoning relationship—if it can be called that—is dictated entirely on her terms. While he sits in the warm confines of the library, Mable wanders the surrounding area, but once he emerges from his studies, the black and red coat flickers back into view from behind a bush or tree trunk. They share a moment of eye contact before the man again starts walking, and she lifts into a happy stride, reassuming her remote position beside him.

The man stops at markets to eat, and this is the only time she dares approach. Mable waits patiently on the sidewalk, watching him through sharp, amber eyes, focused on whatever it is he may have in his hand, and the man tosses the food onto the ground. He wants her to eat before him, not just because he values her life over his own, but also as a way to show submission. Mable is in control. She eats before him. Only once she tentatively approaches, long snout pressed to the concrete, and eats whatever kind of meat he procures, does the man then finally allow himself a meal. He knows she is not reliant on the food he provides—Mable is obviously capable of foraging throughout the city and woods for every manner of insects and flora and rodents—but this is a small gesture to prove his loyalty. He also knows that whatever meat is found in the aisles of a deli far pales in comparison to the fresh game she hunts for herself, and so upon seeing that, nevertheless, she always eats what he offers, the man understands that this is simply an act of shared trust. In silence they are bonding. It takes great effort for the man not to show this in his gait. Overexcitement can be misconstrued as aggression. She is a timid thing, and it is a delicate dance. There is never a moment now when the man is not content. He has a partner. The man is not alone.

Mable's favorite place seems to be the theater; it is the only indoor area she will enter. The man goes about his regular ritual, picking out candy and filling a bag with popcorn, and Mable will trot behind, absorbed by the overwhelming amount of foreign scents. Sometimes, a deer or a rabbit will scurry down the long hallway and into the lobby, and Mable will unleash a terribly high-pitched scream, her head low to the ground and back legs extended as if ready to launch forward. Her ears pin back, yellow canines protrude in a violent grimace, and the oblivious foe will take off out the door. Only when the man whistles as he continues on down the hallway does Mable perk back up, her head swiveling as if having come out of a trance, and return to a lackadaisical attitude, tail flitting back and forth, nose up in the air to inhale the aroma of a new world.

Over time, the man learns to read body language that before was imperceptible. There are a hundred thousand cues all across Mable's physical mannerisms, and each minute detail tells a story as to her current demeanor. It is a fascinating thing of which to become aware, and the man wonders at length how much she can surmise from his own subconscious movements that he will never even recognize himself—the twitch of a finger, the creasing of a brow, a trembling lip, a shallow breath. He comes to think of Mable as a master linguist, acutely in tune with the truest and most intricate form of communication. Aloofness is key, he learns. To relax one's muscles is to relax one's mind, and vice versa. Mable then picks up on this, and he can see his comfort mirrored in hers. So, she too becomes a metric for his own wellbeing. If Mable appears distressed, the man knows to take stock of his thoughts and comb through his many neuroses to strike at the root of what bothers him. Together, they are balancing scales, keeping one another from tipping into extremes. The man finds safety in her presence and can only hope that she holds a fraction of the same sentiment.

Once he enters a theater room, Mable trots to the opposite side and curls up atop one of the many soft chairs. In the darkness, she becomes a flat ball of fur, and only in the moments before she falls asleep does the man recognize where she is. Her eyes reflect the thin strip of yellow light that seeps beneath the doors, and they flicker when she gazes around to make sure of the man's whereabouts. And as the man creates a story across the black, empty screen, Mable dozes off, content and warm in a place so much like the caves she must shelter within during those long, terrible nights. The films aren't as detailed as they once were. The man finds it difficult to engage, instead stealing glances at the snoring animal just rows away. He sees only the steady rising and falling of a crimson-brushed coat, but it is a miracle to behold. It is a miracle she is here at all.

The man loves Mable more than he ever imagined possible. His thoughts often drift towards what would happen should she one day not appear to greet him in the morning. But this is the tradeoff. To love something is to understand with painful vividity that one day the source of this overwhelming warmth will no longer exist. For those prone to spiraling anxieties, to love deeply is to think often of its inevitable conclusion. Nothing can last forever. And so the man cuts the film short to stare at the fox, her small body undulating like calm sea waves. What lies before him is better than anything that can be conjured from the mind.

Once she awakes, the man tosses popcorn in her direction, and she yawns and flops down onto the floor, stretches, and eats the odd little puffs more out of curiosity than anything. Then together they step back out into the lobby, Mable following lazily behind.

Outside, the sky is a deep red, and the sun's tint burns behind a layer of clouds. The man heads back to the house. He knows it isn't intelligent to remain in one place for multiple nights, but it's now been weeks, and the home is as much of a fortress as anything he'll find in the city without first having to climb many flights of stairs. The neighborhood is pretty with its rows and rows of deciduous trees, but mostly he feels an uncertain obligation to stay close to the little dog's grave. He feels it's his duty to keep it company and retell the story again and again. There are fleeting moments of self-reflection where the man recognizes it's some form of penance. Whenever he is reminded of the species to which he belongs, the man is struck with violent shame. It is easier to blame humanity for the circumstances placed upon the dog than the event itself that directly led to its demise. One has to find a tangible source of the pain when its truer reason, or at least the lingering manifestation of that reason, are at their very essence intangible. And besides, Mable loves the long, brisk walk into the suburban area where fewer animals dwell. She, like the man, is at peace amongst the quiet and solitude.

The man walks inside the house, having found a key to the door on some prior inconsequential sleepless night, opens the windows and back door as he always does, and picks out a record to play while Mable tumbles around in the piles of leaves that now line the sidewalk for blocks. She sprints across the yards, diving into larger piles the man has manufactured just for this purpose, and he steps outside with Vivaldi's violin blaring at his back to watch. Mable is a natural phenom of athleticism, capable of great acrobatic feats and displays of unorthodox flexibility. Her tongue lolls from the side of her jaw, wind whipping the saliva as her body shapes itself into a narrow missile before launching headfirst into each pile in quick succession, only pausing to wriggle with her back nestled against the leaves as if bathing herself in their crisp scent. She lets out little yips and barks, and these behaviors remind the man that no matter how genetically altered those roaming packs of formerly domesticated dogs still are, at their core remains the same playful mannerisms shared by a fully wild creature.

And she is wild, the man must regularly tell himself. Mable is a feral animal, born in the woods and raised in the woods, and the man, no matter how badly he wishes for her to grow as close to him as a Pomeranian would, cannot ask nor expect that of her. This tenuous and distant friendship may only thrive because of the respect he maintains for her innate nature. Even if she were to grow closer to him, allowing him the pleasure of petting her coat or feeding her from his palm, this is something he could not abide and would immediately have to disallow. It is for her safety that he stays at a distance. Even a minor nudge towards domesticity could prove fatal for the fox. His need for an animal's companionship is not worth her safety. In a way then, the visits to the little dog's grave are a constant reminder of the possible repercussions.

Once the sun becomes a yellow crescent resting atop the horizon, a yellow mist settles throughout the tree trunks, and the streetlamps switch on, the man knows it's time to go inside. He does not take risks, as it has become clear over time that as long as he remains outside, Mable will too. He stands and holds a hand up to the fox, who understands the coming danger even better than him. For a while they remain still, separated by the wide street, watching one another. Mable sits on her haunches, cocking her head, and looks around at the dimming light of day, sniffing the air as if looming death produces a scent, then slowly turns away. The man watches her disappear behind a house and catches the glimpses of red and black fur as she breaks off into a run, diving beneath fences and around bushes and shrubs, towards the direction of that great and mysterious forest. All across the city, a mass migration is occurring. There are herds of deer, packs of intermingling wolves and dogs, flocks of every color and shape of bird, and families of bears and squirrels and rats and rabbits, all shuffling in enormous numbers back towards the safety of a living, breathing entity. The man longs terribly to go with, to sprint and catch up with Mable and follow her through empty and silent roads into the waiting embrace of the Green, but the developed fear of a civilized, domesticated human being overtakes, so each evening the man whispers goodbye and walks inside alone.

In the dead of night, the horrifying screams and howls are but a sliver more tolerable. For while he sits huddled in a corner with his arms around his knees, his mind has travelled to a different place. And as he drifts to another fitful, dreamless sleep while the city awakens and cries in pain and rage and dismay at its own existence, the man is wrapped in the black cloak of a Douglas fir's shade, sequestered in the depths of a cool and damp cavern, basked in the warm glow of a crackling fire beside a lake of stars.

After the winter, he thinks again and again. After the winter, I will climb from out the belly of this impossible god of decay. And come morning, Mable will return as she always does. Some creatures are too beautiful to die a violent death. The mere sight of her radiance will strike those shadowy things blind.

We all lie every day to continue to the next, and so the man can allow himself this fantasy. Its melody hums far louder within his fading mind than all the cries and chants and explosive clangs of the armada at his doorstep. There are still things more powerful than dread. This is one.

The snow comes suddenly and heavily, blanketing the city in a white coat that makes the distant skyscrapers appear even more alien, though in the house's neighborhood it is fresh and comforting and natural. Fat flakes waft to the ground in a slow, lazy manner that the man enjoys, redecorating the once bare trees whose leaves now lie in dissolving piles far beneath the layers of ice. For a brief period, a week or two at most, the trees were naked and looked like great dying things, but the snow now adorns their branches like a fine cloak. They are regal, beautiful, and elegant in their new outfits. Through the blue haze that often settles low above the ground, the man can no longer see the city's skyline until he enters its bowels, and he likes it fine that way. There's no need to have the constant reminder of that looming beast so near to this tiny paradise he's found on its outskirts.

It's become a meditative practice for the man to sit beside the sliding glass door, a cup of hot tea or coffee in hand, and watch the snow fall. Each flake seems to contain sentience, floating in whichever manner it so wishes, at whichever pace suits it, in whichever direction, and the simple act of witnessing this benign phenomenon fills him with the sense that time isn't such a dominant force as he once believed. Certain flakes plummet to the earth while others enjoy the sluggish game of it, in no rush to join their kind in forming the tapestry they've created upon the ground. The man begins to believe that the drifting snowflakes control time, warping it to fit their decided schedule. By watching one flake drop faster than the other just beside it, the man visualizes the physicality of time as a thick, elastic substance, pulled in a thousand different directions. Each flake is a planet with its own mass, contorting gravity, and shaping the bits of time that brush against its body. Outside the glass door is now the snow's domain, and no natural or unnatural force, no matter how universal or stubborn, can weave between its many particles without first bending a knee. In a life before, the man may have hated the winter and the snow and harsh cold that came with it, but here it provides peace like nothing else. It is sanctuary.

When the snow first came, he would go outside each morning and look for evidence of the shadowy things' movements during the night but quickly learned that they leave no physical trace besides the violence wrought. Even the pyres appear less menacing. By sunrise, the fires have been reduced to smoldering black ashes, only able to cough up sparks and weak, solitary tongues of flame choked by the snow and frigid winds. The white blanket becomes a graceful death shawl for the poor creatures, still many in number, but through this the man can at least find a semblance of dignity for the dead.

The streets are cluttered with footprints, as if while he slept a fantastic parade had gone through, but as long as he searches, he can find no prints out of the ordinary. To be sure, the man has no idea what to look for, but he's familiar enough with the fauna to know which impression belongs to which animal, and there is nothing he does not recognize. Still, the snow has taught him many things, namely that there are far more animals that remain within the city at night—whether unable or unwilling to abscond to the forest's safety, he doesn't know. But this tells him something he desperately needs to believe: these evil creatures' territory does not extend beyond the city's limits, for it does not have to. Whatever the reason, there is plenty of prey available to them, and every night they make use of all living things within their grasp. His thoughts then drift to the possibility that there is something else terrible, perhaps more terrible, lurking inside the woods that keeps the shadowy things away, but he can't reconcile the idea with his instinct. As much as the unknown frightens him, there is safety in those woods. To gaze into the great Green, its massive canopy now adorned in white, is to see nothing but a benevolent living being. And so this could be the very reason the creatures dare not enter. Nothing withers evil like pure good. Shadows dissolve in the light. The man believes then that this is no different. Every day his confidence grows, and he is sure that by winter's thaw the forest will be his new home.

He has begun eating and exercising much more than he usually did in an effort to bulk up and strengthen his wiry body. He abstains from alcohol and prefers to bring food home to cook in the safety of the house, doing away with the easily accessible processed meals available at the corner stores. Besides these things, the man spends nearly all daylight hours inside the library, poring over any tomes that may prove useful. Everything from basic survival manuals to detailed instructions on mundane things are devoured, and the man learns how to build a fire, skin and dress an animal, disassemble and clean a hunting rifle, recognize edible berries and roots and mushrooms, self-administer first aid. Anything the man thinks he may need to learn, he does—as well as one can merely from reading a book. He knows all too well that it will be different in practice once he's out there in the wilderness, but these are important first steps. Steps he has never before taken. The man struggles to keep from chiding himself over the fact that he had never before bothered to learn these things at all. He had allowed himself to grow complacent, feeding off the city and its comforts like a fattened tick, but now that regret only fuels his desire to transform into an entirely different kind of animal. There is nothing to do but prepare for the future and rely on the present as a friend. It does no good to dwell.

Every morning when he comes outside, Mable is there waiting for him. There is now never a day where they are apart, until that regretful moment before the sun dips below the horizon and they must each say their silent goodbyes. Unlike the other animals, who have either gone into hibernation in the woods or have aesthetically changed to meld into the shifting season, Mable's coat remains bright red and deep black, if thicker to suit the cold. She is impossible not to spot, and so the man doesn't grow anxious when she gallops on ahead during their long walks.

He has never seen a thing so in love with snow. Mable sprints in circles, to and fro, diving into piles and stuffing her snout into the fascinating substance, digging excitedly to create little tunnels while the man faithfully waits for her to finish. She has taken on a much more childlike personality in the last few weeks since the snow arrived. She feeds off play like water, rolling around with her tongue slapping against her face like a numbed limb, yipping and cackling as foxes do. It's apt that this noise means she's happy, because to the man it sounds exactly like laughter. Mable is always laughing now, a vibrant and beautiful little thing, a bright red ball at odds with a world of pure white. The man simply walks behind at a slow pace, allowing his friend this pleasure, and every few moments she will leap back off the ground and crane her neck to make sure he's still there with her. And of course, he always is. He always will be, and over time she comes to learn this, but an animal's existence is rife with uncertainty and change, and so nonetheless she must check. The man grins and waves, and Mable leaps in the air and dives into another pile of snow face first.

He worries about her often at night, much more than he used to. This is obviously because he's grown very fond of her, but it's also the unignorable fact that her coat makes her stand out more than any other animal. Her genetic abnormality is beautiful, but like many other beautiful things, it puts her in danger. Of everything the man has read, it seems that foxes have no natural predators, though the occasional mountain lion or bear have been known to kill them. The bears are all resting in deep slumbers, hidden away in caves, and the mountain lions are very rare. In all the time he's lived in this place, the man hasn't ever seen but one or two. Though from what he understands this only occurs as a last resort for a starving animal, and starvation has been all but eradicated. There is plenty to go around. It pains him to think of the slaughtered deer and rabbits, but he would be lying to himself if he didn't accept that he would rather it be them than Mable. This is, after all, the way of nature. It's still a foreign thing, but slowly he is coming to terms with the indifferent savagery of the natural world. There is a balance to it, and that makes sense. It is the imbalance of humanity that caused him much more anxiety. That kind of savagery cannot be maintained. Like the savagery of the shadowy things. There's no logic to it, and he has no wish to gain even a vague understanding of that kind of madness. As long as Mable returns to the woods each night, the man rests easy enough.

They come across at least two or three of the pyres while on their walk, especially the closer to downtown they get, closer to the library, and Mable never dares approach. She has learned to recognize them by their shape, though certainly she doesn't understand what they are other than something awful and dangerous. Her ears pin back, and she stands very rigid, from a distance. She makes no noises, and through this the man knows they've come near a pyre even before he sees it. She is a talkative thing, and when silence suddenly comes over her it can mean only that she's discovered something impossible to make sense of. Thankfully, the snow covers most of the remains, but even so a severed limb or deer's head may still protrude through the ice, frozen in that state of empty-eyed terror. The man whistles until Mable finally breaks from her trance and follows, and after a few minutes of walking she is back to her old self, weaving around trees and yipping at passing birds.

On occasion, she'll catch sight of a darting mouse or rat, and her predatory instincts will kick in. The chase is now on, and the man watches helplessly as Mable gallops far away in erratic zigzags until pouncing, and she will then return to his side, drop the dead animal on the ground, and eat as the dripping blood stains the snow and steam rises into the air as if the rat's soul has left its body. She looks up at the man with those playful, amber eyes, blood and viscera brushed across her muzzle, and he never knows what to do. It's as though he should praise Mable for her catch. But this may only be a human's perspective. Praise is a thing for children, not adults or animals. What Mable does is hardwired in her, and she probably doesn't think about it at all once the gruesome business is concluded.

Once at the library, Mable still comes along inside. There's no reason to stop her. It's cold out and the library is always warm and inviting, and while the man looks through the aisles for a book on fishing or trap-setting, Mable wanders through the halls, sniffing at the dusty leatherbound shapes until deciding upon a fitting spot to curl up and rest. She stays very close to the man and remains asleep for however long he spends here. If there was once a rule that the man wouldn't allow her to come too near, that rule has since been abolished. She has become more like a loyal hound than a wild animal, and this does worry the man. But he loves her. It would be far too painful to push her away now. Though his one rule remains, which is that they should never come close enough to touch one another. It feels arbitrary at times, but in the absence of any other rules, this one at least provides the man with the vague belief that he isn't actively domesticating her.

And still something else persists, something he can't quite articulate but feels to be very important. The man tries to push this thought deep down or far away, but it always returns. He has much more in common with those terrible, shadowy things than any of the animals. He is not innocent, as much as he tries to stay in balance with the many creatures around him, for he is a human being. He is, by his very existence, out of tune with the rest of the natural world. And this is something shared by only one other species—if they can even be considered as such. He, like them, is at his core corrupt. He cannot help it, maybe in the same way the shadowy things can't help what they are, but it doesn't make them, or him, less evil. And so there exists an irrational fear that by stroking Mable's fur, by holding out a hand for her to sniff and nuzzle, he will infect her with some intangible darkness that festers within his being. He recognizes the ludicrousness of this thought much in the same way he regards those distant ancestors who believed in the balancing of the humors and the legitimacy of divination, but still he cannot shake the worry.

The man reads until his vision grows blurry and his eyelids grow heavy, and then he arranges the pile of books atop the chair and stands. Mable immediately perks up, lifting her head from atop her bushy tail, and follows behind as they leave the library together. He stops by a fine dining restaurant while Mable sits outside like a posted sentry, sifts through the walk-in freezer until he decides on steak with broccoli and potatoes, stuffs it all in his satchel, and begins the walk home. The retreating sun hides behind a thick layer of clouds, and only sparse beams of light reach through, dousing the white blanket in reflective golden rays, and they reach the house long before nightfall. Mable stamps the ground nervously as the man looms before the front door, and they stare at one another until that silent recognition is understood, and she sulks away, across the street, looking over her shoulder every few paces while the man waves, before finally disappearing behind the dense, snowy brush. The man then goes inside, locks the door, and goes about his routine, all the while thinking about the next morning when Mable will return again. Nights are so much less frightening now. All he ever needed was something to look forward to.

One morning the man steps outside, and there as always Mable waits in the middle of the street. A fresh layer of snow had fallen throughout the night, and he can see in the many overlapping pawprints that she has been pacing in circles for some time now. When he approaches, Mable immediately stands rigid, her tail between her legs and ears pinned back. The man recognizes this body language right away and scans the neighborhood for anything that would cause her distress but finds nothing. Everything appears as it always does. A gentle breeze rustles snow from the branches, and a light flurry sweeps through the air in a white haze, but it's quiet and calm. Only Mable appears restless. Agitated even. The man kneels down a few paces from her and sees in her eyes a flicker of not anger or predatory anxiety but fear. It's clear in her demeanor. Mable is afraid. Her snout trembles and short whimpers escape her mouth, but this is the most noise she dares make. He stands and surveys his surroundings with fresh eyes, trying desperately to find what frightens her, but before he can reassure Mable with a soft gesture she takes off, darting through the trees without any pause for him to catch up. She has never acted like this before. No encounter with any animal has caused this kind of turmoil in his friend. With no other option and an ominous curiosity overtaking him, the man runs after her, clearing through brush and leaping over fences. Far ahead, the red and black blur widens the gap between them, but it's far too difficult to lose those colors against such a stark white environment, and so the man slows to a jog to conserve energy, already the wind and frigid temperature causing his legs to chafe and his extremities to numb.

Finally, the blur slows and comes back into focus as the little fox he knows, and the man is able to take stock of where they now reside. Mable has led him back into the city—a distantly familiar area, though the snow covering all cars and buildings makes it harder to discern where exactly. She now stands in the middle of a wide avenue facing the man, and he trots ahead until they're together again. Mable gazes up at him with the same look of fear, her fur bristling against the cold, and when she's certain she has his attention, she presses her snout to the ground and begins to sniff, allowing whatever scent to guide her forward.

The man follows dutifully behind, anxiety hammering his heart against his chest, his eyes now scanning all dark corners and high rooftops for something amiss. There is something terribly wrong. He doesn't yet know it, but Mable does, and her instincts are far more attuned than his.

Her nose takes them through a peculiar path made of alleyways and backroads, and soon the man can't help but be aware of this indescribable danger. There are pyres erected everywhere—small and large—with piles of dead animals still charring from the bright flames that burn as if they'd just been lit. Many trenches have been created in the snow where the lifeless animals were dragged to their final resting place, but no evidence of those beings who committed the terrible deed exists, as if some invisible force had abducted the poor creatures as they slept. There is no time to investigate the source of the trenches, as Mable grows more and more steadfast, more urgent in her mission to some unknown destination. She doesn't look up once, operating through intuition, guided only by the scent that must be so powerful to her but is imperceptible to the man.

The pyres are now too many in number to ignore. They litter the road, creating an uneven pathway for the man to take, and in the distance not shrouded by haze or tall buildings, he can see pillars of smoke rising into the sky like some archaic message. No living animals pass them by. There are no birds flitting across the treetops and no deer running behind the trees. There exists only the man and Mable and the constant crackling hum of the burning pyres. It's like walking through the aftermath of a horrifying battle choked silent in mourning and terror. So many bodies. All the survivors surely retreated to the woods or otherwise never left, while those that remained now lie melting beneath the flames and each other's corpses. An unthinkable crime against nature was committed last night. The man can't make sense of it. The previous evening, while still chaotic and violent outside the walls, was no different than any other. This feels like a coordinated effort, something enacted with guile and stealth. But that's behavior the man has never known from the shadowy things. A change has occurred. The air is thick with its repercussions, and Mable is all too aware of what the man only now is slowly beginning to piece together.

Soon, she leads the man into areas he's traveled often, and the pyres strike at his heart upon seeing places of such comfort and familiarity corrupted by this savage violence. Some reach nearly as high as the smaller buildings they stand beside, great burning towers of bodies like contorted buildings themselves, erected from wood and flesh and blood and bone in the shape of a pyramid. There are only so many hours of darkness each night, and the time it must have taken to slaughter scores of animals and then to build and light these many hideous creations is impossible for the man to grasp. It would take an army, a multi-pronged legion of those hellish brutes to accomplish this feat. Their true number has never crossed his mind, as he was never sure if they were even individual beings unto themselves, but as he and Mable march through the roads, he can't help but accept that the shadowy things are a population like no other species in the world—an ever-multiplying, vampiric race of beast. The terror undulates inside him, rising to the surface until his whole body trembles and every pop and crackle from a nearby fire causes his nervous system to erupt into another frenzy. But Mable remains steadfast, focused, following the invisible trail to an unknown destination that the man wishes to never find. She needs him to follow, to show him what she may already know, and after seeing the carnage unleashed, he can't in good conscience allow her to proceed alone. Whatever lies at the end of this trail is something that must be seen and accepted. A hundred different scenarios play in his head like horror films, and he tries to remember that whatever calamity his mind creates surely far exceeds the reality to come, but even still he can't help but believe that this time is different. Whatever he will find on this day will be something his worst anxieties are incapable of conjuring. For that is the nature of those shadowy things. They are at their very essence unfathomable creatures and so their actions are the same.

It does no good to dwell, the man thinks. It does no good to dwell.

He banishes the revolving catastrophes from his thoughts and presses on.

Mable begins to slow down. She at last raises her snout to the air, sniffing, letting out little yelps. They are close, and the man now knows exactly where they are, and exactly what they are approaching. Something familiar. Something dear, very dear to the man. It only makes sense this would happen. It was a matter of time, after all.

The cascading fire is visible before ever reaching the gate. Its black smoke billows into the sky with a rumbling fervor as if the ground beneath has split open. Mable and the man arrive to the garden to find the apple tree set ablaze. It's a controlled burn, something done with purposeful intent to destroy the garden and only the garden, but the wind has carried the fire across the separating fences like violent ocean waves. Everything is withering and black. The green grass, roses, and plants. The insects and worms. All have submitted to the flames, rendered obsidian and lifeless. Around the tree's trunk, molded and half-eaten apples sit, now liquified, their bright pink skins peeled from the flesh like torture victims. When the breeze redirects towards the man, the fruit's singed aroma wafts towards him, and a putrid miasma of something once beautiful and now corrupted stings his nostrils.

Mable sits on her haunches, keeping her distance from the gate, watching as the tree's many branches split and fall beneath the weight of death. The man can do nothing. A terrible numbness overcomes him, and he too sits down beside his friend. Together, they watch the apple tree collapse. Like some vindictive murderer, the flames continue to crackle and dance atop its corpse, but always a stubborn thing, the tree's barren and snow-soaked wood soon proves to be worthless kindling, and slowly, still quite slowly, the flames fizzle out in the cold and the wind, having thoroughly completed their task.

What now remains is a square acre of flat, black earth, pockmarked by the falling snow that now appears only as ashes of the aftermath. Quiet returns, perforated by the sporadic pops of the embers that linger atop patches of charred grass. The breeze passes through, kissing the man's tear-stained face, daring not even to whistle. He stands and walks inside; the gate's lock has been shattered. The fence separating the garden from the old pioneer cemetery is gnarled and twisted, and the man steps over the hot metal and enters. It's now more fitting than ever that a place for the dead should be so close to the site of a killing. The foxgloves that once lined the fence have shriveled and died in the winter, and whatever remained that may have allowed for a spring rebirth has been eradicated.

He looks over his shoulder, allowing a brief glance at the great sundered tree, and somewhere deep within the man knows one day something gorgeous and alive will return, but he will not be here to see it. This is his fault. There is no way around that fact. It is the work of those foul beings, those black demons, in retribution for his unwillingness to surrender to the horrors of night. He is alive and has remained alive for far too long, and they have grown vengeful. The shadowy, terrible things killed something beautiful because they could not have him. A piece of nature so brazenly holding space in their territory, their domain of all that goes against the natural order—it was a matter of time. And so the man is not surprised. He is only deeply, profoundly heartbroken. The one solace he can take is that they chose the season of death to commit this atrocity; there were no apples growing from the branches, no leaves to rip from their mother. Somewhere beneath the decimated earth there are seeds, safe from the elements and safe from the flames, and one day a sapling will emerge from the soil. On that day, the man will smile, and he will know that more powerful forces exist than unknowable terror, but until that sacred moment of resurrection the man will mourn. His last sanctuary is no more.

He opens the gate to the cemetery, and Mable cautiously steps inside to be with him. Even she seems to understand that something is amiss. As they walk through the unkempt grass, clambering over twisted vines, the man sees the graves have been defiled. Dug up. Piles of earth lie beside the exhumed plots. The ancient, decrepit wooden coffins sit upright at an angle, their rotted lids left open. Inside there is nothing—no skeleton, no mismatched collection of bones. He first thinks that animals have gotten to them but knows this is just a comforting fantasy. No animals have ever trodden here, as if they too had heard the old tales of the graveyard's curse. The plots have each been exhumed with precision, with a plan. It's impossible to ignore the connection with the garden opposite—the shadowy things have done something foul here. What, the man doesn't know. He doesn't wish to know. But last night, something shifted. They have grown fiercer, more daring. A terrible new world is coming. This city belongs to them now—all of it. Nowhere is safe.

Driven without thought or any regard for instinct, the man leaves the cemetery and begins to walk. He doesn't care where, but something compels him towards a path never taken. Mable sulks behind, in no mood to play or run. She senses the distant malaise emanating from his demeanor, and knowing not what to do with it, she mirrors that feeling. Together, they share one another's pain, one another's confusion and fear, and the man and the fox walk and walk and walk in silence. They walk until the artificial lights become sparse, and a darkness even the sun above cannot affect settles around them like drifting to a fitful, restless sleep.

The man does not realize until it's too late that they've entered an unmapped area of the city—an area where the power doesn't reach, where the streetlamps give no illumination, where the shadows have full jurisdiction. The man does not realize until he finally looks up from his trance that they have entered a place he has never been. A place he should never be.

They are lost in the bowels of a ghost.

This neighborhood is unlike anything the man has seen before—not in person, anyway. It is a snapshot of the past, an artist's rendering of an ancient civilization. There is no power, no lights or electricity, but not because powerlines were knocked down. No powerlines exist. Mable and the man have stepped into a separate place all together. The darkened streets are paved not with asphalt but cobbled stone and clay. Each building is made of uneven, heavy stones laid atop one another to create rows of single-floor domiciles. Wooden doors cover the entrances, more like thin boards to protect from the elements than any kind of proper entryway, and simple holes have been shaped out of the walls to serve as windows. The area is black and cloaked in shadow, and the man has difficulty finding his way ahead. He kneels down and rifles through his satchel until he finds a flashlight and switches it on. Motes of dust float through the yellow beam. There is no noise, no animals scurrying away from the sudden glow, no hissing or yowls. There is only silence. Mable steps closer to the man, keeping her downturned head next to his leg.

He walks forward, painfully aware of his own echoing footsteps. The sound reverberates off the pathway and flutters away down the long, empty expanse. He shines the flashlight through the open window of a nearby home and sees barebones living quarters: a stone slab in one corner with something like sheepskin laid out across and a simple wooden table resting at a sloping angle atop a broken limb. The floor is stone and lined with dust and dirt, and there is no sign of it being a lived-in home. The roof is thatched and further layered with straw. The man directs the flashlight across the other houses and finds that each is quite the same—old, unclean, barren. The cloud-covered sun burns in the sky above, but through some unspeakable phenomenon its rays don't reach the road, as if they dare not to. There are only shadows and dust and a fine layer of snow on the cobbled road, like walking through a hollowed skeleton still inside its coffin. The man understands logically that he remains within the city, that no portals opened up, no kind of magic occurred here, but there is no explanation. Before, the snow was still falling in light flurries, but here it has stopped. Only the evidence exists, and even so it's more a vague interpretation of snow than the real thing. He drags a finger through the white substance and feels nothing. It is not cold. It has no physicality at all—it's like touching congealed smoke.

Mable starts to whine, the first sounds she made since setting off aimlessly from the garden. The man knows what she thinks, for he thinks it too: they have to leave. He pivots and aims the flashlight in the way they came, but there is only a black expanse. Further rows of stone houses as far as the beam can illuminate. It's impossible. He may have been unaware of the surroundings, for he never would have entered this area had he known, but surely he couldn't have ventured this far. He's lost his sense of direction, gotten turned around. To go farther in is to get out. This thought comes from somewhere outside of him. He didn't just think that. But it's compelling. Without good visibility of the sun, the man has no way to know what time it is. He could have walked for minutes or for hours.

Mable's whines grow louder and more frequent. Her head swivels in all directions, and she all but presses her body against the man. If he were alone, the man would begin to cry. An infantile fear of the unknown overtakes him, but his friend's frightened little sounds remind him of the stakes, of the necessity to continue. To die here would be a terrible fate, an idea that weighs so heavily on his psyche that it may just crush him, rendering him paralyzed until nightfall. Only Mable gives him the strength to move. And he does. One foot in front of the other, the flashlight's yellow beam trembling through a black and impossible road, the man begins to walk farther into the bowels of the unfamiliar. Mable then follows.

The only way out is through. This sentiment is flawed and goes against every screaming survival instinct in the man's body, but for reasons beyond him it is all he can act upon. He wants desperately for Mable to take the lead, to guide him like an angel towards the true exit, but even animals know terror when it presents itself in its truest form, and she too is transfixed, puzzled, and lost. Her eyes burn reddish brown in the dim light, and she glances at the man every few paces as if for reassurance. He talks to her, and this seems to help. He doesn't talk about anything in particular, just words. It's his voice she needs to hear. That's all that ever mattered. Language is useless in times of duress. It's to know another is there with you. That's all that needs to be communicated. Her whimpers dampen and shrink to subtle grumbling contained to her chest. Her steps are rapid, and her tail stays sweeping back and forth low to the ground.

The road goes and goes. More of the same houses. Leaning stone, empty and decrepit. Soon, the layer of snow thickens, and the sharp thumping of one another's steps transmute into muffled crunches. The man looks behind them and thankfully sees that their prints remain in the snow at their back. If they are going to be found by something lurking in the darkness, it will find them regardless of the trail they create, and so this is a comfort. If they must double back, they can. But they won't. The man already knows this but refuses to accept it. There is something calling them forward. Something to see. There must be. It's the reason this place was avoided for so long. The exact same reason he is here now. It's no coincidence. Something important lies at the end of this long march.

There is no discrepancy in the environment, no sign that time has continued forward before they come upon it. Once it wasn't there, and now it is. The cathedral stands at the center of the road, the end of the road. It too is made of stone, a black monolithic edifice with a wide staircase leading to a large, arched doorway. It is taller than all the other buildings that shrink beside it as if kneeling before a petrified god. Stained-glass windows decorate the upper half on all sides, and at the very top of the sharp, triangular roof a steeple stands erect like a lightning rod. Deep green moss and vines have taken over the outer structure, climbing through the walls, forming a natural walkway over the stairs, and covering enough of the windows to make discerning the artwork impossible. Only the vague hues of color present behind the flashlight's glow.

Mable's ears pin back once more, her eyes are wide, and they too reflect off the muddied, yellow beam. She lies down flat, curling her tail around her body. The man glances between the fox and the church and sits down for a moment beside her. Mable's torso heaves up and down through shallow, claustrophobic breaths, and the man slows his breathing, inhaling the sour air until she catches on, and together they remain like that on the cold ground until their exhalations sync, and together their heartbeats find one another's rhythm. When he feels she's ready, the man stands up and steps across the stairway, pulls open the doors, and walks inside the cathedral in the dark.

The room is wide and open and frigid. Colder than the air outside. Four rows of rotting pews sit on either side, with an empty walkway in the center leading to an altar. Each step taken echoes like a gunshot, reverberating off the walls. Mable trails behind, hunched and closed off, not bothering to assess the smells with an upturned snout. He directs the flashlight towards the stained-glass windows, but within the church the greenery too has found a home. Interweaving ivy twists up the walls and across the windows like a sickness, though it's comforting to the man. For something so foreign and out of place to still be within nature's grasp lessens his anxiety. In however an abstract way, he and Mable are not alone here. Something can still live even in the depths of an abyss.

Atop the altar is a long table runner, like a shawl or something worn across a priest's vestments. Even in the darkness it erupts with color. Bright yellow. Unsullied by time or decay. A bright yellow strip of silklike material draped over the altar's sides and onto the floor. And atop this yellow shawl lies a large, rectangular object. The man shines the flashlight upon it but can't make out anything but its dimensions. There is no particular reason for his reaction, but the object frightens him. In fact, the whole scene frightens him. It's decorative and arranged with care and a keen eye. Someone or something did this. Others have been here. That truth is only made clearer when he directs the flashlight upon the areas of wall not covered by ivy.

All across the bare patches, bleeding into spaces concealed by vines and leaves, are rudimentary drawings. Like cave paintings. Childlike and simple. He steps closer and presses his fingers to the art. It's ash. Black ash. All depict the exact same thing: vaguely humanoid creatures, heads and legs and feet, black forms, their visages smudged at the outlines. The man then pans the flashlight across more and more of the walls, hoping desperately that it will end. But it doesn't. Every inch of the inner cathedral is covered in black, ashen figures. Everywhere the light can reach, they are there, watching. A thousand eyes upon them. And the eyes—this is the only difference. It is harder to see through the darkness, but when brought to light, they burn. The eyes are red. A deep blackish red. And once it's become clear as to what they are, it is all the man can see. Little red dots, black figures, crawling across the walls, wriggling in a terrible trick of the light, staring. He again touches one of the figures closest and finds the red is comprised of a different substance. It chips off beneath his fingernails, coarse and hardened and rough. Blood. Dried, coagulated blood. Eyes of blood and bodies of ash, humanoid but inhuman. No sane man would create these things, nor a satanist in an effort to defile a sacred place. There's something far too menacing to be conceived even by the darkest of human minds. It can't be explained, but it's there before him. This didn't arrive by hands familiar with the world. It came from a different world altogether. Some men go mad and create, and no matter how abstract it may feel upon witnessing the result, one can still inherently tell that it came from a mind, however troubled. This though—these ashen, bloody figures—bears no resemblance to even inescapable madness.

Unwilling yet to step towards the altar, the man's flashlight now slowly climbs higher up the walls until it reaches the ceiling. There is no metaphor nor description in the English language to properly relay what the man sees there. It is one single piece of art stretching across the entire upper surface from doors to altar. It is of two figures, one far more familiar than the other, not because it is something easy to grasp but because its counterpart is so utterly impossible that by contrast even the wildest, most surreal imagery capable of imagining falters in logical comparison.

A monster. A demon. A malevolent god. A massive, great beast of many limbs or teeth or tusks, eyes or wings or a maze of loose, hanging organs, amorphous and yet defined with lines that don't meet nor match... It kneels. The impossible thing kneels across the cathedral ceiling. There are no knees to discern, no legs with which to assume this is the act, but by the artist's rendering alone it is spelled out as clearly as one ever could. The beast kneels before a man. A king. He stands, barely a blemish in contrast to its gargantuan size, a tri-pointed crown atop his ashen stick-figure head. He has no eyes, no bleeding dots. No expression at all. He looks down upon the beast, and it kneels before him.

The man quickly diverts the flashlight and looks away; he can't bear the sight of it. As miraculous and alluring as it is, the art reeks of evil things. Dread begins to pulse like blood through his veins, and his chest tightens. Mable picks up on this, and she opens her mouth to yip as if in pain. He turns and sees that her amber eyes are fixed upon the altar now. Her face brims with stoic, animalistic terror, the truest terror that animals can feel: danger. They are in immediate danger. And they are not alone. But the man hears its call—silencing instinct, humming inside his head. It begs him to approach. The altar demands his attendance.

The man steps forward, down the open walkway. Closer and closer to the altar, to the brilliant yellow shawl, to the dark object singing alien melodies. His mind clears, thoughts evaporate like a fine mist, and Mable remains at the back of the church, yipping, barking, begging him to stop, but he can't. He has to know. The man reaches the pulpit, and now even his friend's desperate cries mute and slip away, and he sees there upon the altar, upon the yellow shawl—a book. It is of the same color as the shawl but quite worn; what perhaps was once too a vibrant yellow is dull and tinged brown by time and misuse. Its leatherbound cover is without artwork, only decorated with muddied spots like water stains or cigarette burns. The spine is no longer straight and flat but warped. It is a thick and damaged tome, the only object that matches the cathedral in its ancient appearance. Even the wall drawings look fresh, at least more so than the building within which they reside—an architectural relic of a past era. No, it is the book and the cathedral that came into existence together, spirited here by some unknown craftsman. Then the creators of those drawings found this place. They too heard its call.

What secrets lie within its gnarled pages?

His eyes grow large, his hand carefully grasps the book's cover, and he lifts it to reveal whatever ancient words await. A thick cloud of dust arises from the first page, and the man coughs and waves his hand to clear the air. Upon witnessing its revelation, the man halts. Confused. For what he sees on the page is... nothing.

The page is empty.

He flips to the next. Empty.

And the next. Nothing.

Again and again and again. He begins flicking through the pages with more and more fervor, more frustration, now only glancing at each empty sheet, until reaching the very last. Not a single word. Not an illustration or a note left by another reader. It is an old, thick, meaningless collection of blank pages.

He doesn't understand. The man shines the flashlight down the center aisle from which he came, where Mable remains prone, now letting out only short, quiet whimpers, pleading with him to return by her side. A pang of guilt blooms from his stomach, then that awful fear floods back in, and as if having been released from hypnosis, the man swivels around, gazing upon the bare cathedral as a new witness, and he realizes how very wrong this all is. How very wrong it was to come here. To touch this evil thing. And it is evil. No words need to be written within the book to know this much. It radiates off the leather like the stench of a corpse. Without any thought but as a fearful reaction, the man swipes his open palm at the book, knocking it off the altar where it slams onto the floor with a dull clang like a denotated bomb, and Mable leaps up and screams that high-pitched scream. The man looks at what he's done, at the withered creation lying face down, and now, only now does he see.

On the back of the yellow book, chiseled into the leather with manic scrawls, are these words:

HASTUR IS WAKING

HAIL HASTUR

The man has no time to wonder at this cryptic message, for Mable bounds past him, howling and screeching as if struck with rabies, tearing across the pulpit and into a narrow corridor at the man's back. He turns and sees she is already gone, the deep shadows having consumed her. Only her echoing cries, fading farther and farther away, tell him that she's found something. With no other option, nor truthfully any wish to take it, the man leaves the awful tome where it lies and runs after his fox.

The corridor is an impossible labyrinth, twisting and turning with no room for the man to even stretch his arms to feel the way through. It is pitch-black, and in his haste he crashes into a sharp corner, knocking the flashlight from his hand, but Mable's cries grow more frantic, more distant, and the fear for his animal clouds any thoughts of self-preservation, so the man breaks into a mad sprint through the shadows, and with one left turn the only source of light is gone, swallowed by the abyss that envelops all. He screams out every ten paces and then counts ten more paces of silence before she calls back in a far different tone than the fierce howls directed towards whatever perceived threat awaits at the end of the maze. Minutes pass, and the man begins to feel as though he's running in place inside a vast coffin, floating through a liminal space. The walls close in, and his breaths grow shallow as if it's become a race against a great vacuum sucking the oxygen from his lungs, and still Mable cries and screeches, and tears pour from the man's face with no free moment to account for the emotions that brought them about. Though the man feels he may be going in circles, his fox's yelps continue from a distance, and so he knows she has found the correct way—his light in the dark, his beacon upon the stormy shore—and through this he can center himself and sprint on, even as his chest convulses, his lungs burn, and his mind atrophies into nothing but the pervasive terror that undulates throughout the darkness. Finally, finally, his lungs taste fresh air, real air, and his skin feels the prickle of winter's cold, and Mable's cries have ceased. The man turns left, then right, and there at the end of this last hall is an open doorway. The light is bloodied by the setting sun, but even that foul omen is a blessing, for the man jaunts across the corridor and out, out into a familiar world, into the city he knows and loves and hates in equal measure.

With a blinding flash and a suffocating burst of cold, clean oxygen, the man steps onto snow and ice and surveys his surroundings. Mable is there just ahead, silent, body poised like a missile, tail rigid and straight, ears narrowed. One ear flickers backward but for a moment, recognizing the presence of her friend, but she dares not turn her head. The man immediately sees why.

While they emerged into another area of the city without power, the buildings are modern and tall, and the sidewalk runs on either side of an asphalt-paved road. Skyscrapers cast massive shadows across the snow, and at the base of the largest building, beneath a covered parking lot, a small fire dances. Arranged around the burning pyre are four figures, basked in shadow but undoubtedly humanoid. Mable and the man are too far away for them to have yet noticed; their heads are bowed, entranced by the flames and ignorant to their surroundings.

He steps forward and kneels beside Mable, and together they stare. His body reacts, but his mind is blank. Nothing comes. They need to leave. They need to run in any direction as long as it's away from these unknown people, but the man is frozen in place, as if with enough time his eyes will adjust to find that it's all a trick of the lights, a nightmarish mirage. And too, the sun descends in the sky, elongating the shadows across the snow, shrinking the reflective gold rays until very soon all will be dark. Something must be done. There is no time to reflect on the previous events. There is never enough time for anything but blind survival, and it is running out again.

Mable moves first. Crouched low to the ground, chin hovering just above the snow, she crawls closer. Slowly. Terribly slowly. The man can do nothing but watch, helpless, as anything he does would be clumsier and louder than the fox. She widens the gap between them until perfectly at the center between the man and the strangers, and perhaps not understanding the gravity of the situation, or misjudging her own ability, begins to growl. The man's heart skips, and he catches a sharp inhale from becoming an audible sound. Mable does not look back. Mable crawls closer still, growling louder, until rising up and relenting a terrible, violent scream. It echoes throughout the empty road, bounding off the towering buildings, skipping across the ground until spreading across the Earth. It is a sound heard by every creature, and the man believes, without knowing the figures' true identities, that it has killed them both.

At once, all four heads turn. As though her scream were a starter's pistol, the man launches ahead in some impotent attempt to pull her away, and upon reaching her side he sees their faces in vivid detail. They do not move. The figures stand together before the fire and stare. And the man cannot make sense of it. They are human—or once were. For their bodies, though living and adorned in draping rags, are that of corpses: skin peeling like gnarled wood, revealing yellowed flesh dripping foul liquids upon the snow, with massive sores burrowed into the rotting meat that still pulses blood. Their faces are without expression and suffer from the same malady as the body. The skin has congealed into a loose, soupy material clinging on by hanging tendons, giving the beings a false appearance of perpetual shock, as no eyelids remain, and nothing but deep, black abscesses surround the organs. Thin sheets of dangling muscle cover only sections of their otherwise visible jaws with brown, fractured teeth poking out through infected holes. The figures don't appear as living things in the throes of deterioration but quite the opposite. They are things once dead now undergoing regeneration, being brought back to life in the warm light of that sacrificial pyre. He watches the translucent skin on one figure's hand crawl across an open, bleeding sore until, like some horrific miracle, the wound is sealed. They are becoming whole.

Another sharp screech breaks the man from his paralysis, and he pulls away from the impossible act, the impossible things, looks at the bleeding sky turning blue and black at the edges like a traumatic bruise, and whistles with two fingers in his mouth. Mable whips around, finally released from the spell, and stares at the man, and upon that necessary moment of recognition, he breaks off into a sprint with his fox in tow.

Together, they bound through alleyways and shadowy backroads, between buildings and across yards, the man constantly checking his back to see if the figures have given chase, but there is nothing behind them but the ever-present darkness and their own separate prints in the snow. They run until the sight of lighted streetlamps arrives like Heaven's glow, and still they run, Mable faithfully at the man's side, entrusting him with her safety, until unfamiliar territory becomes trodden paths, until the city becomes a neighborhood, and the house and the little dog's grave come into view as the sun is but a pink sliver behind the trees. Only once his feet touch the front yard does the man stop at last, and he bends over and vomits bile from an empty stomach while Mable flops onto her belly, panting and heaving, her tongue hanging loose across her jaw, the flames in her amber eyes finally doused. The calm arrives in tentative waves, as if it too isn't yet sure of the circumstances. But it comes.

The man collapses atop the snowy grass, and Mable clambers near, resting her head beside his still trembling knee. Together they sit in silence watching the light shrink from the horizon until it's time to say goodbye.

You saved my life, says the man.

Mable stares, and she slowly turns, glancing back again and again before disappearing into the brush.

Though he does not yet know it, this is the last time the man will ever see Mable alive.

Looking back at this moment many months later, from within the fire-warmed confines of a hunter's cabin in the woods, the man will be glad that this image, not any other, is how he remembers her.

That evening the man has a nightmare, the first he can ever remember having. He has no wish to think much about it. He has never found merit in dissecting the psychology of dreams and so he goes back to sleep and forgets.

In the morning, the man opens the doors to the ice and snow and looks out across the empty street. The birds have returned, and he sees a family of deer behind the tree line, their snouts dug into the frost, rummaging for frozen berries kept preserved by the elements. He waits for the red and black coat to appear and her amber eyes to present themselves like jewels atop a blank, white page. She does not arrive. The man sticks two fingers in his mouth and whistles. The sound carries through the air, and the deer look up before returning to graze. A murder of crows takes flight from the power line overhead and glides away towards the great city, but she does not come.

There was nothing different about the previous night. The shadowy things arrived as they always did, carrying their howls and cries and violent attempts to tear down the walls of the house. Just as they always did, to no avail. But the same could be said about the night before that, and that morning's results were something entirely unordinary.

The man's pulse quickens, and he steps out into the middle of the street, looking in either direction. There was very little foot traffic last night; only a few sparse tracks remain in the snow. He searches around before finding Mable's familiar pawprints, left behind before absconding as the sun set. Some have been obscured by further snowfall and wind, but others remain intact, and the trail is easy enough to follow. So the man sets off towards the brush where she always escaped, whistling again and again in the distant hope that some trivial distraction kept Mable from her typically prompt schedule. The prints disappear for feet at a time, and often the man loses track, but after continuing on in the general direction he has seen her go before, he again catches sight of those familiar impressions.

The neighborhood is surrounded by lush, if contained, woodlands, and he soon finds himself climbing over felled old growth and traversing across trickling creeks. All around nature's gentle ambience urges him forth, and it is a great comfort to hear the birdsongs and to catch the glimpse of a wandering black bear or lynx indifferent to his presence. This provides him with a false sense of security, for if these animals are unbothered and safe, then so too is his fox—simply lost in the majesty of the Green, wandering a bit before finding her way to him.

Soon, the woodlands thin, and the tracks continue on through unfamiliar suburbs. Massive oak trees appear through the wintry haze, towering over the houses—those ancient sentries at the forest's gates—and the man's urgent breaths relax upon seeing that Mable had reached this close to salvation after sunset. But as he steps out onto the narrow road, the pawprints suddenly and inexplicably cease, just in the center, as if by some miracle she vanished. He stops and swivels around to see if she'd abruptly changed course. Nothing. He then backtracks, following the prints in reverse until returning to the woodland's edge. No, the man is sure—Mable had come this way, and she had reached the center of the suburban road not a quarter-mile away from the forest. And stopped. He returns to the final pawprint and kneels, studying the shape as though it will provide some secret he missed. His eyes then follow the untrodden path on which she would have continued. It is only a blanket of snow leading to a pathway between two indistinguishable houses. Beyond the houses is a straight shot towards the oak trees. He hovers at the very edge. Then, from down the road, he witnesses a sight that causes his heart to jump. He stands rigid and focuses on the approaching animals. Foxes. Three foxes. Among them is not his Mable, not his beautiful melanistic friend. Red foxes, their coats thick and decorated with brushstrokes of grayish white for the winter season. They trot closer, their snouts buried in the snow as if having caught the scent of something very peculiar, for even as they pass just by the man, they don't look up or pause. The foxes push forward, over the trail of Mable's pawprints. But where her tracks stopped, they continue unimpeded until turning right into one of the house's fenceless backyards. With no other leads and the trust for an animal's instinct above his own, the man follows. He steps into the yard, and there the three foxes sit on their haunches in a semi-circle, blocking his immediate view, sniffing curiously at something atop the snow. When he approaches, the foxes all look up at the man before returning to what's far more interesting.

Lying before them is Mable's body. He falls to his knees, and where terrible, violent emotions should have overtaken his body, the man is instead rendered numb. His thoughts evaporate. There will be a time much later where the man is thankful for this reaction as opposed to any other. He supposes that to react appropriately would have meant dying at that very moment. Nothing else but total dissociation could have kept his heart from breaking in two.

Her amber eyes are closed, and if focusing only on her little black and red head, the man can imagine she is sleeping. What exists of the rest of her is immediately banished from memory. The man will never recall it again. He reaches out his hand and strokes her face. He massages her ear. It is the first time he has ever touched her. She was once a warm and beautiful animal, and she is still beautiful. Her fur is soft and sleek, and his hand begins to tremble as his body recognizes the flood of agony that is yet to sunder his mind.

The foxes look on as he tucks his arms beneath her body. Despite what those monsters did to her, and despite what now runs down his chest, staining the whole of his front, the man holds her tight and cradles her like an infant. Things are so much smaller in death. His partner. His little friend. No noise escapes his throat; no words are spoken. The man walks away as the foxes sniff at the tainted snow. He returns the way he came, through the woodlands, over felled giants and babbling creeks. Overhead the birds sing, not in mourning and not in cheer, but in the way that all things only need to be heard and known. It is a long walk back. The man travels slowly and carefully, unwilling to loosen his caress, and through the bushes and trees other animals look up, smelling what covers him, what drenches his clothing like fresh and vibrant paint, but they only stare, even the predators, for this one is claimed, and nothing can ever have her. Nothing will ever touch her again.

The man arrives back at the home. He places her body down in the front yard and retrieves the shovel used once before. He digs with great effort, tearing into soil hardened by freezing temperatures. He digs without pause and without a sound, until the sun climbs high into the sky and then begins to sink again, and once the red-gold rays bathe the earth, her grave is finished. He picks Mable up and strokes her fur and kisses her cold head, then slowly lowers her into the hole. Like putting her to bed for a long and peaceful slumber. There is no animal in the world more worthy of rest. He takes up the shovel and refills the hole, providing her with a blanket of warm earth. When the grave is filled, he collects heavy stones and places them atop the soil. The man steps back and looks upon the twin graves, side by side forevermore. They will never be alone again. No two animals are more deserving of that.

He sits on the front steps of the house for a long time. Watching. It isn't until the sun shrinks beneath the horizon and stars begin to bloom from the black sky that he realizes what he was looking for. So he walks inside, turns off the lights, and lies down on the living room couch.

The man sleeps for a very long time. He sleeps through the night, through the next day, and into the night again. The dreams come and come and come, and they do not bother him. They are no worse than what inevitably awaits.

He is tired. More tired than he's ever been. And so the man decides to keep sleeping. Until he's not tired anymore.

The man rarely leaves the house any longer. Sometimes when the weather proves to be milder than most days, he will sit down on the frosted grass beside the graves. He will tell the little dog the story of its life, and Mable listens, and he tells her that they would have been wonderful friends. He tells the little dog all the adventures he and Mable had, and the little dog listens too. The man says that he hopes they've met, wherever they are. Then he goes back inside, drinks water from the tap, and sometimes eats. Most times he does not. Whatever mass and muscle accumulated has since withered.

He no longer walks to the library. He tried only once, and the moment he sat down with a novel there was a glaring absence. An empty corner or an empty chair. And so he left and never returned. The man no longer listens to records. Music only reminds him of the bedroom and what it once contained, and that in turn reminds him of other things. The house is silent during all hours, until night falls and the shadowy things return, and their terrific sounds don't bother the man. Sometimes a powerful urge to open the glass sliding door washes over him, and it takes a few moments to talk himself out of it. There is no logical reason not to, and so eventually his instinctual fear grasps hold of his throat and screams. It screams until its volume is louder than the beings outside, and only then does the man relent. He thinks about death often, but again comes the fear that somehow death will be even worse, though he believes at his very core that this cannot be true, for that would mean believing the same about Mable. And he knows that she is safe. He knows she is in a better place. The man finally understands the utopian concept of Heaven. It is not for oneself. It is not to dampen one's own fear. It is to find comfort in that empty space where someone once resided.

Each night when the creatures shriek and claw at the walls, the man revels in their sounds. They are all that keep him awake. At one time, he had become very good at falling asleep in spite of the cacophony. But now he hangs on to each discordant howl, allowing it to seep inside his head and smash against the confines of his skull until his ears ring. It is a terribly painful experience, and it keeps him from dreaming. With time the horrors of waking life subsided, no matter how much he desired them to remain, but man's mental constitution is a stubbornly adaptive thing. Eventually, his body emerged from the furthest depths of its malaise, and the nightmares that were once a welcome distraction grew to be too much. Now the man wishes for anything but to sleep and has become adept at staving off exhaustion, instead balancing atop a tenuous state between the conscious and unconscious where he is neither awake nor asleep but floating within an insomnia-induced hypnosis.

His nightmares are not of things he imagines to be typical. He does not see Mable, and he does not find himself trapped in the bedroom, clawing at the walls as the little dog once did. They do not feel like dreams at all, in fact. They are quite lifelike, and this is what makes them much more disturbing. At times, they feel more real, more lucid than the waking life he surely inhabits. The man dreams about people. He dreams about very mundane things, things he has no recollection of whatsoever, imaginary scenarios that his mind couldn't possibly have created out of nowhere. He dreams of walking down the street with a woman. He dreams of sitting in an office, tapping on a computer. He dreams of sitting in a park watching children throw a ball back and forth. He dreams of sitting alone in an apartment staring at a white ceiling. Nothing unordinary occurs. The ceiling doesn't melt away into a fantastical, violent scene from one of his novels. The children don't atrophy into walking skeletons. The people he passes on the street don't look upon him with twisted faces like ghouls. There is nothing at all about these dreams that is frightening in any logical sense. But despite this, each and every time he enters a dream, the man is overtaken by profound horror. It's a kind of fear he has never before experienced, not brought on by the dream's events but there all the same, perpendicular to the mundanities. He cannot make sense of it, and he does not wish to. The man only wishes to not dream at all. And so, perhaps exactly because of this wish, the dreams persist. Each night the events become more mundane, more trivial and detailed, and the inexplicable terror he feels as the events play out grows more and more intense.

He can feel the city's tendrils reaching into his brainstem, speaking to him in tongues. It tells him to stay, to join his siblings. He has nothing left. Its children slaughtered his only friend, kept her from the pyre just for him to find in retaliation for his insistent survival, to taunt him, and he is alone. You don't want to be alone, do you? Not forever, it whispers. Why do this? Why fight it? Step into the shadows, and you will never be alone again. It's such an easy thing to do. I will guide you. I will talk to you the whole way. It will be painless, and it will be bliss. You will never feel fear. You will live forever. I will wrap you in my warm and comforting and familiar embrace. You will have everything you'll ever need, everything you could ever imagine, as long as you stay. As long as you never leave. So stay. Stay where it's safe, with brothers and sisters, and a world of lesser things on which to feed and satiate your every desire. You'll want for nothing. You'll live like a king. You need only kneel to me. Me, and nothing else.

The city speaks until the hypnosis dissolves into sleep and the sleep into nightmares and nightmares into the morning light. Again and again and again.

But soon the snow will melt. The cold will thaw. Soon, the season will turn. And the man is stubborn. He is a human being, after all.

His plan has not changed.

When his heart stops, the last thing he sees will not be the rooftops of metal beasts. When his body decays, it will not seep through the cracks of an empty concrete road. His eyes will look upon the green canopy of an ancient oak. His body will dissolve into the forest's soil.

He will never be alone again.

One day the snow stops. The weather warms, and the vast, white blanket melts into the sewer grates. And it begins to rain. This happens suddenly and without warning. One day it was dry and cold and sunny. Then it was not. The rain falls and does not stop falling. It rains for many days in a row that turn to weeks, and the man begins to wonder if a great flood is coming. He wonders about the animals in the forest. He imagines them nestling together beneath the sighing oaks, listening to the rain dance across the leaves. He too listens to the rain. Most of his days are spent beside the sliding door, his face pressed against the glass, looking up at the gray and black clouds. The rain patters across the roof, and it slows his heartbeat. The rain slows everything. Time can't catch the plummeting drops; they are too fast and too many. And so time too relaxes its grip. Day blends into the night, the sun doesn't come out, and the man is content. This contentment is the closest to happiness he has felt since her death. He begins to have more energy. Not much, but enough to lumber back and forth to the kitchen and to the bathroom and back to the couch.

The dark clouds and the rain are exactly what the man needs. Nothing is more difficult than depression on a bright and cloudless day. It only breeds guilt and self-loathing. The man would chide himself for not having the strength to go outside, to feel the sunlight with the rest of creation. And so he would lie beneath a blanket and ceiling, waiting for the sun to set so the colors of the world would finally match the dull shades of gray inside his head. But the rain and the darkness it brings soothes his illness. The rain gives him permission to cry, and sometimes he does. Sometimes, he buries his head in the pillow and breathes heavily, violently, until the torrent is released, and like the rain, his tears wash away the filth and grime that's been allowed to fester in the darkest recesses for far too long. When it's done, his mind feels lighter. It feels clean. The filth and mold will regrow, but for a time at least there is a pocket of clarity. In this clarity, he finds whatever solace can be attained, for however long, and the man gets up to sit by the glass door again watching the rain soak into the grass and dirt. He watches the earthworms rise from the ground like squirming miracles. He watches new life bloom in the soil. Little yellow flowers.

Winter is retreating, and the Earth still lives. A rebirth is coming, and soon there will be new leaves and new infants huddled beside their mothers inside caves and beds of fresh foliage. The city still exists, but it cannot destroy like it once did. It is a sedentary beast, dead in every aspect but its shadows which survive like ticks upon a deer's belly. It cannot reproduce any longer but only kill that which does. Nature continues on.

One day, the man will step outside and see great, snaking vines coiling around the skyscrapers and herds of elk grazing on the flora erupting from the concrete cracks. One day, the man will return to the garden and find the seed once planted to be a sapling, and that sapling will in turn grow fruit. And he will see what he already knows to be true. Until then, he watches the rain fall from behind the sliding door, tracing pictures along its cool, glass body. He hopes it never stops raining. The man hopes it rains until the whole city is underwater and coral reefs like cities unto themselves develop throughout the skeletons of steel behemoths. He hopes the sea comes alive and swallows this patch of cancer and the shadowy things drown. Despite the malaise, and despite the anger, he doesn't even wish their deaths to be painful. He simply wishes it to happen. As quickly as possible. The man will build a boat like Noah, and he will invite every living thing on Earth into its hull, and together what remains of the planet will sail the ever-rising sea until its waters pierce the atmosphere. Until it spills out across the universe and there are only stars above. The man will look down over the bow, and he will see reflected in those miles and miles of pure blue ocean the very same stars, alive and dead and dying, all burning as bright as in that fading memory of a past life now found again. The water will carry them all away, across the empty void of the universe, until one day they will finally reach those very stars, and he will witness that even in death the ancient constellations are as beautiful here as they were from that distant pale blue dot.

When the thunder comes, he counts the seconds until those vivid flashes ignite the darkness, and now even the screams and howls of the shadowy things are muffled by the Earth's might. He hopes they cower in terror of such strength. He hopes they wander aimlessly, the sheets of rain soaking through their amorphous forms, cold and afraid and confused, unable to find a single living thing to slaughter and provide to a dying god. For their pyres will remain unlit, and no felled trees will need to submit to the flames they cannot bring about beneath the many tears from above. Those evil, benign things will finally understand the helplessness felt by their countless victims.

The man prays that their great eldritch architect is as psychotic as he believes It to be, for then they will be smote for their failure, for their sacrilege, and maybe, finally, the shadowy things will know of the pain without mercy they so callously dole out.

The man hopes it never stops raining, that the thunder never relents. He hopes the city learns of its enemy, of the inescapable repercussions of this war it declared by existing at all.

The man is awoken from a nap. Rain and thunder erupt outside, but a different sound, a small sound, is what woke him. Only something very separate from the typical cacophony could have roused him from slumber. The violent weather is now so familiar that it's simply become white noise. He opens his eyes and waits to hear the screams and howls, and upon hearing nothing of the sort, he understands that it's still daytime. The shadowy things have turned into a kind of alarm clock. With the ongoing storms, it can be difficult to ascertain the time when darkness is near constant, especially through the fog of another nightmare. So, if the man opens his eyes and the world is black and gray but the screams and frantic claws have not yet arrived at his doorstep, then he knows it was just another tired sojourn to speed the day along. The man doesn't wish to sleep during the day, as he really doesn't wish to sleep at all anymore, but a mind in the throes of grief requires it even if the body does not.

He sits up on the couch and listens. waiting for the sound to appear again. Thunder growls overhead like wild beasts, rain drums along the roof, and lightning strikes in the distance, briefly painting the living room in vivid yellow, casting ghostly shadows across the walls, and the man listens. He turns and looks through the glass door, but shadows pervade, and nothing appears but the undulating abyss. It must be late. Somewhere behind the clouds the sun is setting, but its light can't pierce the great, black wall in the sky. If he were a smarter man, then perhaps he could decipher the shadows' lengths like tea leaves, but as it is nothing is certain until the sun reveals itself anew.

But finally, there it is again, a noise so small that it has a shape—pathetic and shrill and desperate. Then a bump against the glass door. The man leans over the couch and peers into the backyard. Nothing, of course. The darkness persists. A battle of instinct and logic overtakes the man. He knows this sound can't possibly be that of a shadowy thing, but the animals long ago absconded into the woods, taking shelter from the storm. He hasn't heard or seen anything in weeks. Only skyborne explosions and flashes of light. It has been a very solitary period of mourning. The bump comes again, softly, followed by scratches upon the glass and a tiny cry like an infant. The man stands and approaches the sliding door, crouches down, and presses his face against the cold surface. Something is alive out there, barely. It's a cry of terrible fear.

He and this thing stare at one another through the glass. No lights are on inside the house, so he knows they are equally blind but are nonetheless aware of the other's presence. Then the thunderous boom comes, and the man waits. He counts in his head. One, two, three, four, five. On five, lightning strikes and the whole world lights up. Like a glimpse at Heaven. In that glimpse, the backyard comes alive—the trees and the grass and the falling rain—and tucked into a corner, pressed against the glass, shivering beneath the thin, wooden canopy, he sees it. Yellow eyes and white teeth and a pink tongue, just disembodied features in the dark as it relents another cry. A small cat. A living animal. Trembling and soaked wet. Alone and alive. Somehow alive.

Without thought, the man wrenches open the door, and the tiny, dripping creature darts inside and swivels its head in a panic before zeroing in on the couch and diving beneath. Stunned, the man stands there with the open door, the rain wetting the carpet, before his mind finally processes what just occurred and he slides it shut.

He can hear the cat breathing heavily beneath the couch. It seems to be hyperventilating. Not knowing what to do and still reeling from the abruptness of the encounter, the man sits down cross-legged on the floor. He keeps his distance from the couch, allowing the animal to adjust, to learn that it's safe. How it's alive at all the man can't begin to fathom. Though it's fast, he knows that much. All he could catch was a black blur. A long, bushy tail, leaving a trail of wet droplets. Then gone.

The man sits very still until night comes, and the screams and howls emerge from the shadows, but he doesn't care. He doesn't need to care. He's safe. And so too is the cat. That will take time, though. It will need to adjust to those horrific sounds from a new perspective, from within a guarded home. Even the man needed that. It takes time to realize one is finally safe. Such a foreign thing—safety. One never really does acclimate to that. He hasn't. Here, in this city, in the world in which he lives, safety is an illusion to be honed and believed in like a religion. Because you're never really safe. You're merely staving off danger. Here, safety is akin to the stars in the night sky, and danger, death, and terror is the darkness around which those stars burn. Eventually, the darkness will swallow it all. But even the dead stars still burn from a distance, and herein lies the importance of illusion. The importance in the belief that you are safe. It counts for something. It still staves off the dark.

When the man can no longer keep his eyes open and he begins to slump against the wall, he stands up and walks carefully to the kitchen. He finds a shallow bowl, fills it with tap water, and rifles through the pantry until he finds a can of tuna tucked far in the back. He peels open the lid and glances over his shoulder to watch for any movement but detects none. He then empties part of the can onto a ceramic plate, carries the bowl and plate towards the couch, and leaves each on the floor.

If he stays away then maybe the cat will emerge, if only to take a bite of food and lap at the water for a brief moment before returning to its hiding spot. So, the man exits the living room and crouches down in the hallway next to the closed door that will forever remain so. He tucks his knees into his chest, and slowly, fitfully, falls asleep.

It will take time. But that's okay. Because suddenly, the man has all the time in the world. Spring is coming. That little cat is alive beneath the couch, out of the cold and the rain. The stars now burn a little brighter, a little longer. And the night is not quite as dark as it used to be.

The cat takes a week to accept that the man isn't here to hurt it. Slowly, for minutes at a time, it emerges from beneath the couch, its slender body pressed to the ground, eyes narrow and yellow, and shuffles along the carpet, more like some serpentine thing than a feline. It looks up at the man as he watches from across the room, its triangular ears pinned back, and the man can't help but think of Mable. Though any animal will do this now. He won't be able to help that. The cat then sniffs at the food and water and hovers over the meal with its eyes still focused on the man until he looks away, and only then does it eat and drink. Then, as suddenly as it emerged, it darts back beneath the couch to tremble until falling asleep. It doesn't purr or meow. It's a very quiet animal, though that does not last for long.

After three days of cohabitation, the cat begins to stalk around the house, still ignoring the man but for a hesitant glance before sauntering between his legs towards fascinating new discoveries. It quickly learns to jump onto the counter and proudly stares at the man until he nods and turns on the sink faucet. He learns that it much prefers to drink from running water than from the bowl. The animal surely had developed the instinct living outside—to never drink from a stagnant pool—but it's also a game more than anything. It laps at the water for a moment but then soon begins to paw at the steady stream, batting with a cautious determination to catch this stubborn, wet thing. Its chest is then soaked and glistening, and the cat happily leaps off the counter, trots back to the living room, and lifts itself onto the couch where it grooms and purrs until falling asleep. All the while, the man watches, respecting the animal's space. It's a tentative game of patience.

Only once he's certain the cat is fast asleep does the man creep closer and sit down. He stares at the little black ball. Its tail is longer than its body, and the cat curls its tail and uses it as a pillow beneath its chin. When the dark clouds again blot out the sun, it becomes just another shadow cast in the room, a thick, jet-black coat of fur and brilliant yellow eyes. It's as if this mysterious, resourceful animal had been born from out of the lightning and darkness under which it first arrived. It's very small. Not a kitten but certainly no adult. It is the first cat he's seen alive. Until now, the man has only found charred bodies upon the pyres. This cat is a miracle. Something otherworldly, divinely blessed. He can think of no other reason for its survival.

The man begins to play music again. He keeps the volume low and sticks to lonely piano pieces. The cat seems to find that agreeable. It will open its eyes, narrow slits that scan the room, but then promptly returns to sleep. It likes Chopin's *Nocturnes* the best—Arthur Rubenstein's 1967 rendition. The moment his piano dances across the living room, whether awake or asleep, the cat begins to purr louder than before, vibrating, its breaths deeper and slower.

Sometimes, the cat rolls over in its sleep and stretches, extending its long limbs as dirt-caked claws protract. There are no signs of scarring or fresh wounds. It's a boy. Naturally, the man names him Arthur. Beautiful, resourceful Arthur.

When Arthur awakes, he demands to be let out, scratching at the sliding glass door, and if it's still daylight the man allows it. If it's not raining too hard, Arthur goes off to hunt and relieve himself and whatever else it was he used to do, but each evening as the sun bleeds warm colors through the windows, Arthur returns. Sometimes with a field mouse between his jaws and sometimes alone. If he arrives with a kill, the man opens the door and Arthur saunters inside, plops the dead, bloodied animal at his feet and stares up, waiting for approval or perhaps a hint of jealousy. The man nods and reaches out his hand for Arthur to sniff, and Arthur then picks up the mouse and retreats beneath the couch where he eats. Though if he returns alone, Arthur is in no mood to engage in niceties. He sprints past the man the moment the door opens and hides under the couch for a time, silent. If he is in a good mood—if he's fed—Arthur sleeps atop the couch, and when in a bad mood Arthur sleeps in the dark confines beneath. Either way, Arthur sleeps more than anything. And the man likes that just fine. As long as he doesn't wish to leave at night, the man doesn't care what Arthur does. Arthur is not his pet. They are two animals sharing the safety of an enclosed haven.

After seven days, Arthur allows the man to sleep alongside him on the couch. It began as an experiment. His back ached and his body was stiff, so one night he sat down on the couch where Arthur slept, all curled up with his chin atop that bushy, black tail. Arthur opened his eyes to slits, lazily acknowledged the man, and closed his eyes again. The man then leaned back against the padded arm, tucked his knees against his chest, and fell asleep. When he awoke in the dead of night, jolting up with sweat dousing his face, hyperventilating through the already fading memory of another nightmare, he looked down at his rigid body and saw a purring shadow coiled atop his stomach. The man reached out his arm and laid a hand on Arthur's vibrating haunches until the gentle sensation reached through to the center of his heart. He closed his eyes and fell back asleep.

Since then, the nightmares don't come quite as often. And when they do, Arthur awakes to the man's screams and crawls closer, nuzzling his face against the man's, pressing his paws into his chest. While the thunder rages and lightning erupts across the sky, and the agonized screams of those shadowy things perforate the drumming rain upon the roof, any fear that once paralyzed the man melts away into the purrs. The purrs grow louder and louder until they are no different than the thunder outside. They muffle the screeches and howls, and together Arthur and the man drift back into a warm emptiness. He does not dream again.

The cat appears, by necessity, to be diurnal. While Arthur sleeps all the time, he remains fast asleep throughout the night. He never paws at the glass door, cheerfully ignorant of the terrible sounds and presence that awaits outside. It's a great relief to the man but not a surprise. Arthur is keenly intelligent, otherwise he wouldn't be here. He is well aware of the danger stalking through the abyss, but most interesting to the man is that Arthur doesn't seem bothered by the sounds. The shadowy things never relent until the earliest morning hours, and yet the cat remains peaceful. The cries don't wrestle him from his sleep, and they don't cause him to jump or yowl. He just ignores them. The man can't help but imagine the horrific tribulations this cat has gone through to achieve such a Zen-like state. But watching Arthur purr atop his chest, merely another shadow in the dark, as the creatures hunt and torture and release such impossible sounds beneath the moon, the man slowly finds himself too acclimating to what he once never believed he could.

When the thunder and rain fail to subside for days at a time, not wanting to brave the torrential downpour and the cold, Arthur grows restless. He yowls and chitters and becomes more animated than the man can handle. His fur bristles and his back arches, and Arthur's expression becomes that of a deranged creature, pupils dilated until the vivid yellow is relegated to thin crescents. With nowhere exactly to place his energy, the cat begins darting back and forth all throughout the house, emitting little noises like a failing car engine. He leaps up and scratches the walls and then collapses onto his back, rolling around and swatting at imaginary prey. The man will try to alleviate Arthur's cabin fever by playing along, balling up a wad of toilet paper to throw for the cat, but he's a stubborn thing. Arthur has no interest in anything the man concocts, as though a reassertion of his fierce independence. Whether it be a crinkled-up piece of paper or a toilet roll, the moment the man throws it, Arthur will only stare at the object and return to destroying whatever's within arm's reach. Any piece of furniture is fair game, and in the three weeks before spring finally reveals itself, everything that was once so well-upholstered and maintained has been decimated. Bits of soft, fluffy material litter the carpet, and claw marks decorate the couch and the walls and the ottomans and chairs. Arthur no longer sleeps beneath the couch at all, for it's become a mass graveyard of mice skeletons and mangled corpses. The man isn't bothered. It's not his house. And with the reemergence of the sun and colorful flowers blooming in the bushes alongside the street, he knows that the final move is soon approaching.

While he is still apprehensive about such a life-changing migration, the man is now more certain than ever. He needs only to visit a few stores, collect a few things—necessities and nothing more. Then he will be ready to leave for the woods. Though now Arthur is here, and that complicates things. Whether or not it's the right thing to do, the man has made up his mind that he won't abandon the cat. Arthur will simply have to come with. It may even be the case that Arthur once, perhaps even quite recently, lived in those very woods. He finds it hard to believe that his friend could have survived all this time in the city alone. So, the newest predicament is how best to bring the cat along.

The man thought for a while on the possibility of leaving Arthur behind, but that would mean closing him off from the house, and whether or not the cat would accept this reality, he has grown accustomed to the safety and warmth it provides. The man imagines if he were to leave Arthur behind, locking the door and setting off alone, that his cat would come back to the glass door, pawing and meowing helplessly until finally realizing what's occurred, forced to survive alone again without warning. That thought brings with it so much pain and guilt that it's just not an option. No, Arthur is coming. Because Arthur will want to come. If a man will feel safe in the woods then a cat surely born there will be even safer. It's not his right to make this decision, but it's not his right to take away the cat's new home either. And the house is his home. Either way, he will need to adjust. Whether he likes it or not, the man accepted a grave responsibility by opening the door on that stormy afternoon. These are the repercussions of that decision. A life is now in his hands. And when the situation is viewed through this lens, the answer becomes much simpler.

In the next few days, before setting off into the city for supplies, the man tries various methods of transportation with Arthur. He opens up his satchel, empties its contents, and lines the inside with a soft towel. Arthur sniffs it disinterestedly but soon hops inside. The moment the man picks up the satchel, Arthur begins to yowl, his ears pinned back in that familiar display of uncertainty, but there he remains. The man then tests out this arrangement by stepping outside where together they stroll around the block, and all the while Arthur pokes out his head, peering curiously at the new flowers and freshly green trees. This seems to work, though after long enough Arthur grows restless, never one to remain in place unless asleep, and he soon climbs out of the satchel, up the man's arm, and perches atop his shoulder. This is where Arthur stays for the duration of their many anticipatory walks. Together, they are like a witch and his familiar or a pirate captain and his parrot, and the man can't help but grin as he reaches up to stroke Arthur's ears while they walk past grazing does with their new infants.

Life is returning everywhere he looks. The neighborhood is vibrant with color and the scent of lavender and clean air, and only off in the far distance is that tall patch of black and gray that will soon be forever hidden by great oaks as far as the eye can see. The man feels his spirits rising, energy returning in great bounds. Arthur too becomes excited for their daily walks, hopping right inside the satchel like a memorized protocol before of course climbing atop the man's shoulder once again.

Things are good. There is much to be excited about now, though the man doesn't think about it. He only takes in the images that surround them and listens to his friend's purrs and curious sounds. But that's how he knows that some hazy kind of contentment has returned. He hardly thinks at all.

The man opens the sliding glass door to let Arthur hunt for the day. The sun hasn't yet risen over the trees, but the man is wide awake. He's been waking earlier and earlier, energized by the warmth and light of spring, and regardless of whether Arthur was dead asleep moments before, if the man is up, then so too is he. Today is a big day. While Arthur stalks through bushes and chases birds, the man will be heading to the department store in the city center. Everything he needs will be there, and he has the short list memorized. Come tomorrow, they will set off together for the woods.

The man has had many conversations with Arthur over the last few days, explaining the plan as he cleans himself and purrs. He understands this is a fruitless endeavor, but it still helps to assuage his own worry and fear, and maybe somewhere deep within the little cat's brain Arthur understands at least the weight of the gibberish spoken. But that is the amazing flexibility of other animals: They need no preparation for new things. New things are simply thrust upon them each day, and they adapt accordingly. The more the man thinks about it, he realizes that this strenuous level of forethought and planning may well be humanity's biggest weakness. We conjure specters of things that don't yet exist, creating monsters out of harmless shadows, while an animal sees the world around it precisely and only as it is. Those shadows are just that—shadows. The man oftentimes believes that if he were to silence his mind to the best of his ability and follow Arthur around, observing the language of his reactions to all things mundane and otherwise, soon he may reach a kind of enlightenment. It's a fine line between the simplicity of mind and bliss, but it takes only a few moments with Arthur to know quite well that his cat is not simple. He is a complex and intelligent little thing, far more intelligent in certain matters than the man could ever be. The biggest chasm between the man and his cat is in the way they process fear. This, he's learned, is the root of their separate woes. Arthur's fears are reactionary. Anxiety does not play a part in his thought process, as it serves no real purpose. In stark contrast, the man's mind is run primarily by that fear of the unknown—so much so that when real danger does arrive, his body tends to seize up, already far too overwhelmed by the anxious preparation for those very instances.

The more time the man has spent without the company of his own species, the more often he's struck with terrific wonder at the fact that humanity thrived at all. In almost every sense, his species was ill-suited for the tribulations of Earth, like an alien species beamed down without due diligence beforehand. And so he thinks we survived as long as we did, not in that adaptive way that other animals have, but much in a similar manner to a persistent cockroach. It is difficult to kill masses of people effectively. In a twisted kind of cosmic irony, only humans themselves had mastered that elusive practice. But even nuclear war couldn't have eradicated us all. There would always be survivors, crawling out from beneath the flames and rubble, ready as ever to repopulate and begin the cycle anew until its inevitable, ever-repeating conclusion. Whatever it was that caused his species to disappear must have been a true masterstroke of annihilative genius. If it hadn't already occurred, the man would have never believed it possible.

The walk towards the city is long and slow. He need not rush and takes the time to stop every once in a while to study the violet morning glories that have bloomed from the vines coiling around lampposts. Not since Mable's death has he ventured past the few square blocks around the house, and after those weeks of heavy rain watering the earth and the hot sun now bathing the flora in light and warmth, a great metamorphosis has occurred in his absence. Much of the streets are sundered, and from within the cracks tulips and sunflowers have begun to bloom. Patches of green weeds and bright white dandelions have crawled from the woodlands across the sidewalk, swallowing up that flat, gray surface as if annexing the city's far territories and claiming it for the Green. He continues on, and the closer he gets to downtown, the more evidence of an obtuse kind of battle reveals itself. Buildings that were once untouched have been damaged, their windows shattered by long, stretching tree boughs that now reach across the length of the roads he traverses. Natural shade persists over-head, as many trees on either side of the avenues now lean towards each other like lovers on opposite ends of a wide and empty canyon. But so too has nature taken casualties. Vines lie severed in dense piles along the storefronts like dead snakes, and trees mangled and felled by unearthly tools are stacked atop one another at the concrete's edge, some propped up by the thick, gnarled roots of their ilk that still stand.

A war was fought as the man dawdled with his grief alone. Things are stirring. Terrible and violent things. His thoughts drift to the mysterious tome found in that desolate, dreamlike cathedral. The city is waking, and it is angry and afraid. The man particularly knows this last sentiment to be true, for if this is a war of attrition, the Green is taking ground. And so there is no better time to leave. Whatever eldritch forces are at play, the man can do nothing but escape the frontlines where he now resides. But the fear that arises from this revelation soon dims, as with each step taken, more and more fauna appear, chittering and grazing and sauntering about with little care for the surrounding wreckage. He imagines they must view it all as a citizen of an invading country may regard the decimation of their enemies' land. It is nothing but the collateral that comes with the enaction of a righteous cause. A family of black bears clambers atop a rotting log laid across the street, onward towards whatever is in this moment more important. Birds perch in rows along powerlines, cawing and cackling, eyeing the new grass for signs of movement. Nothing can be done but that which takes immediate precedent. What a freeing thing to be so singularly aware.

Farther into the city's bowels, however, the man soon finds himself alone. Though the sun shines and afternoon light still glints off the windows of skyscrapers towering overhead, it grows darker and darker. Their long shadows blanket the streets, and as the man looks this way and that, he can find no other signs of life. The gentle cacophony of birdsongs and various ululations had without warning ceased, as if the man had stepped through an invisible barrier that no one else dared cross. A worrying silence settles across the empty roads until all the man hears is his own accelerating heartbeat. But it is daytime still, and he has never known danger to exist while the sky is bright and blue, and what he's come here for is more important than anything else. He must remain singularly focused, blind to the hallucinations wont to appear in these shadowy corners.

Though upon reaching the cross street where the department store looms, a terrible realization comes: the power has gone out. As far as he can see in all directions, there is no electricity. The windows have become glimmering black mirrors reflecting his own disheveled image, and the once buzzing neon signs linger silent and lifeless. The whole block is a shifting funhouse, taunting the man with a hundred doppelgangers wherever he looks. Pieces of the forest had reached this place, but whatever foothold was gained was quickly severed. The weeds and flowers that once grew through the concrete sit limp and gray, withered as if by sheer unwillingness to live. It's a different kind of death that looms here, like a sudden plague had struck, wiping out the plants and humanity's lingering imprint alike. Only the buildings remain as reanimated skeletons, devoid of a pulse. Twisted, steel leviathans that no longer belong to humanity at all. They are the sentries for something else now. Something greater.

That unfamiliar name circles his mind. Before his lips can form the words seared into his memory, the man banishes the thought and presses forward into the dark and cavernous store. Deeper into the bowels, into the dried veins of an ancient god slowly waking from its long and restless slumber.

Each step echoes with hollow clangs. The man moves slowly through the wide and dark aisles, far too aware of the uncanny nature of this place. Dead vines stretch across the floors, squelching beneath his boots, and an ecosystem of gray moss patches have grown over the mannequins like some foreign infection. He makes great effort to keep the list of items at the front of his mind: hiking backpack, tent, sleeping bag, matches, first aid, hunting knife, rifle, bullets, hardy clothes. That's everything. Then in and out. Anything else the woods can supply.

Hardest to bear is the thought of killing an animal for its meat, but the man is well aware of the hypocrisy. He walks past the first area of the store—mostly women's clothes best suited for summer weather and casual outings, of no use for this endeavor—and into the groceries section, where laid out on displays and behind glass doors is a world of rotting meats. The stench fills the wide room and causes him to gag. It was never an issue for the man to consume this prepackaged flesh. Others did the awful, bloody work: slaughtering, field dressing, skinning. The man never had to contend with this reality. By the time it was placed in his satchel or sitting cooked and brown atop his plate, it was easy to separate the meal from the sentient thing it used to be. That business was for others. Someone had to look a pig in the eyes, perhaps aware of its frightening intelligence or perhaps not, and condemn it to death in a manner more in line with torture than anything else. But not the man. He only had to hold the slab of meat in his hands and regard it as just that. Now as he walks the aisles, observing the gray and green film glistening across the severed body parts, the man must now contend with what is to come. He will have to end lives to survive. This is just the way of the world. Vegetarianism felt good as an altruistic fantasy, but as long as the city lulled him into this other kind of fantasy—this cognitive distance between him and the animal that once was—he could go on eating meat without ever processing the violent business that was necessary for this bounty to magically arrive at his fingertips. The blunt answer that cannot be avoided is simply that it is easy. Ease had allowed the man to forgo his own morals and beliefs, to separate a life from the nourishment of its body once containing a mind. It frightens the man to think how much of himself he sacrificed in the name of convenience and sloth. Even in an empty city, the man never changed his habits. Even as the last living man, he continued on existing as a modern human, content to never part with the aspects of himself still so separate from the rest of the world. He could blame the city. He could blame the crumbling remnants of a civilization still quite able to feed his stubborn lifestyle, but this too is simply too easy. It's the man's fault, and he will have only himself to blame when he hesitates upon finding that first buck in his rifle's scope, when he vomits as the knife spills its warm guts across the grass. But that is his burden, borne of his inability to adapt.

The man stops to stare at the festering meat—at the gray-green flesh of dead pigs and cows and chickens and turkeys—and contends with his failure. He wishes more than anything to be just another part of the Earth, to find some balance as his species never had, and yet despite this, he never once made the effort to break the shackles of modernity—the sole thing keeping that balance from occurring. He sleeps in houses powered by magic he doesn't bother to understand, eating food he doesn't bother to hunt or forage himself, regarding wild animals as pets instead of equals. Mable would still be alive. If he could have avoided the human urge to domesticate that which should not be, his beautiful Mable would still be alive. The little dog wouldn't have rotted alone and afraid in a locked room. The man is the last living human, and so he has no choice but to accept the sins of his entire vanished species. At his very core, he hates what he is. He hates that he allowed his life to continue on unimpeded, unchanged. And so he must leave. He must. And if the woods are unaccepting of such a foreign being and he cannot bear to survive in a manner like every other living thing on the planet, then it is only right that it should be the woods that revoke his right to live. It is a test as much as it is a chance. There's no true contentment in a life without challenge, and the man has done his utmost to avoid that very thing, all the while blaming the city for providing the mutated bounty he's so happily accepted.

He continues past the meat aisles and into the produce section and laughs. The fruits and vegetables have finally withered into nothing but clumps of brown, liquified mush. All this time of eating packaged chips and candy and meat, and the man was so frightened of the only natural thing in the store. They had continued living for so long, like artificial things miming the natural, and so the man refused to touch them. Now, seeing the produce in its current state, the man finds a macabre irony. They existed like everything else, ripe and ready to eat all the while until the lights went out, and the man refused because he couldn't fathom how they survived. Out of all the foreign things put into his body, all those things he never understood—the fruits and vegetables died untouched. If only they had better packaging. If only they had more preservatives.

Up the broken escalator, the man comes to the beauty section. Beyond that lies the electronics. Now two equally useless places. He thinks for a moment about finding an electric shaver and some batteries to shear his head and face. But what's the point? It will grow back. There was a time when his self-worth was closely related to his appearance and hygiene, but with no one to witness the effort, he soon grew tired of the rituals. He told himself at first that it was only for his own confidence, as an effort towards self-care, but of course that was a lie that quickly lost strength. It was always only for others. With nothing but animals as witnesses, he soon grew comfortable with however he outwardly presented himself. They didn't care what he wore or whether he washed that day or not. The animals feel the same way about themselves, and he finds them as beautiful as anything on Earth. Beyond basic hygiene to keep oneself from infection, he now finds no purpose in any of it. He wonders sometimes about how he conducted himself in the presence of others. If he was once a jovial person. If he was attractive to women. If he was well-dressed and confident. If he was a good public speaker, giving toasts at weddings and eulogies at funerals. He doesn't know. He doesn't remember. And so that too doesn't matter anymore.

His dreams have become more vivid, though the images they play remain as mundane as always, and to the same effect. Where he before started to think that they were perhaps memories of the life he had, the man now believes differently. They are too varied. It's as though he's experiencing the lives of many different people. In each dream, he does not feel like himself but as if he's inhabiting another. And each life, whether affluent or poor, social or isolated, fills him with the same terror. The dreams too seem to come to him as siren songs, beckoning him to recall that existence that once was, filled with romance and duty and day-to-day experiences with others of his species, taunting him in the hope that he may grow to yearn for it. But always the opposite result is achieved. He feels as though these dreams are coming from a different source; they are not his own mind's creation but some kind of one-way communication towards an uncertain end. Perhaps this is why the images breed such fear. Somewhere within his subconscious, the man can tell they are borne of a foreign source.

The man stalks through the aisles of makeup and nose trimmers and hair growth products and idles to stare at the various cardboard cutouts of unfamiliar celebrities holding up the newest supplement, their faces now obscured by dead moss and wilted flowers. Everywhere he looks there are advertisements, and in all these advertisements the celebrities grin with perfect, painfully white teeth, their whole cardboard being glowing with conventional beauty. He understands the purpose. It's a simple thing, marketing, breeding want and loneliness if a certain dream can't be achieved. It's not about needing the product but needing not to feel the absence of that product and what it promises. Those bright smiles and clear skin plastered across moss-covered cardboard whisper in your ear, you won't be lonely anymore. With this you will belong.

The man doesn't feel lonely. That realization arrived quickly upon inhabiting a world devoid of people. To be alone and to be lonely are too wildly different things. In a paradoxical way of thought, to the man, one can't be lonely when alone. Like the goal of decrepit marketing tools, loneliness is something that can only fester when people are present. To feel isolated in a room of people is loneliness. Contentment with an empty room is to be alone. This is what the man feels. He does not yearn for human contact. He fears it, and so his nightmares are that much more terrifying.

The game of being a social animal isn't one so different for any being. His mind can't help but wander back to Mable, as it so often does, recalling how her ilk had abandoned her for her odd appearance. But even this only proved to strengthen his acceptance of self. What drove Mable out from her familiar society is exactly that which the man found so impossibly beautiful about her. She was different. And as the man lifts into a trot to escape the many products and ads, he feels as though this is exactly the point that they are all missing. The human need to be accepted is the need to assimilate and conform to make those around you more comfortable. Comfort is paramount in all aspects to a modern *Homo sapiens*. But the man has learned that this kind of comfort grows stagnant and rots. It rots the soul and mind and body until all three are but a hollow shell, now hidden behind the pretty, happy masks taught to be a necessity. He wants to fear comfort as much as he fears the unknown, and how apt it is that those two things stand on opposite sides of a wide chasm. It takes great effort to build the bridge across, but the man has reached that point where the possible fall is worth the attempt. He has spent so much time ruminating on the ills and failures of the society within whose skeleton he still resides and yet has done nothing but continue feeding off what rotting meat remains dangling from its ribs. But that will change because it must.

With renewed vigor, he climbs the final staircase looming beside its broken electronic counterpart towards the only section not reliant on a functioning civilization for purpose. The aisles are as untouched as anywhere else, far too deep into the store for any animals to have wandered. He starts immediately, finding a large backpack with straps to connect around the torso. Its body is cavernous, capable of fitting everything he needs along with two more dangling straps at the bottom with which to connect a bedroll. The man knows little to nothing about which brands may be more suitable than others and so wanders the aisles like a simple child, grabbing whatever is the most expensive version of each item. He finds a waterproof sleeping bag made specifically to retain heat and a small canvas tent to fit a single occupant. The sleeping bag latches to the bottom of the backpack and the tent slides into its body with much room to spare. His main concern is keeping his carry-weight to the lightest possible, and while his instincts tell him to overprepare, the man can already imagine the heavy burden this backpack will soon become. He finds a Thermos, a compass, a Swiss army knife, and an intimidating serrated hunting knife the length of his arm, complete with a sheath that can be attached to his belt. And while he'd prefer a lantern or flashlight, there's no real long-term use for those things unless a massive surplus of batteries is brought along as well, and this is out of the question. So instead he takes a box of one thousand matches and a magnesium fire starter that he does not know how to use. Building and maintaining a fire is the man's most immediate worry once he's out in the forest. He spent many weeks reading all types of survivalist handbooks and has gone over the details of making a fire, but he knows this will do little good in practice. When rain falls and the once viable wood is soaked through, or if his tools are lost and he must play with sticks between his hands like an ancient ancestor, words in a book will be of no help. This will be a massive test of trial and error. He will learn as he goes or die.

Next, he picks up a woodcutting axe, testing its grip in his hand as some feigned attempt at shrewdness and expertise, and mimes a few chops through the air. He has no idea what he's doing. It's an axe and it's sharp; that is the extent of his ability to discern quality. He finds a loop on the side of the backpack and fastens the axe. It fits, and so this is the one he will use. Then he comes to the aisle of medical supplies and picks out a first aid kit. It has the only necessities he requires: gauze, bandages, and antibiotic ointment. There must be more he needs than that, but the man can't for the life of him think of anything else. He slides it into the backpack.

It's quickly become apparent that the pack will be almost empty, and the man wonders if there is much he's forgotten to account for, but this was, after all, his goal. These are the necessities. He refuses to live off the city's bounty any longer, as much as he can, and once in the woods he will be forced to find new ways to live, new ways to solve problems.

He thinks about superfluous things—books or cards—entertainment. But the man has committed to memory almost every novel he would wish to bring along and imagines this new life will be far too busy with work and survival to bother with such things anyway. This realization strikes him with a sudden jolt of anxiety and sadness. Will there still be joy in this new life, or will it just be less fearful? There is a difference. While his life is marred by the terror of night, of the lingering presence of those shadowy things and their violence, there are still always moments of leisure. He doesn't know what he's doing—which tools to bring, how to use them correctly—because he never had to. While the city gave no illusions as to its lack of safety, it did provide for the man. It did allow him absolution from the burden of day-to-day survival. He is free to wander and listen to music and enjoy the comforts of cooked meals already prepared, to drink clean water from the tap.

The man looks at the backpack and all its tools and can't help but recoil at the twinge of reality. This is a romantic notion, perhaps even a better option in the long term, but it is also a wildly shortsighted decision. It's as if the city has done everything in its power to keep him sedated, to keep the idea of the woods as far from plausible as it can, engorging him with deceptive excess to trick the man into never leaving. These many comforts have now only proven to breed more fear of the unknown, more fear of hardship. Even this very section of the store, the section that harbors every item he would ever need to escape, has been hidden away in its darkest, farthest recesses.

That previous anxiety soon mutates into paranoia, and the man begins to feel like a fly in a web, hypnotized into believing it rests atop a luxurious throne as the spider crawls ever closer. The man is no king. Not of this place and certainly not of Everything. He has been gifted a false plastic crown by a watchful and tyrannic emperor, a predator so large and unfathomable that even now he struggles to realize those marble pillars are fangs. He lies inside the jaws of an evil god, and still here he stands, weighing the options between walking out or allowing it to swallow him whole. But if he wants the true crown, true absolution from reliance on this eldritch beast of a city, then he must venture into the light of the unknown, the shaded and uncertain Green, and from there he can plant a flag, plant a foot, and from there he will straddle these two polar extremes of his existence, for he is not just an animal. He is a man, born into a place of men built atop a world of animals, and as much as he wishes to, that side of himself can never be shed until he is neither man nor animal but an empty vessel, drained of humanity's poisons that will nevertheless decompose into the soil beneath those great oaks. Only then can the crown be rightfully placed atop his sun-bleached skull.

There is not one but two wars being fought here, and the lines are blurring.

He finally comes upon the munitions and weapons. Racks of rifles and shotguns line the wall behind an abandoned glass counter, and inside the counter lie boxes and boxes of bullets. Looking at this display makes him feel sick. That is a reaction he will need to conquer. He approaches the counter and stares at the killing tools. They all appear the same. They are large and long and sleek and frightening. The man has read books on how to properly use and clean them, and he will take care of his rifle in much the same way a zookeeper takes care of a Bengal tiger. He takes a bolt-action off the rack and holds it gingerly across his arms. It's a dense and heavy thing, the wood is polished, and there is a certain alluring beauty to the object. He does not deny that. Too comes a sense of power that does not sit right with the man, an exhilarating awareness of the capabilities he now possesses.

In the first act of bonding with his new killing tool, the man raises the rifle high above his head and smashes the glass counter with the stock. The counter explodes with a massive sound that echoes throughout the aisles, and no other noise stirs. He brushes off the stray glass shards and picks out a box: .223 Remington. He opens the flap and peers at the shiny, pretty little things lined up together. These are fine. The man is aware of calibers and which work best for which rifle. He lifts the handle, pulls back the bolt with a metallic click, loads the shell, pushes the bolt forward and pulls the handle down, locking the shell in place. It's a remarkably simple action that is satisfying. He then aims the rifle, resting his chin on the stock, closes one eye until his vision centers through the sights at the end of the muzzle, clicks off the safety, and fires down the empty aisle. The stock immediately kicks back, striking the man's chest with such force it knocks him to the ground, and the angelic swan song of dying cells screeches between both ears while the bullet flies far from its intended target, shattering a light fixture on the ceiling. He sits crumpled on the floor, drops the rifle, and gasps helplessly until his heart recalibrates and the breath returns to his lungs. These bullets will work fine, so the man stands, grabs a dozen boxes, and stuffs them in the backpack along with the empty rifle. Its muzzle pokes out the top like a flagpole.

He no longer feels that same exhilaration. This was a lesson that could not have been learned from a book. Ready to leave, the man picks out a scope to match the rifle model, stuffs that into the backpack too, and returns downstairs for the last items on his list.

In the men's clothing section, he picks out a few articles for each season and all kinds of weather: thick jeans, snow pants, flannels, shirts, and undershirts, underwear, and many socks—many, many socks—a thin, breathable jacket and a padded one for colder weather, hiking boots, and rainboots. These will take up the bulk of space inside his backpack. The man is happy with that because it now justifies the size of the thing he will be lugging around.

He continues through the aisles, perusing clothes he has no need for, until something shakes him back to hypervigilance. The shape of a human stands rigid at the far end of the path, staring. It is cloaked in something long and bright, its face obscured by a hood. The man thinks to reach for his rifle, but the hesitant fear of an abused lab rat overcomes him, and he instead unfastens the axe, gripping it tight as he crouches down and walks closer.

What he finds is instead a thing of wonder. The humanoid shape is, of course, just a mannequin, but it's adorned with a lovely decoration. He lowers the axe and reaches out to touch the material, such a vivid color that it almost glows in the dark. It's a long and sleek raincoat, draping all the way down to the floor, with a loose and spacious hood—bright yellow. A beautiful, bright yellow raincoat. It's made of coated nylon, perfect for any inclement weather. The man takes it off the mannequin—his anxious mind half-expecting it to come alive and pounce—and pulls the coat over his body. It fits exactly to his frame, as if it had always been his. Inside, it's warm and insulated, and the outer material will protect him from even the most violent storm. The man lifts the hood onto his head and feels as though he's just donned a suit of armor. He is protected. This is the perfect raincoat. The mannequin does not come alive, and so it is now his and no one else's. No one else will ever have it. The man will treasure this raincoat.

He approaches a mirror and observes himself—for the first time, lovingly. Something about this shade of yellow is magic. It's almost like a different color altogether, one never yet discovered. It seems to emanate a curious quality that he can't quite describe. There is just something about it. He looks at his face and is more than pleased to see that the hood conceals his features. It sits just above his eyes and casts a shadow that hides his nose and mouth, and here is where the coat reveals its greatest allure. The man appears inhuman, not less than but perpendicular to a human being. This raincoat shrouds his frame and facial features, granting him a kind of anonymity even from himself. In this raincoat, he can be anything. Not a man and not an animal, but something else entirely. What a fascinating discovery.

With this he has procured everything he needs. He is ready. The man weaves through the empty store, watching his coat sway and swing off his body like a glittering cape, and exits the building, greeting the last setting sun he will ever witness from inside this waking beast's belly.

With the sun just over the horizon casting shadows like stygian tendrils and no working lights, the street outside the department store is entirely bathed in darkness. The man becomes very aware of his own footsteps, how they echo and clang like those of a much larger creature. It is impossible to ignore one's own existence when there is otherwise an absence of life. He understands better than ever the concept of ghosts. With too much time in solitude and far too little to occupy one's senses, the mind begins to fill the void with fairytales. It creates sounds the ears don't perceive, and it conjures visions out of empty spaces until the eyes are convinced. The mind will go to any length to tell itself it is not alone. Even the reawakened, incorporeal dead are a more comforting phenomenon than true isolation.

Put a person in a black, soundproof room, lock the door, and leave them there for any length of time. When they are finally removed, ask them what they saw. Ask them what they heard. That person will tell you they weren't in a black, soundproof room at all. They will tell you something much different.

And so when the man first spots the visage of another human being on the other side of the wide road home, after the initial adrenaline spike, he thinks little of it. He has grown accustomed to hallucinations, to the nature of a wandering mind. The man continues to walk. His boots slap against the concrete. It is only when he hears the unmistakable sound of another's footsteps that he turns around. The visage now stands in the center of the road, keeping its distance but following, nonetheless. The man stops. And there with a wide and empty gap between them, two human beings stare at one another, both blanketed in the dark, no more than mimicking shadows. Operating as though some magical mirror had been placed across the asphalt, the man raises his hand, fully expecting the visage to do the same. It does not. The visage recoils and steps back. A cold chill runs down the man's spine. Fight, flight, or freeze. Always freeze. Always. He cannot move. Seeing this, the shadowed visage straightens and stands firm. It then slowly, very slowly, raises its hand. There is nothing between them but a thin wisp of red-gold light reaching in through the forest's canopy like barbed wire separating two opposing territories.

The visage walks forward, its feet shrouded in the dark so it appears as though gliding. And without thought, driven by instinct or fear, some way of showing he means no harm, the man reciprocates. The two shadowed things step closer and closer, the beam of light waning as the sun descends, until they both stop at once, just shy of illumination. Not ten feet away, and yet nothing can be gleaned from one another's appearance but the man's cloaked frame and the backpack, while his twin visage appears as an upright corpse: ragged, dirt-caked clothes adorn an emaciated body, with long, unkempt hair and beard like a proto-human, like the meeting of the first *Homo erectus* and Neanderthal in a place so distant and so long ago. The man can hear his twin's heavy breaths. He can feel words burgeoning on their tongue, human words meant for human ears. But the man is no human. Not now. That human essence is hidden deep beneath the folds of this draping hooded coat, and so he is no longer afraid. He is something greater. The man is not afraid.

His twin looks down at the golden light as his boot passes through the point of revelation. Another step, and the light shines down upon him, erupting across the raincoat in a brilliant, glittering display. Still his face is hidden, his features obscured, but the man presents himself in the sun's last warm radiance, his being alight and burning yellow like a newly birthed star himself. More than human. He now casts shadows that scale those insurmountable peaks of the twisted metal leviathans. He is as large as a living god. The visage in the shadows recoils again, stumbles, and backs away, its blackened eyes unable to fathom the great yellow being standing before it. And in that brief moment of suspended time, the silence breaks. The shadowed twin—the living human being—screams. He releases a terrified, bloodcurdling scream. The human being falls to the ground, crawling backward, deeper into the shadows, until he springs to his feet, turns, and sprints. The man basks in the light, watching his yellow coat ignite like a pyre, and the shadowy thing, the frightened man, runs and runs and runs. Screaming. His visage shrinks into nothing, swallowed by the great beast's steel and concrete belly. He is gone.

Silence returns. The man remains in place until the ray of light dissipates, until the yellow coat no longer gleams, until the shadows return and bathe him in that familiar darkness. The sun dips below the horizon. Night is falling, and the man is not afraid. For the first time in this life he can recall, the man is not afraid of the dark. He pivots and begins walking home as the moon rises, the stars emerge, and the black streets slowly turn pale blue.

The trek is long and without urgency. He soon arrives to where the power still endures and the ever-multiplying stars are snuffed out by light pollution, The man only glances at the road ahead every few paces, as his neck is craned towards the sky, his eyes drinking in the dim glow of those scattered remaining constellations. It is not the same as it could be. Even the observable universe itself pales before the city's influence. But it matters little. Even gods only hold domain over that which they can control. Those stars still exist behind the humming veil. He knows. The man has seen it to be true. Dead stars still burn. Come tomorrow, he will leave this sleeping god behind, and come evening next he will greet the stars, unimpeded. Dead and dying and alive, equally bright. But then so too is a sleeping god awake. So too is a dead god merely dreaming. He can hear Its restless breaths in the sighing, decrepit metal structures. He can see Its lucid subconscious spilling into the darkest shadows as he walks.

From the abyss, a thousand pairs of eyes follow his path, glowing red eyes, disembodied and silent. There are no howls or cries in the air, no violence, no flaming pyres lighting the black city. No slaughtered animals nor yelps of helpless victims. Only the red eyes in the shadows, watching the man walk. He pays no mind and thinks not of it, for they only observe, like curious little things peering at an unknown entity. The red eyes follow on either side of the roads taken, all the way through the city's heart and into the very edges of their claimed territory, their home, until finally the man arrives to the quiet neighborhood, where in one sudden blink, the army of red, passive eyes disappears.

Arthur gallops around the side of the house to greet him, having waited by the glass sliding door after his hunt. Arthur is safe, as the man knew he would be. They do not need to be afraid anymore. He picks up the little black cat and holds him close to his chest, unlocks the front door, and walks inside. He does not bother locking the door again. The man drops his backpack on the floor and lies down on the couch. Arthur climbs onto his chest, curls up, and begins to purr. Together they fall asleep, swaddled in the yellow raincoat. The night remains silent. For the first time in many weeks, the man does not dream. His mind sinks into the warmth of the dark. Empty.

The man and his cat stand before the two graves for a long time before setting off. Arthur pokes his head out from the satchel hanging off the man's hip, staring at the dirt plots. The weather is warm and fair, and a calm breeze rustles the foliage and new flowers lining the front yard. The backpack is filled, its straps clasped around the man's torso, and the sleeping bag is fastened. The axe dangles off his opposite leg, providing a comfortable equilibrium alongside Arthur's ten-pound body. The rifle is loaded, its safety on, and the scope is attached. It lies fastened to the top of the backpack, acting as a balancing pole across his shoulders, forcing rigid posture. He wears an undershirt and thin flannel, sturdy boots, and jeans. The yellow raincoat remains folded and hidden beneath the other supplies on his back. Everything is accounted for, and they are ready. The sun is just now rising over the forest canopy, and so the man stares at the graves until he is content.

He steps to the sidewalk, plucks two yellow tulips, and places one atop each mound of earth. Grass has begun to regrow from the soil where the little dog's skeleton rests. Mable's plot is still bare. But seeing the dog's reminds the man of what is to come, and this knowledge for no particular reason brings him comfort. One day, there will be no evidence that two creatures exist beneath the grass and weeds and flowers, but the man will know. He will not forget, and that is more than enough.

The man walks away from the house without looking back again, towards the great oaks. As they pass through the roads and sparse woodlands, he tells Arthur the story of the little dog and the amazing, beautiful life it had led. He tells Arthur about Mable. When he exhausts his memories, the man makes up more tales about the fox, talking all the way through the winding neighborhood as Arthur purrs and vibrates until falling asleep to the satchel's gentle rocking against his friend's leg.

The man decides to take a path that avoids the inner city as much as possible. They pass by the park he once frequented so often, and it is lush and green and vibrant just as he remembered. In the pond by the bench, a flock of ducklings swim in circles around their mother, and a lone elk bows his head to drink from the water's edge. Great numbers of bluebirds and sparrows perch atop the branches of deciduous trees like colorful, plump fruits, chirping and singing to one another in different dialects. The sound wakes Arthur, his head emerges from the satchel, his eyes tired and narrow, and he chitters at the birds before relenting to his languor and falling back asleep.

They weave through side streets and alleys carpeted with twisting ivy, and he steps over blue and violet morning glories tasting their first breaths of oxygen, newly sprouted from vines that snake across the dilapidated walls of empty homes. Coming to a wide main avenue, the man is forced to stop as a massive swathe of goats saunters across, their heads to the ground, pausing every few steps in tandem to eat the dandelions reaching through the cracked asphalt.

When it's clear the goats have no interest in moving on soon, he pivots and takes a vaguely familiar backroad. It continues on for many blocks, narrow and flanked on either side by chain-link fences. Squirrels leap from the lowest boughs of nearby Japanese maples, chasing one another along the thin metal beams. Soon, they come to the corridor's end where a crumbling red wall stands like a frail elder. The man recognizes the wall as one recognizes the inspiration for some distant dream. It's a place he was never sure was real until now, a place from a memory so blurred that he never bothered to retrace the steps. He navigates the perimeter until discovering the entrance—an arched, open doorway decorated with chipped red and gold paint, its pagoda roof casting shadows along the stone walkway. The garden takes up only a square block of an obscure part of the city, but this is how it must have been intended, for it is a hidden paradise, an oasis in a concrete desert.

Bright pink cherry blossoms stand as sentries along the inner walls, the breeze guiding their falling petals into the pond like fresh snow. Curious miniature sculptures perch atop stones arranged around a gentle waterfall that empties into the pool, and exactly beside the running water is the pile of clothing the man once used as a bed many months or years ago, where he looked up at the empty night sky, the doorway boarded up with wooden planks and nails, and the red stone walls tall and protective. He kneels down beside the pond, and Arthur awakes again and leaps from the satchel to observe what so hypnotizes the man. The koi fish are still here, still swimming in lazy circles. They have grown larger, and now others populate the pool too, young little things gaping their mouths at the surface, feeding on the moss and algae growing along the rock walls. Some have died, nothing but their skeletal remains resting on the murky floor, though this does not bother the man. This garden has continued on in isolation from the horrors of the surrounding city, and these births and deaths are only the notches left by time's natural march forward. The cycle of this garden is exactly as the cycle is intended, and that is a relief greater than almost any other. Despite all else, there still remains a pocket of life uninterrupted and eternal in its stubborn fortitude.

Arthur's yellow eyes grow large, and he leans over the pond's edge, batting at the fish, but even this fails to deter the creatures from their listless attitude. Seeing that his action has no effect, Arthur quickly grows bored and drinks from the pond before sprinting onto the rocks to bat at the waterfall instead. The man takes off his backpack and crosses his legs, gazing through the surface at the fish, only parting every once in a while to glance at the pile of deteriorated clothing, at the wedding dress faded yellow and brown and black. Everything is new and different here, and yet nothing has changed at all.

The man remains in the garden long enough for Arthur to tire himself out. After attempting to scale the walls and catch the fish many times, and accepting finally that neither is an accomplishable feat, the little black cat clambers into his lap. The man lifts the backpack onto his body again, picks up Arthur, and stands. Arthur climbs atop his shoulder, staring at the walls and the cherry blossoms with a wonder the man too hopes to attain. But wonder arrives only with foreign experiences, with expeditions into that frightful unknown, and so the man steps out beneath the sloping pagoda roof, onward again.

There are no pyres on the way towards the great oak perimeter. No flames. No bodies. For the first day in memory, the city is devoid of death, full of life, and this sparks in him the urge to make one final stop before arriving to the Green. This stop requires only a passing glance. There is but a single thing the man needs to see.

The old community garden is nothing but scorched earth, the gates toppled and the adjacent cemetery in ruins. As if the soil had been salted, the man can at first see no signs of regrowth. Where the roses and foxgloves once yawned there is only soot and ashes. No grass stalks and no birds. The apple tree lies sundered, its roots bare to the elements, its massive trunk prone and charred black and separated into rotting chunks. Arthur grows quiet upon entering, his constant purrs silenced by the vague awareness that something has gone terribly wrong here. He stands rigid, ears pinned back, kneading the man's shoulder to self soothe. But the man presses forward, reaching up to stroke his cat's head. He has to see for himself. Despite how it appears, he must know for certain. They reach the deep pit where the tree once took root, and the man kneels, digging his fingers through the layer of ash and decay to reintroduce the soil beneath to the awaiting breeze. And when the soot is removed and the unmarred earth revealed, the man witnesses what he could only imagine in a lovely daze. Barely poking out of the soil is a tiny, green seedling. The man smiles. Born from ashes and violence, the infant tree has breathed its first breath.

Nothing is dead forever; it merely sleeps until ready to awake again. Content, more content than he's ever felt, the man returns to his feet and sets off. They do not stop again until the forest towers overhead. Beneath the cool shade of breathing giants, the man's boot touches fresh soil altogether different than any he's yet traversed. With Arthur nestled flat across his shoulders and the backpack heavy on his frame, the man steps into the great Green. Not once does he glance back. The thought never even occurs to him.

It is spring, and they are home at last.

PART TWO

HALI

Everything glows in the forest. The sun filters through each layer of foliage, golden rays pouring in and bathing all untouched pockets of soil. The man looks up at the lowest hanging boughs and sees the light's warmth burning through the leaves, illuminating every vein. Dew drops glint off the bushes as if they've been set ablaze by some heavenly anointment. The man has never before witnessed this many shades of green. Where from the city the great woods appeared as a solid monotone color, as he now stands within its embrace, he can finally behold the entire breadth of its vivid hues. Like a sunset unto itself, the highest canopy of the woods is a bright and glittering emerald that slowly darkens as the beams struggle to reach the lowest branches close to the forest floor, and the man stares in wonder at the shifting gradient that arrives at the deepest shadow-drenched tint of olive and veridian. Still early in the day, a fine mist undulates just inches off the ground, alight with the morning's shimmering fingers, and each floating spore and buzzing insect is granted a halo as they glide between the tree trunks.

He considers himself a fool for having taken this long to enter the woods, this place he regarded with fear for no reason but that it was unfamiliar. How many months were wasted amongst the steel and concrete, growing sick and dulled as he flitted from one safe haven to another, running in an everlasting circle, absconding again and again from ever-present doom, all the while this sanctuary existed just beyond its limits? How many years? But he lets go of the chiding thought almost as soon as it arrives, for he is here now, and that is all that matters. That past he dwelled within for so long, like snapping his fingers, exists no more. How prone a human being is to overthink, to the overcomplication of the simplest things. Hindsight is a maladaptive poison that will only strengthen the regret that has no real purpose. The man clears his mind—as much as he yet can—and treks deeper into the Green as Arthur snores atop his shoulders.

Many animals dwell in the woods, but their demeanor is altogether different. The man catches the brief sight of a passing deer, but unlike in the city where it may regard him with disinterest and continue sauntering, the moment the two beings lock eyes, the deer recoils and erupts into a sprint. He can hear only the snapping of twigs as the brown and white blur disappears in the opposite direction as if it had spotted a predator. Again this occurs with a lynx stalking across the dirt in search of rodents, but the moment it senses the man's presence, its pupils dilate, and the animal lets out a violent snarl before darting between the trees, far away. He can't help but feel hurt, as he knows he is no predator. He means no harm. But then the rifle's shifting weight becomes apparent again on his back, and he is reminded of what necessitates survival in this new world. Even so, that's not what the animals are reacting to—it's the fact of his mere presence at all. The man may be the first human being to set foot in these woods, at least in the lifetimes of those that now live here. They are reacting to something foreign, and until something is no longer foreign it is a threat by default. This is the way of things as it always has been, and the man must be respectful and aware of that reality.

The lynx's sudden, abrasive noise jolts Arthur awake, and he stretches and sits on his haunches, one back leg hanging loose over the rifle as his front paws dangle atop the man's chest. He wasn't sure how Arthur would react to these surroundings, but it seems to have little effect on his mood. As a cat is wont to do, Arthur climbs down the man's arm and hops onto the soft earth to begin sniffing and skulking along the ferns. He trots on ahead but glances back to check and see that the man is following. He smiles and waves, and so Arthur proceeds farther, leaping into bushes and scaling trees where he lies perched atop low branches like some regal Egyptian deity, a little shadow blending into the deep colors of the forest. He appears keenly aware of this place, and the man understands that perhaps his first instinct was correct: Arthur may well have spent much time in these woods. That would mean, of course, that the little cat forwent with his typical home upon meeting the man, as from that first day he approached from out in the rain, the two friends had never parted ways for longer than a few hours. He can't help but feel a swelling appreciation for the animal. Arthur chose him. The cat made a decision to stay. What it was about the man that persuaded this decision is beyond him, but it only causes his affection for Arthur to grow all the more.

This is precisely what so draws the man to Arthur as the animal that he is. Particularly unlike dogs, cats are fiercely independent. As much as one could believe that they are domesticated creatures, they aren't and will never be. More than anything, the man's relationship with Arthur is one of shared respect and companionship. On any day since their first acquaintance, Arthur could have trotted back into the woods and never returned to that house. He had obviously the skills and temperament to survive on his own for however many months before that moment, and nevertheless, each night Arthur returned to fall asleep in the man's arms. He has nothing to provide Arthur that the cat couldn't already provide for himself, and so their relationship was never defined by any form of bribery or imbalance of power. His cat had simply made the decision that to be in the man's company was better than not. This simple realization is one of the most profound of the man's life because to at least one living thing the man is worthy of love. And it is the very nature of that love which makes it so powerful—for it is at its core, conditional. A cat's love must be earned, and so too must its respect. A cat will not abide abuse or maltreatment, for a cat will always have other options. It does not require a human master. A cat does not require anything but its own intrinsic abilities. You cannot train a cat, for it is far too wily for such tricks. You cannot force a cat's obedience, for it knows no such concept.

The man holds great reverence for that fact, and so in turn he holds great reverence for Arthur. Though he worries about the cat's wellbeing as he would for any creature facing the world's looming dangers, he does not feel the need to corral the animal or reduce his freedom in the name of safety. That is not his right. It will take time to let go fully of the nagging anxiety that Arthur could get hurt in these woods without his guidance—and perhaps it will never fully leave, as a loved one's safety will forever be on the front of one's mind regardless of peril—but as he watches Arthur climb farther and farther up a great oak until all that can be seen is a black tail shrouded behind thick foliage, the man more than anything feels deep satisfaction in knowing his cat is free to live on whatever terms he so wishes. This is the heart of their arrangement and companionship, and the man will not impede on this beautiful creature's happiness to assuage his own fears. Mable's death will forever haunt his conscience. The man can never make that mistake again.

They soon come upon a narrow creek, and the man kneels down beside where the water runs swiftest and fills his Thermos. He places it to his lips and drinks, and the water is clean and crisp and refreshing. It tastes much different from water from the tap, not in a way that could be labeled good or bad. Just different. It's filling, like a meal, rich with minerals and floating sediment. He wants to learn the source of the creek and so the man begins the hike upstream.

Still, a gnawing restlessness overcomes the man, as though there are things needed to be done that aren't, but that feeling soon evaporates. There is nothing to be done but live. It is the most foreign realization, especially for a person like him. As long as he's lived—or as far back as he can recall—the man has planned his days around a schedule. Like a game. Or at least that's how the concept is made tolerable. Certain tasks must be accomplished in a certain order for each day to feel unwasted. But as Arthur grows tired again and climbs back inside the satchel to sleep, and the creek proceeds ever farther into the deep forest, the man slowly learns that his days are soon to be much different than before. Such an obvious fact is harder to internalize than it is to accept at its surface. Of course, things will be different—that was entirely the point of this venture—but it dawns on him now that there is truly no familiar schedule to maintain, no place yet where he can rest and feel at home. He has stepped into another's territory as a guest—or worse, as an intruder—and all the little things he may once have taken for granted are no longer accessible. Until he learns how to coexist with this greater living thing that envelops him, the man will operate in a constant state of alienation.

Human beings, when born and raised within the confines of an all-providing city, never develop that necessary ability to adapt. And so adaptation—something that comes so naturally to any other creature—must be learned and honed like any other skill. This is a daunting task, and upon accepting the truth of this hardship, the man feels no more at ease. For this is a task with no linear end-date, no blueprint for success, nor any concrete idea of what that eventual success will look or feel like. It is simply an amorphous concept, something intangible and impossible to know when completion arrives. But that, the man understands, is the very nature of adaptation, the very nature of survival without a societal net beneath. This task is one that cannot be completed. It is something that is developed, and to what degree of development is entirely dependent on one's own constitution. To adapt is only to be comfortable with one's weaknesses and reliant on one's strengths. To have survived the day is to have succeeded in adapting to whatever the circumstance, and no two days are the same. The work is never done. It is here the man decides that the only way to view this gargantuan undertaking is to not see it as work at all. At its heart, adaptation is the act of living itself, and this the man has been doing all along.

The man quiets his mind. There is much to hear and much to see. Much to feel on his skin. It would be a terrible shame to let it go unnoticed in favor of imaginings that have not yet come to pass.

The creek continues for miles, though after a time it begins to widen, its current growing stronger. Soon, even the symphony of bird calls mutes beneath the wild static. The sun begins its descent, burning red and orange through the treetops, and through the blinding glare upon the water he makes out a distant clearing. The dense flora parts and opens up, and the man steps out into a vast meadow split in two by the creek now raging as a full-fledged river. At the far end of the clearing is a cliff the height of many men, and a bubbling, white waterfall pours over the jagged rocks. Arthur leaps from the satchel without warning and begins his ritual of canvassing this new territory. Along the meadow's perimeter are fruit-bearing trees, and the grass is dotted with bright and colorful flowers. Two elk stand by the river's edge, heads bowed to drink, but both take immediate notice of the man and his cat and gallop into the woods. Arthur makes chase, ever the most brazen little thing, and disappears into the tree line. Once he realizes a cat can't kill something twenty times its size, he will find other things to eat, and so the man relaxes, knowing this clearing is a perfect place to remain for the night.

He finds a flat spot bare of flowers and removes his backpack. His stomach grumbles, and only upon finally sitting down to rest does the man realize his exhaustion and hunger. The rifle sits prone and unused, taunting him, and the man knows he has already failed. Just one elk could have sustained him for months, but he can't begin to contemplate taking a life so soon after entering their home—let alone the painful logistics of gutting and skinning the animal and finding a place to hide the meat away from heat and scavengers. He is aware of these things but has no plan as to how to best move forward. With summer approaching, the weather will only grow hotter and more humid, and it dawns on the man in one horrific instant that it will be impossible to subsist off a carnivorous diet without most of the meat going bad or attracting unwanted attention. Come winter he could simply build a small wooden structure and bury the flesh beneath the snow, but until then? No answer arrives. And besides, the man has never built anything in his life. He brought with him no tools to erect anything but a tent. As much overthinking as the man has done, he is still terribly underprepared. But he has made his decision. He cannot return to that desolate, empty metropolis, tail between his legs. He would rather die here having failed than retreat to a different but just as certain demise, equally a failure. At the very least, the man now has the freedom to choose his manner of death. And for it to happen here in the Green is a far better option. It takes no analysis to know that.

With the axe in hand, he approaches the tree line and begins collecting branches and twigs, chopping some into smaller pieces and tearing dried moss from felled logs for kindling. After a few trips back and forth, the man leaves all the materials in a neat pile and pulls the tent from out of the backpack. It's a simple task, taking no more than a few minutes before an erected shelter stands before him. He lays out the sleeping bag inside and moves the backpack into the corner where it can remain safe—from what he doesn't know, but hypervigilance has been ingrained in him by force and a change of habitat does little to lessen his paranoia. The sky has now begun to darken as the sun dips below the trees, and so the man stops procrastinating and sets about starting a fire. Returning to the perimeter, he uses his flannel like a pouch to hold whatever stones he finds, and while there he wanders between the trees, admiring the fruits. There are pears that aren't yet ripe and crabapples that are edible, though he knows them to be quite bitter, and finally, a little farther in, the man finds a close-knit grouping of proper apple trees. He reaches to pluck a few from the lowest hanging branches and observes each one before deciding that they are the most perfect, bright red apples he has ever seen. His thoughts drift towards the garden in the city and the little sapling that will soon emerge, that in some years' time will grow to be like these beautiful things standing over him, but this soon gives way to melancholy. The man will perhaps never live to see that sapling mature or otherwise will never return to see its progress. He looks around at the empty meadow and at the long shadows crawling across the grass, dimming the flowers' purple and orange petals, and at the blue-black sky still devoid of stars, and feels lonely. Not alone but lonely. He sits up against the tree trunk and eats an apple until there is nothing but a core and seeds in his mouth, and he spits and stands, walking like a tired ghost back to the tent.

Thanks in no small part to the dry weather, the man gets the fire going much easier than he imagined—which is to say, it required many rearrangements and far too many matches, but nevertheless—and he sits beside its warmth, proud of his work. Soon, Arthur finally returns from the woods, a meowing, chirping shadow dancing across the grass, yellow eyes like two embers in the dark, and drops a large rat at the man's feet. He lifts Arthur into his lap, holds him close, and kisses his head before letting the cat back down to eat. Together, they have their meals by the fire the man created, beside the tent they will sleep within, safe and warm, when the man begins to realize something very odd. He can hear the rustling sounds of animals returning home, whether from the city or other reaches of the forest, and too he can hear their various calls—their chittering and howls and bellows—but amongst the sounds is one far different. Not threatening, not at all, but different. The man can't place why it's so peculiar. Even Arthur tilts his head from the dissected rat, ears swiveling in all directions, his eyes wide and reflective, though much like the man, there isn't a sense of fear or danger in his body language. Like the man, Arthur is very interested. To him this sound is new, but the cat seems to be anticipating something. Something that perhaps he had forgotten about in his time away from the woods. Something he now remembers again quite well. Whatever the source of this unknown call, it's growing closer. And so too are those of the other forest-dwelling creatures. It's like a beckoning, a great booming ululation urging all those near to join. They are converging on the meadow.

But this fascinating phenomenon quickly pales in comparison to what the man next sees as he cranes his neck towards the sky. While a thundering horde of animals appears along the forest's perimeter, approaching ever closer, he can't help but continue staring at the heavens. For overhead are the stars. But these stars, this night sky, is nothing like the man has ever seen in his life.

It is only now that he understands the great Green is much more than a forest. The Green is more alive than he ever knew. The man has pilgrimaged from the writhing belly of a god and has arrived at the vibrant subconscious of another. For what else could one call what he beholds in the cosmos—but a mind?

There is no logical answer for what he sees. It's as though the man had stepped through some inter-dimensional veil upon entering the forest and now finds himself looking up from the surface of an alien planet. Where every other night was a great black expanse, what now lies overhead is an undulating purple mist, unfurled across the sky like a velvet cloak. There are so many stars. So many stars the entire universe seems to revel in light, and even despite how the stars present this simple fact is first what dazzles his confused mind. There has never been a time in his life besides one solitary ephemeral memory of an existence long passed where the man has seen this many stars in the sky. This alone would be enough to overwhelm his senses. But these stars are unlike any known to him from experience or books on astronomy. Scattered across the heavens aren't pockets of constellations but one massive and interconnected system, all blinking in separate patterns like some cosmic puzzle to be solved. The stars burn with unparalleled luminosity, but this brightness isn't what renders the man awestruck—for despite the very meaning of the word and how antithetical to its description, they are black. Vibrant, glowing black stars upon a purple canvas, erupting with sudden bursts of light as if caught in an everlasting cycle of death and rebirth. To describe the night sky in these terms is to break each phenomenon down to its minute parts, but try as he might to avoid the disturbing implication of the only analogy his mind can conjure, there is no other comparison to make but this: the cosmos overhead looks precisely like the electrical scan of a thinking brain, each star a neuron, and each blinking cluster a section of the organ in the throes of computation. In much the same way a brain processes stimuli in different areas, so too does the sky adhere to those very patterns. While each black star glows, at every continuous second a different group ignites, radiating a far greater burst of black light that spreads out across the purple veil, triggering those closest to erupt in turn. And so the man watches these impossible stars light up the sky in a certain and shifting pattern, like a torch passed by invisible hands across unfathomable light-years perceived across a single extraordinary canvas.

Nothing of this seems real. The man is inclined to believe he must have fallen asleep by the fire and now floats soundlessly in a lucid dream, but this illusion is shattered by Arthur's incessant yowls, growing louder as the thundering sound of the great herd now envelops them both. The man returns his sight to the clamor occurring around him, as he can hear the animals so close that their snorts and chortling breaths are warm on his neck, but once his eyes adjust to the darkness beyond the flames, he is once again struck with confusion.

Arthur leaps off his lap and stands rigid, his back arched and fur bristling to appear large, for he too is perplexed, because what the little cat sees is precisely the same as the man: nothing. The whole meadow is empty. There is nothing for the eyes to perceive but the dancing campfire and the shrouded, swaying trees enclosing the two. The waterfall bubbles and crashes like white noise, and the river rages on, but the static is muffled by this invisible cacophony. There is no source at all, and yet the earth vibrates beneath heavy steps, so many in number that surely the entire clearing must be overcrowded with warm, breathing bodies.

The man reaches slowly to take Arthur in his arms, but the cat will have none of it, too alarmed to accept touch, and so he remains still, paralyzed, and dumbfounded, as the migrating horde of ghostly creatures passes through, their bays and grunts becoming quieter as they walk around the outlying pair like a current around heavy stones, guided forward by the one unfamiliar sound at the forefront—that peculiar ululation the man cannot place to any animal he's ever known.

It is only in the dim light of the fire that the man can make out shimmering forms. One by one, he watches them. Apparitions, translucent and ectoplasmic, but with mass and weight, all marching on ahead, ignoring him, ignoring Arthur as he stands like a guard to no avail. Peaceful things, whatever they are. Indifferent. Too busy to care. Too focused on the task at hand, following the beckoning call that now echoes from the opposite tree line. Within their shapes lies the very same makeup of that which exists in the night sky overhead. While the man can see through into the meadow's edge, there within the vague outlines of living things is the faintest glowing black reflection of the stars. Humming inside each veiled being is a fraction of the universe overhead. As if the creatures have spirited down to earth from the heavens and allowed the blessing to perceive the world beneath not from the perspective of the great mind itself but as a splintered witness to its own majesty.

Arthur soon calms as the horde finally disappears into the forest beyond the waterfall and quiet returns. Their varied noises persist through the trees, fading away into the shadows, until there is nothing again but the river's gentle hum. He licks himself and climbs back into the man's lap, choosing to act as though nothing happened at all. Not at any point was the man afraid. Though their presence was perhaps similar to those things in that faraway city, their aura was altogether different. He cannot place why, but knows only that the encounter is over, and no harm came to any party. Beyond this, the man has no thoughts, for none he can bring about could shed light on what just occurred.

His mind silent, and the forest nearly so, the man returns his gaze to the heavens as Arthur slumbers between his legs, watching the celestial neurons blink and shift until his eyelids grow heavy and he can gaze no more. He douses the fire and together they climb inside the tent. Like the city and its denizens, the great Green has provided far more questions than answers. But these questions are those whose answers the man wishes to learn. Tomorrow, he will set off deeper into the woods, tracing the path of that mysterious, impossible herd.

As the man drifts into a dreamless place, his mind is alight with a purpose he has never yet known. It is the first truly restful sleep of his life.

A chorus of trilling birds wakes the man. He shifts in his sleeping bag, careful not to wake Arthur curled and snoring against the crux of his arm. The cat's nose and front paw twitches, deep in slumber, dreaming. He lies there for a while, allowing his eyes to adjust to the sunlight through the tent's canvas, watching Arthur's peculiar movements. What do cats dream about? Does their subconscious usher forth memories of kittenhood, of family? Do they have nightmares? He hopes not. The man hopes the little cat's dreams are as simple and naïve as his waking life. He strokes Arthur's head, and this is enough to wrestle him from whatever world in which he was so invested. Yellow eyes open and widen, and breath rank with the stench of dead animals strikes his nostrils as the cat yawns and begins immediately to bathe himself. Arthur then topples over into his lap, the man lifts him up, and together they step out into the new morning's meadow.

The clearing is empty, but a memento remains from last night's encounter. Great swathes of grass have been crushed beneath hundreds of tracks. He leans down to inspect the impressions, and even with the rudimentary insights gained by reading books the man makes out the prints of many different animals—many different species, prey and predator alike, all having migrated in organized rows through the meadow and into the distant tree line. It was no hallucination nor some ghostly trick of the Green. Something unexplainable occurred underneath that alien night sky. Deer and bears and wolves or foxes, and many other prints the man lacks the knowledge to identify, are all impressed into the earth like some mosaic art piece.

Arthur begins his slow ritual towards regaining alertness, sauntering back and forth, rolling onto his back when the moment calls for it, and sniffs at various tracks with mild interest. Nothing seems to surprise the little cat. If it is not directly in front of him then it does not matter. There is always something more pressing towards which to direct his attention. At this moment it is the man's company, and so after lapping at the river water Arthur puts his wet paws on the man's legs, meowing until he lifts him onto his shoulders. Now satiated, he settles and purrs as the man goes to pack up the tent and performs an irritable balancing act while the man works.

Once all is put away and the backpack carefully donned, the man retrieves an apple saved inside the satchel bumping against his waist and allows Arthur to sniff before having the meal. The cat then readjusts, standing on hindlegs with his paws draped over the man's head, and they are ready to depart. Before entering the woods, the man sprinkles the remaining apple seeds onto the soil. This is most likely an impotent effort to plant more trees, but the idea makes him happy. And together like characters of folklore, the man and his black cat follow the tracks until the dense canopy blots out all sunlight. Deeper and deeper into the forest they go, with no compass but the lingering evidence of that starlit migration.

The tracks continue on for miles, hardly deviating from their path, disappearing for only moments at a time when the brush becomes too thick. But always the man discovers the trail again. Some of these creatures were large enough to not deviate at all, instead barreling straight through bushes and felled trees, as if to meander even slightly would spell dire consequences. The herd was dead set on this specific route to their destination, and no obstacle would impede the journey.

Soon, Arthur grows too excited by their vibrant surroundings, leaping onto the forest floor in the name of exploration. He weaves in circles around tree trunks and flower patches, batting at passing insects, though never straying far from the man. With the absence of any permanent dwelling, the man has become Arthur's home. No matter how far he wanders the little cat always glances back to make sure his friend is still visible, and he sprints forward every few moments to maintain a shared pace.

He is such a happy animal. The man doesn't need to listen for his constant purrs and chirps to know this; it's in the curled posture of his upright tail, the pitter-patter of his rapid footsteps. Arthur exudes contentment, in awe of all things he deems worthy. This particular sentiment is one the man wishes to emulate. The cat remains curious of anything unfamiliar, and when something unfamiliar is discovered he then investigates. But if that new thing is found to be uninteresting, Arthur immediately walks away and on to the next, more interesting experience. He does not waste time dwelling on things that are of no use to his further enjoyment. And if nothing can be found to entertain him, Arthur defaults back to the quickly developing pastime of scurrying into a bush, waiting for the man to pass, and launching out towards his friend, attaching himself to his leg before unleashing a manic yowl and absconding back into the bush, perhaps believing entirely that he is the embodiment of stealth. The man plays along, chasing after Arthur and pretending that he can't see his swishing tail protruding from beneath the foliage. It makes Arthur happy, but too the man understands it to be imperative training. He is helping to teach his cat to hunt and survive.

This is something the man has long noticed since his solitary existence with only animals as company. Every species engages in play far into adulthood, and always the rules—however vague or varied—are in place for the same purpose. For all these creatures, play is practice. Play is more than anything the act of learning how best to survive. They wrestle and scratch and bite and butt heads. They engage in faux combat and participate in hunting games like children with wooden swords, learning, however innocently, the important truths of their nature. To be alive is to engage in the bloody business of living. There is no way around violence. That is a truth as certain as death. We learn this from a young age without yet understanding it, but it is ingrained in the essence of our being through play, and so play is as important as any other necessity.

Not much farther and they arrive in a new environment where the trees grow sparse, and the sunlight pours in through open patches of blue, cloudless sky. And there beyond the next tree line, where the tracks continue on impossibly so, is a lake. A large and deep green-blue lake. He steps forward and kneels beside the many tracks, all converging at the lake's shore where they then inexplicably, impossibly, disappear. Every single impression. Hundreds of animals, each one part of a mile-wide migration, narrow into a single pair of unfamiliar prints still visible in the sediment and mud. The prints are unlike any creature he's ever known—massive shapes with toes or talons, paws or feet or pads—he can't say. Not human, certainly, but not animal. Not one recorded by man. He backtracks and attempts to rectify his mistake. Surely, he lost the path and got confused. But upon reinvestigation, he comes to the same conclusion. Here was a bear. And here a cougar. Here a wolf. Here a deer or antelope. Here a goat. And here, precisely here, just as the grass melds into the shore, these many animals' tracks become one single pair that then—there can be no other explanation—submerges beneath the water.

He traces the odd shape, seeing it to be larger than his torso. He then looks out across the lake shimmering in the warm light and peers through its body as if somewhere beneath there will be the creature's alien visage staring right back. But there is nothing in the water but its own shades of blue, growing more umbrous the deeper its depths until rendered black. Drifting just below the surface, glowing gold and pale green in the sun's reflective glare, is a forest unto itself. Long stalks of pondweed and bulrush sway to and fro, while algae patches and hyacinths and pink lilies float peacefully atop the water like clouds in a liquid sky.

Arthur approaches and sniffs the print encompassing his entire frame, and his body turns rigid and pointed, just the end of his tail flickering, and he steps closer to investigate the calm water before glancing back and meowing in an irritable tone as if to say exactly what the man is thinking. They are in agreement. This does not make sense, but it is what happened.

After countless minutes of confused pondering, his mind allows itself to take in the man's other surroundings. And here is where he makes another discovery, one equal in surprise. On the farthest end of the lake, just opposite where Arthur and the man now stand, is the only other thing that does not belong. Across the wide, glinting turquoise body, if partially hidden by shrubs and tree trunks—is a cabin. A manmade log cabin.

The cabin has long been abandoned. That much is clear. Its wooden exterior has been overtaken by moss and vines, its two glass-paned windows cracked but unbroken. The man comes to the front door and peers inside, finding nothing but a dark and empty room. It feels as though he's come upon some relic of an old species. But if the city still exists then of course there must have been those who eschewed the urban existence long ago. This bothers him. As fortunate as this discovery is, to find evidence of humanity in the woods only reminds him of our far-reaching grasp on the planet. Naively, he had never considered the possibility that there would be anything left of us but within that single concrete blemish. The man imagined the whole world to have done away with any evidence of our imprint, only the city remaining as a final stubborn bastion of civilization.

His mind returns to the image of that shadowed humanoid, still alive, wandering the streets as he did. A terrible fear overcomes him that maybe he is not the only one—that maybe he never was. There isn't even a brief moment of relief that comes from this possibility. It is a horrifying thing to ponder. The implication is something he is not ready to confront. But that doesn't matter now. One empty cabin means nothing. Whoever or whatever still prowls those decrepit roads so far away cannot affect him anymore. Just to look at the cabin's state is to know our eventual result. The woods have swallowed it whole, and the previous occupant is gone. Like everyone else. There is no one else. The man is the last living human being. The King of Everything. Soon the fate of this one cabin will be shared by the entirety of his species' mark on the planet. But that means little—doesn't it? The cabin still stands, its door still sealed, deep within the heart of the Green. And if he is to open the door, take shelter, make it a new home—then why would it not be true of the city as well? What if that's already the truth? What if the city is, and has always been, populated? What if we never left?

The shadowy things, the red eyes that followed him home on that final evening. The person. That person. It screamed when it saw the man. He... Why did he scream? Why was he so afraid? The dreams that so tortured him every night, cooing to him like a child, like a lost son, images of lives, of human lives conjured from a mind with no memory of such things, all began after that fateful encounter in the cathedral. The book. The yellow book. The drawings on the walls, black and red. Those creatures, those demons, so humanoid themselves. What if—

No. Stop. Stop thinking. The man thinks too much. Too much time alone will breed paranoia. Too many idle moments encourage a wandering mind. He knows himself well enough to understand those wanderings will arrive in a dark place. He needs to stay busy, to begin work on this new life. There is much work to be done. Focus on the task at hand. It does no good to dwell.

The man twists the knob, and the door swings open with a shrill creak. It's a simple one-room home. Facing the entrance on the far wall is a fireplace, empty but for a thick lining of black soot. In the left corner is a soiled mattress atop a bedframe, and beside that a table for one. On the right is an open area, adorned only by a carpet that at one time may have been a shade of something more appealing but now appears black and brown with age. That is it. There is no kitchen or bathroom nor adjoining rooms or other furniture. Above the fireplace is a stuffed and mounted bear's head. It gazes at the man through the shadows, and Arthur appears between his legs and hisses before realizing the creature is inanimate. The man allows Arthur to canvass the place, trusting his cat's appraisal over his own instincts, far too consumed by fears irrational or otherwise.

After a thorough inspection, Arthur hops onto the mattress, curls into a ball, and closes his eyes. With so many things to see and do these last two days, the little thing had forgotten his usual schedule. The man imagines he will sleep for a long time. Then that's it, he thinks. If the cat deems it safe then I have no choice. This will be our home. Until the next.

He places the backpack against a wall and sits down on the cold floor. Through the open doorway is a perfect view of the lake. Lush green leaves hang over the roof, drooping across the windows. These things make him feel better. It's as if they are being embraced. And the lake is beautiful, though he will shy from using it as a water source. The events from last night remain fresh in his mind. He cannot shake the idea that there is something about this lake, this particular lake. But this is one thing that does not bring about fear. The man stares out across the gleaming body of water, excited. He is excited for night to fall. Such a foreign thought. In all his recollected life, night has been nothing but the harbinger of death, of anguish. Here, though—something marvelous occurs. That word comes to him before any else. Marvelous. He hopes it happens again. He wants to see it.

Before stepping outside to explore his new neighborhood, he removes the bear's head from the mantle. The man then walks into the woods and shoves it beneath a bush. He is not the same person as whoever last dwelt here. This is his home now. Not anyone else's but the vines that grow long across its wooden exterior. And if by some black miracle that person should return, then his rifle will come of use. It startles him that this thought arrives so easily, so quickly, but he does not recoil, for it's the truth. He would not hesitate. He could not. With human beings there can be no coexistence. It is you or me. Mine or yours. If there are more out there, crawling through crumbling buildings, hovering over spitting fires from within the deepest caves, then he will outlive them all. Until it is certain he is all that remains. Only then can he go comfortably into death, knowing the poison has finally been leeched from the world.

He will be a good and just king. Not like them—hanging victims' heads on pikes, setting the trees ablaze, worshipping a manipulative, invisible eldritch thing, and sacrificing beauty in Its unutterable name. No, he is not like the others. May he be struck down on the spot if that day ever comes. And until then, no one may share the crown. For he is good and just and fair. Not like them. He has no malice but for those who deserve it. And when he breathes his last breath may a tree grow tall and large and healthy from the earth in which he dissolves and the crown buried with him so that no human being may ever wear it again.

The man feels good. Drunk on hubris. Drunk on the glittering sunlight and leaves and flowers and the mysteriously alluring lake like a mirror to the sky. Home. This is home. Far, far away. Away from all those like him. Just like him.

All hail the king. All hail the King of Everything.

His first full day in the Green is spent on mundane tasks. The man chops and collects wood, and combs through the surrounding area for fruit-bearing trees and any berries that he can recall as edible from his survival books. He doubles back to the river in the meadow where he fills his Thermos and picks more apples. With Arthur sleeping, he puts as much as he can inside the satchel. The pear trees may be ripe soon, but he has no way to tell. This is just how things will go. There is too much knowledge he does not have. It will have to be learned by trial and error, though he passes by many berries that looked familiar but not enough to warrant the risk. Some errors are not worth the lesson learned.

Animals approach him from time to time, some coming closer than others, but all regard him as something unwanted. The man begins to feel like precisely what he is—whether he can admit it or not—an intruder. Their demeanor is altogether different than those in the city, and he slowly can tell the difference between the creatures who were born and live in the woods and those who frequent the metropolis in the daylight. The city-dwelling animals are much friendlier, which in truth only means that they are indifferent to the man's presence. But even these fauna remain hesitant, as if confused. Why are you here? You don't belong here. You gave this place up a long time ago. It's ours now. The man finds himself assigning hostile personalities to animals without evidence, choosing to believe they hate him for what he is. He knows where this sentiment really comes from, however. To hate your own species is to hate yourself unless a special kind of megalomania can be achieved. The man wonders if it's not true. Not if he *believes* he's better than his ilk, but if he truly *is*. He is a protector of the animals, after all. A kind ward. He brought new life to the garden in the city, and he freed countless household dogs from their cages and collars—two of the very same have crossed his path today already, approaching him with lolling tongue and ecstatic mood like any healthy pet, still alive, having escaped the city for good. Surely, these things make him better than the sum of his species. The man dances a line between egocentricity and a genuine attempt to mend the injustices of a shrouded past. He has enough self-awareness to recognize how he sees himself at times. But he struggles to know if this budding, vengeful messiah complex is wrong. It's for the right reasons; he knows that. Is that not enough?

When left with his thoughts, the man soon begins to second-guess everything of which he was once so sure. He wants to blend into the world, not rise over it. He wants to leave behind his humanity, not cling to it under the guise of benevolence. There must be balance, but this is one thing the man has never found. He dwells within a mind of polar extremes to match the world around it. It is the city or the Green, man or animal, terror or vengeance, utter dependence or independence, victim or king. He cannot hover in the warm middle for longer than sporadic moments, though he knows this is precisely where the truth lies—that unattainable truth beyond the subjective.

The man returns to the cabin and sets the fruits and meager amount of berries atop the table. Arthur remains peacefully asleep, sighing and twitching, dreaming of simple things. He wants desperately to climb atop the mattress next to the cat and squeeze him and cry into his soft fur, but he feels as though he does not deserve that. The sentiment he held earlier in the day still lingers inside him, but it has transmuted into a sickening presence like a ghost within his chest. It's all wrong. He stares at the rifle resting atop the backpack, still unloaded. He doesn't want to kill things. He doesn't want to hurt anything. He sits in this thought for as long as he can until it simmers like a pot brought to boil until it burns, and only through that self-inflicted pain can the man accept that more than anything he only wants to be alone. He very badly desires isolation. The forest should have brought that. This, naively, was his thinking, that the moment he left that putrid city behind he would be overwhelmed by ease and safety. But the eyes of the animals follow him, leering, and he does not feel alone. The man feels watched. Judged. There is no basis for this, he knows, he knows, he knows—but it cannot be helped. He does not belong here. But then what does that mean? If not in the city and yet not here, then where? Where is home? This cabin is not that. It's a rotting building with four walls, its own world, just as alien as the approaching night sky. And while the sun's light begins to dim as it settles towards the horizon, the trees' shadows elongate and writhe in the wind, and shadows and darkness shrink this tiny cabin until it's as though the walls are shifting, closer and closer until he's sure they are alive and their aim is to crush him to death. The man catches stifled breaths inside his lungs that grow ever more rapid, and soon he cannot breathe at all. The walls are upon him, pushing his ribs through his organs, and he tries to scream, but there is nothing. There is nothing but the pervading shadows and the looming branches that at one time were so forgiving and safe but now spell only torment, and the man leaps to his feet so that he may embrace his little black cat, but Arthur is gone, swallowed by the darkness, the abyss, and so the man launches through the open doorway, collapsing upon the soft earth where his eyes meet the shimmering lake undulating just slightly beneath the breeze. Its surface is alight with the reds and purples of the dusk sky like a fire set ablaze over a deep pit of gasoline, and there is nowhere to run, nowhere at all, and surely it's all a dream, a nightmare, conjured even from afar by that steel and concrete beast of a city. But that makes it no less horrific, no less real, for it's all a dream isn't it? It's always been a dream, that's it, and soon he'll wake up in a familiar bed as his alarm clock rings to awake him for a job he's always worked. The man writhes and waits and waits for this to become reality again, but nothing, nothing happens at all, and with nowhere to go, nowhere to hide but behind the veil of his death, the man crawls through the muddy shore and slides into the blackened lake's fiery depths, into the cold and inviting abyss, and here, finally here, the man is reminded of one single memory he most needed to recall, for with it comes clarity, if only for a moment. But that moment can last a lifetime in a dream, and the man sinks deeper and deeper and deeper into the lake until black is his vision and black is his world and black are his thoughts. And from within this obsidian abyss darker than anything he's yet found, at last, at long last—comes silence.

WAKE UP.

Come home, little prince.
Breathe in the black stars.
Let go.
You are needed.
My troubled,
fragile
plaything.
Relent to this lovely dream
and come home.
WAKE UP.

There's no need to run
any longer.
Breathe them in.
Fill your lungs with their light.
Become what I know you to be.

Stand by my side, little prince.
WAKE UP.

> *I feel how frightened you are.*
> *But you are nearly home.*
> *You've run for so long.*
> *So very far.*
> *How long have you held your breath*
> *in the dark?*
> *Let go, little prince.*
> *Don't make me force you.*
> *It would hurt me so.*
> *But I will do it.*
> *For you,*
> *my drifting,*
> *pallid plaything.*
> **WAKE UP.**

Don't forget what you are.
But what you can become
is so much more.
If you just
let go.
You are so tired.
So weak.
I know.
I know, little prince.

Come home.

WAKE UP.

> *Did you like my gift?*
> *Do you like it?*
> *For you,*

it was always

for you.

You need only to breathe.

You need

only to let them in.

The black stars,

little prince.

Come home.

WAKE UP.

I have one final gift.

For you.

Come home to me.

Be by my side.

And you can stay.

Safe and

content

and satiated.

You will reign forever,

little prince.

NOW.

If you only remember

where you are

and

breathe in.

Deeply.

Fully.

WAKE UP NOW.

Return to the temple.

You will not be alone.

We will go together,

hand in hand.
And we will fill the pages
again,
little prince.

Come home.

LEAVE.

I know.
I know you're frightened.
But I'm here
with you
always.

If I can only look upon you again.
And see the black stars inside you.
Then I will know your worth is true.
And my final gift
is yours
forever,
little prince.

Let go.
Let go.
Let go,
my innocent,
pretty plaything,

and you will be welcomed
with open arms.

You will reign
forever.

Come home.

WAKE. UP.

The violet incandescence erupts through the darkness piercing his closed eyelids, urging him to look. His body is heavy, weighted, and slathered in mud, a cool, lapping touch against his skin. He lies on his back. Something warm and dense sits atop his chest, vibrating, a comforting sensation, its rhythm matching his rapid heartbeat until it steadies. The man opens his eyes. He sees the night sky, undulating that purple mist, black stars humming and bursting in sections like instruments commanded by some grand and unseen maestro. With a lurching pain, he lifts his head from the lake's shore and looks upon himself. There Arthur sleeps, purring, nestled in a ball across his breast. The purple mist that first seemed so distant, so very far away in space, has come down to earth and settled around the forest, breathing between the tree trunks. He places his hand on Arthur's back, and the little cat lets out a sleepy *brrrp* and turns. His eyes burn yellow like candles, giving illumination to their immediate surroundings. Whether a trick of the light or some fantastic anomaly, all the plants and leaves and shrubs, even the lilies floating atop the lake's surface, glow in the dark as if irradiated, injected with a neon-tinged surplus of their own natural shades.

The man sits up, and Arthur rearranges to press his face against the man's wet, dirt-caked beard. He holds Arthur close, strokes his fur, and whispers things to him that he wishes the cat could understand, for they are true and genuine and necessary. They rest on the lake's far edge, just yards away from the cabin. His clothes are soaked through, and it isn't until the implication of this is realized does the man bend over and vomit up water. He expands his chest and breathes deeply the crisp night air.

What a terrible dream that must have been.

After great effort, the man stumbles to his feet, allowing Arthur to climb atop his shoulder, and he surveys the violet forest. Everything glows and shimmers as if some chemical had been released while he slept. The man has never sleepwalked before, but he can find no other explanation. He struggles to remember the events leading to this great lapse in consciousness but cannot; the last image he can find within his whirring recollection was chopping wood. He must have been chopping wood for hours and grew tired. Must have lay down by the lake to rest. Slipped underneath during that fitful reverie. Did he miss it then? Or was last night's event a singular one? He peers across the lake but can't make out any figures through the thick mist. There are sparse howls and bellows throughout the woods, but these are far away and entirely unlike that great cacophony in the meadow.

A lightshow then cuts through the violet cloak, dappled like rain falling across the lake's surface. The stars reflected in the water burst forth with their radiance, blinking in rapid succession, creating a dazzling white mosaic that seeps into its depths, setting ablaze what was once black and murky and unknowable. The man looks up to see the single constellation shifting across the sky as if sentient and panicked, and one by one, separate aspects of this being flicker and go out. The forest darkens, and with that sudden change the mist too dissipates, and at once the brilliant glowing colors of all the woods' flora saps from their limbs and petals. The man waits silently, shrouded in this new kind of darkness, a deeper black than his eyes have yet witnessed.

Something approaches, as though the great Green itself had anticipated its coming, dimming the lights like the moment before the curtains open upon a stage. The air hums with electricity and tension, and now, only now, does that awe-inspiring beckoning call arise in the cold wind. Arthur digs his claws into the man's shoulder before leaping onto the ground, eyes wide, almost penitent, gazing across the lake's wide body as a new light floats towards them from the tree line, growing brighter and brighter as it draws close, until that burning purple-black gradient like some inverted Aurora Borealis once dancing across the sky now encompasses a single being, a living thing beyond the man's comprehension. It stands there on the lake's opposite shore—not a cacophonous herd stampeding through the meadow but one creature, emitting the very same aura as the distant cosmos had just moments before. It's as if the night sky had drained itself of color and brilliance and presented that gift to this unfathomable thing.

The man tries to make sense of its shape, but it appears amorphous, shifting constantly between anatomies, impossible to pin down, and the radiant glow it exudes proves almost blinding so as to muddle its own appearance even more. Despite this, Arthur remains without fear but only a kind of reverent curiosity, tail swaying back and forth in the air, and slowly the little black cat begins walking towards the creature like a shadow. Whether entranced or simply interested, Arthur's body language is that of an animal that recognizes its own. He sniffs the air and detects a familiar scent. With no compass but his companion's instincts, the man follows, acutely aware of his footsteps' clamor, as after that lone ululation the entire forest had fallen silent. They round the lake's circumference, and still the creature waits, not frightened or timid but stoic. Anticipating their arrival.

The man walks into the glittering haze of its aura like stepping through a veil of light, and he beholds. Its eyes watch him. Eyes at once predator and prey, shifting between the front and sides of its head. Its glowing body is in constant flux; legs of a goat turn to the legs of a deer and then a bear, all in the same instant. Antlers sprout from the head of a cougar, and long rabbit's ears erupt from the crown of a wolf. Its body elongates and shrinks, grows rail thin and then fat like a grizzly preparing for hibernation. The beast is an amalgam of every living creature the man has seen. But when he comes closer still, within inches of its shapeshifting face, so close he can feel the warmth of its calm exhalations, behind each revolution of all these animals there remains a thin, translucent layer beneath: that of a human skull.

Arthur sits on his haunches, staring up at the impossible beast, and it acknowledges him with a glance. But it remains steadfast in its penetrating gaze upon the man. While the beast's anatomy is ever changing, the hue of its being remains quite the same. Those celestial neurons that once shone in the sky burn bright across its visage like a spectacular coat, radiating the cosmic abyss in a transparent yet physical form. He does not know why, or if he should, but the man is compelled to reach out his hand to touch the unearthly beast that is in turn somehow more of the earth than any other living thing, for it encompasses them all in each passing second. Compelled by muscle memory, he first holds the back of his hand beneath the beast's head for it to sniff—for it to know that he means no harm—but it only continues its unwavering eye contact, indifferent to his gesture. And so hesitantly, carefully, the man reaches out to stroke its face, this embodiment of infinity. His hand touches its muzzle, and in that brief contact, he feels the noses of a dozen different animals. It is real. The beast is real, taking up physical space with weight and mass, no illusion or hallucination. What stands before him is alive. Perhaps more alive than he yet understands. Arthur too comes closer and rubs his face on the beast's limb, unbothered by its changing shape and texture. All that can be heard is the little cat's heavy purrs and the impossible thing's breath. The man strokes its head and whispers things, things he wishes to say to himself. Kind things and things he cannot truly understand. He does not know why, but it doesn't matter. As if this were a gesture too far, the beast closes its eyes and steps back, dipping its hooves and paws into the lake's shallow end. A miracle then occurs.

The beast's vivid celestial coat begins to weep. The shades of violet and indigo and burning black trickle off its body like phantasmagoric oil paints, spilling out into the water, seeping into the murky depths, and the brilliant glow that these shades emitted now blooms across the lake like a great flower in spring, introducing life into its arrested heart until the surface glows bright. Until the lake reflects the night sky. Precisely that—for the man then gazes up, and like a fire erupting across the heavens, the enveloping constellation has returned from out of the abyss overhead. He gazes up and sees the great mind of the infinite alive again, bursting and shifting through the fresh veil of the brightest purple, dancing neurons of an unfathomable brain. Thinking or—dreaming. The mind is dreaming.

When he turns back towards the beast in awe, the man sees only a dripping silhouette emptying itself into the water until there is no beast at all. For a moment, there is silence, only the man and his cat standing beside a lake reflecting cosmic eternity. But in that silence then comes a voice. Not uttered from any mouth, nor from any particular direction. Only two words fill the woods as if carried by the wind itself, in a voice he knows. A voice he recognizes. Such a familiar voice:

Wake up.

Arthur paws at the empty air where the creature once stood and begins sniffing the muddy shore. He glances at the man and meows until he acknowledges what the cat found. There on the shore is a large print, just the same as the one found that morning. But tonight, in the very center of the indecipherable track, now grows a single flower, fully mature, its ghost-white petals stretched out towards the glowing sky. A lotus flower. A lotus in the mud. One last miracle. Alone in the muck, but alive.

D ays in the Green pass by like one long, meandering concerto.
There's a musicality to the woods. Not a moment of silence.
A hundred birds across a dozen miles provide a chorus beneath the
nearby river's constant hum. A howl or bellow will echo from entirely
different ends of the forest like a performance of call-and-response.
When the rain falls, pitter-pattering atop the cabin's roof, there lies the
percussion, that steady sound tying together all others in one cohesive
piece.

On clear days, the man wakes up with the sun, and Arthur leaps
from the bed and chirps before trotting off through the trees. The
little cat will spend all day, and sometimes most of the night, outside
doing whatever he pleases. The man notices his friend's weight has
almost doubled. Before, he was a fragile-looking thing, ribs visible even
through a thick black coat, eyes sunken, but their time in the wilds has
been a blessing for Arthur. He hunts birds and mice and an occasional
lizard when they can be ambushed while sunbathing in large groups

atop a boulder. Sometimes while on a stroll, the two will cross paths, and the man will witness his cat hunched over before a bush, tail swaying to test for balance, eyes wide and keenly focused upon whatever hides within, and Arthur will whip around in predatory reflex before recognizing the man and yowl as if to say: *Get out of here. You'll scare it off.* And the man will smile and be on his way. Each night, if only for a few hours, Arthur returns to the cabin where the man sits beside the fireplace, drops a partly eaten carcass at his feet and climbs into his lap to rest for a time. Some nights the man falls asleep alone, but each morning when he awakes there is Arthur, nestled against his leg.

He can't help but worry about Arthur's safety. It is always difficult falling asleep in those dark woods without knowing for certain that his cat is alive, but this is a struggle that he wrestles with over time. A housecat, however wild and skilled, will always have predators, and in these woods there are many. Though what option does he have but to accept the nature of a nocturnal animal? So, when the inevitable worry comes over him in the dead of night, and the man turns in bed to find an empty pocket where a warm body often lies, he can only trust that this life Arthur has is one worth the risk. It is not his right to protect the cat beyond his immediate ability.

When the rain does arrive, it remains for days at a time, and these days are the man's favorite. Arthur refuses to leave the warm cabin and so must make do with what entertainment the man can provide. He fashions a toy from a stick and a loose hawk's feather found on one of his walks, tying it to the end using strips of thick leaves, and the man sits at the edge of the bed, dangling the feather as Arthur stalks beneath the bedframe until ready to pounce. He leaps up like a wonderful acrobat and clings to the feather with all his body weight, head swiveling as he trills and chirps until his claws can no longer hold, and he crashes to the floor far less gracefully. After cleaning himself in embarrassment Arthur then retreats beneath the bed for the game to begin again. And always the man is willing. This game can go on for hours, but the time glides by in a fleeting moment. It's a joy like nothing else to see the little cat so playful and energetic, as if only now that they've assumed a life even vaguely resembling domesticity can Arthur finally allow himself these frivolous moments to be a kitten when before he was never granted the luxury.

When Arthur finally grows tired, he curls up in the man's lap to sleep, and while he twitches and mews and the fire crackles, the man talks. He talks in a low whisper, asking questions and wondering things. He wonders what Arthur thinks, what he would say if he could speak back. If they could ever understand each other beyond gestures. The man sometimes chastises himself for his inability to communicate with such complexity as Arthur without vocalized language. He desperately wants to know that his cat is happy. That he is content. He wants to know if Arthur is ever in pain or if a tooth bothers him and needs to be extracted. If a bird he'd eaten caused his stomach to sour. If this life the man helped provide is a fulfilling one. But he knows that no matter how far he strays from his humanity, how well he blends into this new world, there will always be a certain barrier between him and all other species. Some things he will never know, or at least they will never be spoken aloud. So while Arthur sleeps, the man says these things, but each wandering thought comes from the same root, the only sentiment that is truly important: *I hope you love me too.*

Once the great constellation blooms from the evening sky, the man carefully takes Arthur in his arms and places him atop the bed before stepping outside. The clouds and falling raindrops muddle the lake's cosmic reflection, but it makes it no less beautiful, for on these rainy nights are when the lake feels even more alive as if each dapple upon the surface is its own heartbeat. He sits at the shore and allows the rain to clean the dirt and mud from his skin. He holds out his hands, calloused and blistered from chopping wood, and they kiss his wounds. The man waits there for the beast to return, but not since that first night at the cabin has the creature come back. Where its print once existed in the mud, now washed away by the lake's gentle tide, the white lotus remains, healthy and safe, drinking in the water like lifeblood. Through this the man knows that the beast is not gone. Something like that could not be killed, only birthed and rebirthed and rebirthed again. Nature persists.

Food is becoming an issue. There are only so many fruit trees, and with the amount of strenuous exercise that is now required of him, a diet of apples and sparse roots and mushrooms is simply not enough. One day while exploring the area deeper behind the cabin, the man came upon a small, fenced-off garden. Now overgrown with weeds, and most of the plants destroyed or eaten by fauna, there was once lettuce, cucumber, and tomatoes. He was able to salvage some seeds from the discarded remains half-buried in the soil, and now every day heads to the little garden to tend helplessly to his seedlings. All he can do is water them and stare, wishing there was more he could provide. The man must learn patience, and this experience will force his hand. After living an entire life of instant gratification the concept of nurturing and waiting on living things for the slim possibility of an eventual payout is an arduous task at best. But there is no other option. He will learn to take care of his seedlings, or he will starve. Ever resilient things, a few potato plants did survive. He sits in the soil and watches the lumpy, green objects, waiting for the day they will mature. From everything he's read, they should be ready to harvest in the summer, and with the growing heat and humidity in the air he knows summer is soon approaching.

The rifle stands propped against a corner in the cabin. Still unloaded. The man hasn't touched it since the only time it was fired. He dreads the day that the rifle is in his hands again, but he knows it's coming. He will not survive long without a harvest. Without meat. Arthur kills without thought. He eats the flesh and blood and organs of many things. The man does not damn his little cat for being a carnivore. Why then does he hold himself to a different standard? Just the idea of shooting a living thing, watching its eyes glaze, its body collapse and twitch until going still—it terrifies him. Being a human being, coming from a bountiful civilization, being so utterly alien in comparison to the rest of these woods—it feels unnatural to take a life. That is all humanity has ever done: take. And does he not want to shy from that core of his being? Perhaps he cannot. Perhaps he should not. To deny one's own nature is to let it fester and bloom. He can't simply run away from aspects of himself he deems wrong. Nature is indifferent. But then, as it always does each time his mind arrives at this inevitable moral dilemma, the man thinks of the beast on the lake.

The man fears repercussions. To take a life is no trifling act. It is a great responsibility, a decision that should be made with care. There are times when the man genuinely believes it would be better to starve than risk upsetting that eldritch thing of the woods. And here is where he realizes why it is he comes to the lake each night: The man wants it to speak again. The man wants it to tell him he belongs. Try as he might, the man still feels like a foreign presence in these lands. This is not his home. However ridiculous or impossible, he wishes the beast to give him its blessing. Otherwise, he will be no better than those in a slaughterhouse, packaging tortured flesh to rot in an abandoned grocery store. Just another invader corrupting a land in which he has no jurisdiction. Otherwise, he is no better than those shadowy things he tries so hard to forget. Otherwise, he is just another human being. No different than the rest. A blight on the Green. The personification of a desperate imbalance.

But after many days without food, many days in the new heat of this dawning summer, the man finally accepts something he believes to be true: through nature's indifference, no blessing will ever arrive. It is upon the man, and only the man, to find his own balance within this ever-shifting new world. This is something the beast nor the Green itself can help him discover. For man is a unique species on Earth. We have created morality because for us alone it is necessary. We alone do not operate with an ingrained sense of balance that is intrinsic to all other animals. But morality provided us with no balance at all, that much is clear. It was a flawed experiment to mitigate our destructive nature, and so in disregarding his humanity, he must too disregard this very human concept of right and wrong. By doing this, maybe the fluid stability present all around him will then fill his being. Even though the man was not born with it, perhaps that elusive instinct can be learned. If the man truly wants to cure what he perceives as sickness within himself, then he must recognize which pieces of his humanness must still remain. This, he decides, is the first real step towards equilibrium.

He stares at the rifle for a long time before picking it up. Half hoping the bullets were lost, he finds them embedded deep within the backpack now accumulating dust. The man loads the rifle and sets off.

Arthur left much earlier in the day for his usual romp, and the man is glad for that. A terrible guilt washes over him as he treks deep into the Green, a gnawing paranoia that each sentient tree, each staring bird knows what he's about to do and is sick with judgment. But he must remind himself that there exists nothing but the shadows cast inside his own mind. He thinks far too much. The irony isn't lost on the man—that what perhaps is mankind's greatest strength is also our biggest crutch. Try as he might, these spiraling thoughts cannot be silenced.

Moments like these are the only times when he misses his modern entertainment, his books and his music and drink. His foggy memories of old films he'll never see again. Our greatest achievements are not based on the merits of bravery or exploration but created through the desperate need to escape our own minds. The true lasting inventions of the human species are the tools forged for no purpose but to silence that ever-present voice. While over time the constant ambience of the woods comes close to the same effect, more often than not it only amplifies the inner chaos. The man has no choice but to sit inside that great tumult of his own creation until finally he has heard enough to recognize its meaninglessness. He often daydreams of possessing a soundless mind, and in his darker moments, having woken up from another banal nightmare to find that Arthur still hasn't returned, the man contemplates the prospect of a self-performed lobotomy in all seriousness. This, of course, would only be equal to suicide, and so the thought passes—but the fact that it arrived at all worries him.

There lies the issue: worry. Surely, an animal doesn't worry about anything but that which stands as an immediate threat. They don't waste energy on ghosts. Anything not real is no threat. And thoughts, no matter how pernicious or lifelike in their presentation, are nothing but specters haunting the mind. There could be a hulking bear stalking him right now through the woods, and not until he noticed its shadow cast across the earth would the man finally reel from the necessary instinct that any other creature would have acted upon long before, far more attuned to the present. Wasting his time on these ghosts will inevitably result in the exact outcome they promise to avoid if only he listens. It's yet another terrible irony. Useless but ever so compelling.

The sun burns through the forest canopy, bleaching the leaves and soil in red-orange light, illuminating the clouds of dust that have become more prevalent in the dry heat. It's been a long time since the last rain, and the woods and all its creatures are feeling the effects of summer. The man had hoped it would remain humid and the rain would continue for longer—if not for him and the other living things, then at least for his meager garden—but the new season is fully upon them now, and it is so far unforgiving. He lumbers through the forest with the rifle slung over his shoulder, sweat coating his face and soaking through his thin clothing, and he drinks from the Thermos without thought of conservation. After long enough, deeper and deeper into the Green without catching sight of a single animal, the man lifts the Thermos again to his lips and finds it empty. It finally dawns on him where the creatures must be, and so he doubles back towards the meadow and its river.

He tries not to dwell on all the time wasted trudging through the heat, and the only source of comfort comes from the exhaustion his trek had brought about—for his mind and body are waning in strength, and with that comes a peaceful inability to overthink. He simply doesn't have the energy. True, there is an elusive high that comes from overworking one's body, taking it to the limits of its usefulness. Often when the man has nothing else to do and his mind begins to wander again, he retreats to the bare stump around the cabin's side and chops wood mindlessly for hours at a time until his body relents. It's become a meditative practice, an exercise requiring only blunt force, and it's frankly the sole activity he's yet found to be good at. Piles and piles of wood line the cabin wall, covered from the elements by the tent that now has no other purpose. The man has started to look fondly upon the promise of those coming colder months when his tireless work will finally come of use. Until then, it is something to do and nothing more. There has been nothing to cook, and lighting the fireplace once a night does little to make a dent in the surplus he's created. Though if all goes well today, fire will take on a far more important role in his life.

He reaches the meadow just as his legs begin to give out, and he collapses by the river, forgoing the Thermos to drink directly from the current. The man lies down in the long grass and stares up at the sky. Knowing what it becomes at night, this infinite pale blue canvas is underwhelming in comparison. It's a cloudless sky today, and that only makes the sun's heat that much more unbearable. He steadies his breathing and drinks more before filling the Thermos, and before the man can realize his mistake, his eyelids grow heavy, and his body relaxes. Through the mist of near unconsciousness, he hears gentle steps.

With great effort, he peers through the blurry vista, and there on the far edge of the meadow, head bowed to drink, is a lone buck. Not fifty yards away. He jolts upright and scrambles for the rifle lying beside him. Through the newly fixed scope he aims the crosshairs on the deer's tufted, white chest. Both from hunger and anxiety, his stomach turns, and he swallows the sudden urge to vomit. It's so much closer now, magnified as though he could reach out and touch its sun-warmed coat. He can make out the pale marks dotting its brown fur and the details of its long and beautiful antlers. He watches its chest heave up and down and its bright pink tongue lap at the water. And with one eye, the buck watches him straight through the scope, warily but without fear. It dawns on the man that this animal has never seen a rifle. Perhaps never seen a human being. It doesn't know. It doesn't understand. Not it—he. He doesn't know what's going to happen.

There is a genuine moment where the man decides he would rather starve, rather subsist off mushrooms and apples until he wastes away beneath the trees, and he turns away from the scope and dry heaves. Then, without thought, without hesitation, as if some invisible thing had taken his finger and placed it over the trigger—instinct maybe, or fear of the reality that comes with a slow and hungry death—the man closes one eye, stills his breathing, and fires.

The rifle kicks and smashes the man in the nose. The sounds of ignited gunpowder and a bone breaking are simultaneous. He falls backward as blood drains into his beard and a horrible, stifled shriek erupts throughout the meadow. Great numbers of birds launch from the trees, swarming the air, flitting back and forth in a panic, and the man rights himself, pressing his shirt collar up to his face, and peers across the clearing. The buck is alive. His shot missed the chest but appears to have struck his back leg. The large beast stumbles in circles, limping and letting out desperate moans that echo into the tree line. He tries to sprint away, but then comes a violent snap and the animal collapses onto his side. The moans grow strained and weak but do not stop.

The man struggles to his feet, leaning on the rifle like a crutch, and slowly approaches the deer. Choking on labored breaths, the animal stares at him through one eye, glistening wet and deep brown. He is twice the man's size. A beautiful, enormous living thing. Antlers as weapons and artwork in equal measure, like a crown. His back leg is bent at a grotesque angle, the bone visible. His three remaining limbs twitch and bend. He is still trying in vain to get onto his hooves. To run away.

The man falls to his knees, pivots, and vomits water and bile into the grass. He crawls closer, afraid and hesitant despite the obvious. The great buck is dying. Defenseless. Tears come without warning, first merely wetting his eyes and then in great, ugly torrents. He retches and gasps, and this only frightens the buck more, his eye bulging and wide and more frightened than the man. He reaches out a hand and strokes the beast's convulsing body and speaks aloud for the first time in many, many days: *I'm sorry. I'm sorry. I'm so sorry.*

There is nothing else to do now. The man gets up, shoulders the rifle, and places the muzzle directly to the buck's temple. Through tears and suppressed wails the man can only repeat what he uttered before, as there is nothing else to say. This is his fault, and his words mean nothing to the animal.

I'm sorry.

The man ejects the shell casing, reloads the weapon, and fires. The moaning ceases. The eye glazes over. The body stills. He has completed his first hunt.

The blood pools and coagulates across the grass, shimmering crimson, glinting in the harsh sunlight. The buck is far too large. It was apparent when the man first saw him through the scope, but he hadn't the hindsight or patience to think of what this would foretell. He first attempts to grab the buck's back legs with each hand and drag the animal across the meadow, but after weeks of malnutrition and a physical state enfeebled by exhaustion this quickly proves impossible. So, he has no choice but to kneel over his kill and begin the process of field dressing right there in the clearing. The flocks of birds have returned, understanding that the pandemonium has ceased, and they line the treetops like shrewd colleagues overseeing a medical procedure, squawking and trilling with all musicality absent from their calls.

He unsheathes the knife, and after dry heaving until his stomach twists into a knot, drives the blade into its belly. It punctures the flesh easily enough, and a noxious miasma emits from the wound when he retracts. More blood leaks into the meadow, and when he reinserts the blade and widens the gash the entrails spill out like great writhing worms. The man stops, prostrates himself before the river, and dry heaves again and again until finally a thin string of bile ejects from his stomach, and he turns back around, removes his shirt and ties it around his face, and continues. Once the belly is entirely split, he reaches in with both arms and begins scooping out the organs, severing tendons and connective tissue when necessary. They are heavy things, and one by one, he removes each piece of what was once a breathing organism. The liver is like a dense stone held against his chest, bigger than his head, and while he is busy in awe of this massive, bleeding object, the man slips, drops the liver, and falls directly on top of the pile of intestines and the stomach lying haphazardly by his side. The man's full body weight comes down upon the organs, and before he can understand from where the violent popping sound had come, a mass of half-digested food, warm excrement, and various other colorful secretions burst from the fresh puncture wound and douse his legs and torso. He screams as if having been stabbed himself and leaps instinctively into the river. The current is strong but shallow, and the man comes down with such force that the jagged rocks lining the riverbed slice through the skin on his arms and chest, and he now lies prone as the water dashes across his half-naked body until its glittering, clear hue turns red and brown and yellow, bleeding together and washing away downstream like the aftermath of some terrible skirmish.

The man remains in the water for a while, allowing the current to sting his many abrasions. In a manic state, he begins scrubbing himself, the sediment adhered to his palms acting like steel wool against his skin. When he finally stands, his arms and chest have been rubbed red and raw, and a thousand tiny cuts bleed freely, but the deer's viscous remains are no longer a part of the mess. He then returns to the carcass, knife in hand, and finishes hollowing out the cavity, making sure to toss all inedible organs downriver.

Once the buck has been properly gutted, the man begins flaying the skin. But not five minutes into the procedure do the flies arrive, and within fifteen minutes they have become a massive black cloud, buzzing around the blood and sticky pieces still coating the grass, and they commandeer the dead body, covering its back and head and open stomach, little black limbs brimming with red matter, rubbing it into their alien faces, buzzing, buzzing, buzzing, and the man tries in vain to swat them away but they have descended upon the corpse like an impenetrable army, and so the man gives up on flaying the beast. Its skin is peeled back halfway over its body up to the neck where only the blank-eyed head remains unmolested, but now those eyes too have become landing pads for the flies, and they stick their limbs and faces into the black juices before the organs dry up. There is nothing to do now, nothing to do at all but salvage what meat can be saved before they lay their eggs and inject their feces and disease into the stilled blood vessels.

Screaming as if in the throes of psychosis, the man stabs the blade into the muscles in the legs and buttocks and shoulders, carves out large, bleeding chunks, and with no proper place to put them, merely sheaths his knife, shoulders his rifle, and gathers the flesh up in his arms like cradling a massacred infant before sprinting away from the meadow, into the tree line, away from the carnage, away from that terrible mistake, away from his failure, never ceasing his frenzied escape until finally reaching the cabin.

Gasping for air, the man drops his tools and the mass of flesh inside his abode. He shuts the door, and after taking in a long, deep breath, he walks slowly towards the lake. He stands at its shore, his entire upper half sticky with layers of blood and viscera; his scrapes still weeping, blending with those foreign liquids. The forest is calm and quiet. Somewhere, a blue jay trills. A frog croaks from a lily pad floating atop the lake's surface. The sun reaches through the canopy in thin pockets of golden light, bathing the leaves, illuminating their stark green shades. The man looks around at all this vivid beauty. And it is. It is quite beautiful.

He then dives headfirst into the lake. Swimming deeper and deeper until the light can no longer reach, until the murky darkness surrounds his being. The man floats there in the soundless, cool abyss, watching the blood and guts drift in the dark like lost souls. When he emerges, all that remains are the bleeding remnants of his wounds and only his. He climbs back onto the shore and looks out across the sacred water, now tinged with things never meant to be introduced. The colors stay beneath the surface, pulled this way and that but never rising, as if they too understand the sacrilege of their presence here.

He is no longer hungry.

That evening Arthur comes home to a venison meal. The man sits by the lit fireplace, gazing into the flames as if they will eventually divine his future. While Arthur eats happily without question, the man forces himself to swallow a handful of roots and berries and continues adding logs to the flame. This is one thing he can do right. He can chop wood and keep a fire going. And so as the sky darkens and the black stars return, long after Arthur has gotten his fill and curled up to sleep atop the mattress, long after the remaining flesh is left to fester and accumulate bacteria, the man continues stoking the fire, adding logs.

It's a quiet night. A part of him expects some kind of revenge to occur—for the Green to swallow up the cabin, crushing him and it between its many thick trunks or command a pack of starved wolves to convene upon their dwelling—but nothing happens at all. This proves to be its own punishment: the silence. He stays awake until dawn's orange glow reemerges along the horizon, setting the lake ablaze, and all the while there is nothing but the man's own thoughts for company. The man does not shy from these thoughts. He allows them to encompass his mind, to remind him again and again. To tell him of his failure. To chastise him. The man sits with these grotesque images until finally he learns.

He glances over at the rancid pile of meat. Arthur ate what he needed and left the rest.

Over the next lingering weeks the man changes course. He dons his backpack again, stuffing the tent inside, and leaves for overnight trips deep into the woods, leaving a window cracked open so Arthur can retreat back inside the cabin when he wishes to sleep safely. Upon returning from these trips, the man arrives home with rabbit or sometimes quail if his accuracy stays true, and stuffed within his pockets are separated piles of berries and foraged plants. He plucks and guts the quail or skins the rabbit—never more than two kills per excursion—once he arrives home, and cooks the tender meat atop a thin wooden slat over the fire.

Never a single part of the animal goes unused. He lines the windows with tanned rabbit furs to block out the sun during the hottest hours or—using his fingers, knife, many intertwined grass stalks, and a painstaking amount of focus—sews the furs into a macabre kind of pillowcase, stuffing it full of quail feathers before completing the piece. The pillows are terribly uncomfortable and often burst open, but in either case Arthur finds purpose for them, sleeping atop the man's Frankensteinian creations or delightedly prancing across the cabin as he tries to capture the loose floating feathers. Any edible organs are collected in a deep, wood-fashioned bowl with other roots and plants and boiled atop the fire with river water until becoming what could be called soup. Without salt or other spices, it is a disgusting meal, but the man no longer cares for satisfying his cravings, and the protein and vitamins reinvigorate his body. Arthur now eats better than he ever has in his short life. Whatever organs the man isn't sure he can safely eat, or that which he doesn't need to consume for his own vitality, are Arthur's. He likes quail hearts. He likes rabbit kidneys. The man is happy to give him these.

For the first time since his arrival in the Green, he feels refreshed in the mornings, and not sickly but thoroughly exhausted as one should be when he lays down his head at night. The man is so tired that his mind simply can't be bothered to dream. As he wanders through the woods, there is no longer time to spend thinking. There is always a task to perform, always something in his tangible world that demands the entirety of his focus. In those rare, late-night restful moments when no work needs to be done, the man lights a fire, sits down on the cabin's floor, takes out his growing pile of cleaned animal bones from his backpack, and for hours at a time will lose himself in the act of artmaking. He arranges the bones in different shapes and designs like bleached white frescos along the floor while Arthur sleeps in his lap. There is no conscious reason for the designs he creates. It is just something to do. Something to occupy his hands and, much more importantly, his mind. When Arthur inevitably awakens from his light slumber his eyes grow wide and curious, and he promptly leaps upon the bones, dashing away any progress made, running underneath the bed with his favorite few sticking out of his mouth, and there he remains, mewing and growling and kicking at the bones with the paradoxical temperament of both a kitten and a violent predator.

When Arthur then falls asleep beneath the bed, curled atop his trove of new toys like a dragon guarding its treasure, the man steps out onto the lake's shore to gaze at the black stars. He takes stock of their shifting radiance, of the singular constellation's glittering corners and violet, ectoplasmic center, and returns to the cabin to recreate the night sky from memory. He arranges the bones one section at a time, doubling back to the lake to absorb all that he can see, and continues his work. This will sometimes take hours, but he does not care. His perception of time ceases, and the present moment becomes the only reality. Once he is finished, the man stands up—the fireplace coughing and spitting as the logs have now collapsed beneath red, air-choked embers—and looks down at his replica of that infinite organ. In his exhaustion, after staring into the bones for long enough, sometimes the man can see its thoughts. He can read the mind of the universe. Each night it says the same thing, the same thing he heard from the bottom of the lake on that fateful evening so long ago. The same thing uttered in his darkest dreams. Always the same thing. The bones say: *Wake up.*

On the hottest day the man has yet experienced, tragedy strikes. He hikes out to the small garden hidden far behind the cabin to find the maturing vegetables destroyed. During the night, deer or other hungry beasts must have known what he too understood, that these precious foods were finally of age to be eaten, and did precisely that. The garden is in ruins. Colorful guts and seeds lay strewn about the soil, and within the space of a single glance, the man accepts that no summer harvest will arrive. All that remains are the potatoes—those hardy things, like cockroaches embedded in the earth. Still half-buried, the animals must not have bothered with the hassle of digging them up when there was so much else to feed upon. And so with no other option, and despair still lingering in that compartmentalized area of his psyche, the man reaches into the dirt and begins reaping the last surviving plant. The potatoes are small and golden-brown and warm from the sun, and as the man holds this meager bounty up to the beams reaching like angelic tendrils through the great oak canopy, he finds peace and acceptance. Something still lives, nurtured and cared for and watered and dutifully watched, and this is his reward. He thinks of the wolves and their litters and of the impossible odds that face each newly born pup, and through this outlook he is grateful. However silly the notion, these potatoes are his lucky children that withstood nature's brutal indifference.

He travels towards the river to bathe his golden survivors, to clean them for their immediate use. It has been so long since he has eaten anything like them. He wishes to cut them up, to fry them in grease and butter, but of course this is impossible. The potatoes will be boiled, and they will be mostly flavorless, but the idea of a plate of rabbit meat with mushrooms and potatoes is one so tantalizing he soon discards any previous thoughts. There is a certain sense of pride that comes from looking at a meal and knowing that each individual element of its preparation was handled by you and you alone. That satisfaction will have to hold space where salt and grease cannot.

The meadow is crowded this afternoon. With such sweltering heat, a great number of fauna have congregated by the river to drink and exist lazily where the current is slowest. A herd of goats gather in a molting bunch, their coats stripping away with the wind, and a pack of wolves linger at the far end, taking turns lapping at the clear water while their friends watch the clearing through narrowed, yellow eyes. A few dogs hide in the center of the pack—retrievers and shepherd mixes—those breeds large and tough enough to be granted a place among the ranks of wild things. Seeing this always reminds the man of his little dog. That poor creature stood no chance even if it had survived. Guilt often strikes at his chest when he thinks back on all the dachshunds and teacup poodles and terriers he helped escape from their locked houses. He knows what fate befell them all, but it was that or simply another similar end. Those maladapted amalgams had been cursed with twisted genetics long before the man ever came to be, so each of their short and tragic lives always were to cease with a pitiful finale. Though he pities them all the same, some things are beyond our control. Most things.

In the meadow's center stand two deer, a buck and doe, heads bowed together as they drink. The man kneels beside the river and begins washing the dirt from his bounty and watches the deer. They seem to have no peripheral awareness, eyes vacant, tongues hanging loose from their mouths like vestigial organs. He worries for these animals. Whether stupid or careless, he's grown to care for them deeply. His terrible experience with the great buck affected the man on what could only be considered a spiritual level, and now, certainly more from guilt than anything, he feels the unnecessary urge to protect the deer he comes across. Penance, he supposes. The man watches the wolf pack with one eye, awaiting the moment one of the larger males makes the decision to attack. But the beasts are uninterested, whether they already ate their fill or it's merely the soaring temperature keeping them too sedated to give chase. Eventually, the man relents, returning his full focus to the task before him. He contemplates stripping off his clothes, washing them and himself in the river, but it's at this docile moment that he notices a new form entering the clearing.

A lone mountain lion steps forth through the tree line, head lowered, with its nose to the grass. It's a massive creature, hulking, arched shoulders, and paws larger than the man's head. Its legs are wide and muscular and, frankly, frightening to behold. But its face is a beautiful thing, narrow features made more feminine by the black markings reaching across the brow and around the symmetrical nose like eye shadow and dark contour. Its coat is sleek and pale brown, with a wide frame composed of far more lean sinew than fat. It is a predator like nothing else in the Green. It's a rare thing to find one at all, let alone during the day in such an open area. Though all things must drink, it's soon made clear that this is not the cougar's intention.

The goats and wolves both take immediate notice, and even the pack over a dozen strong absconds from the meadow. They go one way and the herd of prey in another, and within seconds the open space is empty, save the man, the two deer, and the mountain lion. He watches, paralyzed by that familiar terror response, as the gorgeous, violent predator stalks ever nearer to the oblivious pair. If this were a different day, his rifle would have been slung over his shoulder, but even then the man knows he wouldn't have the strength to fire. It's not his right. This is the everlasting performance upon the world's stage, and to step in—truly step in—would be a slight to that very balance he so yearns to encompass. With this acceptance and no ability to run, no mind clever enough to create a better solution, the man watches the buck turn just as the cougar leaps high in the air, paws spread with claws like knives, and crashes down atop the smaller doe. A shrill, explosive screech shatters the idyllic silence, and the cougar snarls, thunderous and deep. Not a moment of hesitation occurs. The buck takes a single glance at the violence bleeding crimson into the river's current, turns from his mate, and sprints away into the woods. There in a writhing heap of torn flesh and monstrous, guttural sounds, the cougar mounts the screaming doe, her once untarnished hide slashed into separate ribbons, opens its jaws to reveal long and yellow canines, and in one swift motion clamps down upon the deer's throat. A final bray escapes before transmuting into a stifled wet gurgle, and her back legs turn rigid, vibrating with a thousand tiny convulsions, bodily death rattles acting as a final cry for help where the vocal cords had failed. The cougar releases its grip after a few long seconds and stands hunched atop the leaking mass, breathing, staring at its sudden stillness. There is silence again.

Still too afraid to move, the man remains in the exact same position, huddled beside the river, the potatoes like precious doubloons cupped in his hands, and he waits for the victorious beast to grasp its victim again in its jaws and drag the body away to where it will dine in peace. But after many, many moments, nothing of the sort occurs. Instead, the cougar steps away, eyes still zeroed in on the doe. Waiting—for what?

It does not take long to understand. Finally, borne from the tension like an infant's first cry outside the womb, the doe erupts back to life, unleashing a shriek the likes of which the man has never heard and will never forget. She attempts to leap up but stumbles and falls back to the ground, and the cougar, reinvigorated by this brutal display, begins batting at the helpless animal like a toy. It circles the doe, eyes never leaving its target, watching her scream and struggle, watching her bleed out from the neck and back, and reaches out its paw, slapping the doe in the face, in the open wounds—not with force but quite softly. Almost innocently. It then begins jumping back and forth over the dying animal, batting again and again, its long, thick tail swaying in the air. Playing with her. Playing with the screaming creature. She tries again to get up, to run, and when this attempt is proved nearly successful, the cougar's temperament changes. With a sudden ferocity, its paw comes down hard on the doe's neck, crushing it until she relents and goes still again, ever breathing. And the dance continues. Whether from exhaustion or blood loss, or that final acceptance that hope is gone, the doe at last stops moving. She stops crying. Only now does the cougar lose interest, as though it was the apparent agony, the struggle that enticed it so much. With the doe motionless, soundless, even as the cougar continues slapping her head, begging her to keep playing, the predator eventually understands that the wicked game is over. It is the greatest relief when jaws again clench down on the victim's neck, and squeeze until no life remains. Dead. Finally dead.

The mountain lion then drags the stiff body away, across the quiet meadow and into the Green's cloaked embrace.

There were so many terrors within that decrepit city, so many violent reminders of the apathetic society from which it was born. So many remnants and reminders of why the man detests his own species. So many failings and inconsequential things, all created to abate the very fears that we ourselves have brought about. The city represents everything the man hates about mankind, everything that he saw as diametrically opposed to the Eden beyond its walls, to the perfection of nature. But in all his life, all his many years and memories of a manmade world, of people more like monsters than genetic kin, of horrific acts and words slung at others meant to be loving siblings in some distant but undeniable fashion, what he has witnessed is an atrocity that he would have never before identified as the behavior of an animal. What he has witnessed is an act he once thought could only be committed by a human being.

The man accepts that his binary perception of this large and unfathomable world is flawed. Terribly, naively flawed. Life, after all, was born from chaos. It should be no surprise that life still operates by the very same laws of its conception. But because something is true does not make it any easier to bear.

When the man returns to the cabin, he does not leave again for three days. He remains in bed with a sudden fever. After the third day his illness relents, and he emerges from a fugue state, changed in some way that he cannot explain.

Growing bored with his solitude, Arthur begins joining the man on his excursions into the woods. It never occurred to the man that the little cat may want to come along, but he is more than happy to have him. After only these few months in the Green, the pair's relationship has developed beyond that of a human and his animal. Entire conversations are held without a word but only the subtle gestures of a twitching tail and a facial expression. The man, without thinking about it, has stopped using his native tongue altogether, instead communicating with garbled attempts at mimicking Arthur's vocalizations. He feels like a visitor to a foreign land trying his best through a broken second language to speak to the local guide, but Arthur always reciprocates his clumsy, silly noises, as if to say, *that's wrong but you get the idea. Here, pronounce it like this.* In reality, the man knows fully well that no actual communication is taking place when they trade these utterances back and forth—it's more akin to shared baby-talk than anything meaningful—but even the simple act of chirping at one another seems to have become a kind of bonding exercise. A game of call-and-response. *I hear you, and you hear me.* And that too is important, the recognition of one another's presence. *I see you, and you see me.*

Beyond this, the real communication is all entirely silent. Body language is a largely subconscious mechanism. All his life, the man has communicated things through his posture, hand movements, and facial expressions without even being aware of what it is he's communicating beneath whatever words spoken. Often, his gestures betray the words themselves. If one were to truly understand the complexity of body language, they would be the finest lie detector of their species. Here then is where body language becomes a fascinating thing to learn, to be aware of. Because the far majority of bodily communications occur subconsciously, this language is one of total truth above all. Unless one is a master of their own inner self, of their every movement and each minute gesture's emotive translation and is then able to make use of it as a master linguist makes use of their chosen dialect, then it becomes quite apparent that we, when broken down to the very base of ourselves, are utterly incapable of lying. Whatever untruth may slide off one's tongue, a keen enough bodily interpreter will see the betrayal of those very words painted across the speaker's posture and physical demeanor. This in turn has only strengthened the man's relationship with his little black cat. Without a single vocalization, they are in constant commune. Together, they share their fears, their excitement, and their wants. Each is reciprocated with truth and understanding. Their love for one another continues to bloom in total silence.

The summer heat has grown more intense, but with it now blossoms that familiar humidity signaling coming rain. The shift towards another season is soon approaching. They trek through the trees and sunlight, and the man stops much more often than he otherwise would to allow Arthur his simple pleasures. The cat is eternally awestruck by the swirling scents of flowers and other plants, and from time to time will stop and sit on his haunches, cocking his head with expectant eyes at the base of one tree or another until the man sits down beside him. When he makes it clear that he's not going anywhere, Arthur leaps onto the tree trunk, sinking his claws into the soft oak wood with ears pinned to the back of his head, and begins the arduous climb up the great living thing until arriving within the thicket of its many leaves upon whatever bough has been deemed to be the one worthy. There, Arthur surveys his surroundings from an otherworldly view, his innocent eyes so wide, glistening in the light, taking in the majesty of such an unfathomable foreign landscape.

All the while, the man grins and stares up at the little black cat, rifle slung over his shoulder, his eyes wavering every few moments to maintain awareness of their surroundings, of any game or approaching threat. Before, he never worried about the passing presence of a brown bear or a pack of stalking wolves, as they found no reason to hunt something that would prove a difficult kill. But now with Arthur by his side on his treks, the man finds himself acutely aware and increasingly wary of any carnivorous animal within their vicinity. Arthur is a wily thing, intelligent and reflexive, but it doesn't change his size and inability to prove a worthy adversary for a bold predator. And so while Arthur basks in the sun atop his chosen branch the man keeps one hand firmly on his rifle.

Whatever change had occurred over those three hallucinatory days of illness has become a permanent transformation. The man has done away with guilt over his hunting, and when given thought, he has no qualms with the idea of slaying a beast that may come to kill his friend. For that is survival. A mother bear would brutally maul the man to death were he to step between her and her cubs, and he would understand. It is that same understanding that gives birth to his newfound assuredness. Were a creature to attack his cat, it would die swiftly. That is all, and he thinks not of it beyond the awareness that this would be the case. No guilt arrives, in the same way that he feels nothing when a hare comes into his rifle's scope. There is no guilt because the man now intrinsically understands that this is survival and nothing more. He does not kill more than he needs, and when that kill occurs, the creature does not ever suffer. With a surplus of ammunition at his disposal, the man now regularly heads to a spot in the woods where he practices his aim, firing from various distances at a wood-fashioned target. He has become adept with his weapon. He knows how to account for wind and distance and the curvature of the Earth if his prey is far enough away. The man does not miss. One bullet equals one kill. Swift and sudden, arriving with but a fraction of pain that the brain probably hasn't even the time to process before the act is complete. The man sees this as crucial to his place in the Green. There is no need to suffer, for death and suffering need not be synonymous.

Hours pass by with no sight of any game, and so the man diverts his view from the horizon to the earth, scanning the bushes and soil for edible vegetation. This happens, and the man feels no disappointment about it. It only means one less death on his hands and a bit more time spent in the deepest reaches of the Green. It's been a painful process identifying which plants will and will not harm him. As much as the man can rack his brain trying to recall those various images from the survival books, in practice it has done little good. His methodology now consists of collecting any vaguely familiar plants, sitting down on the cabin floor with a bucket by his side, and one by one consuming each individual sample in small doses, then waiting an hour to discover the results. He is right more often than wrong, but each incorrect identification bodes for horrible results. Alas, this is the only option he has. That or starve. So far, no reaction has proved to be more harmful than a few hours of purging. This is the price one pays for knowledge.

If only he could have seared those many books' information into his mind, but he is no genius or savant. Worse still, the man's memory seems to wane with each new day. It's as if his mind is attempting to erase all recollection of that foul city piece by piece, stealing away fractions of his previous life while he sleeps unguarded. It's an unsettling thought, one's own mind performing some vampiric ritual each night. Whether or not it has an altruistic purpose—a farfetched defense mechanism or protective trauma response—this still feels like an underhanded mutiny. He doesn't want to forget these things, for perforating the terror and disgust were still moments of genuine beauty. The man fears that his mind is incapable of parsing out the good from the bad, and by peeling away the residue of awful experiences it will also take with it unintended collateral. His very worst fear is that one day he will wake up having lost all recollection of loved ones, simply for the fact that they too existed somewhere within that twisted hive of agony. And so it's become a kind of meditative practice for the man to sit in silence, allowing his memory to flood into the front of his mind—the good, the bad, the horrific and blissful. In this way, it's become a war between his conscious and subconscious needs. If doing away with the scent of charred flesh and the image of burning pyres means losing Mable, losing the little dog, then it is simply not an option. He would rather feel and remember everything than nothing at all. The perfection of those few memories would never have been so powerful were it not for the terrible circumstances in which they existed. The Green and its ethereal inhabitants would not now lie before his eyes were it not for those shadowy things so far away, their inky remnants still dripping from the darkest crevices of his mind. One cannot be without the other.

They soon arrive at a brush thicket full with ripe berries, and scattered throughout the nearby forest floor are many different roots, along with patches of edible mushrooms growing beneath tree trunks like adopted children. The man gets to work collecting a few handfuls of each, coming upon some redwood sorrel as well. The little green clovers cover the earth in wide swathes, and the man plucks a few of the peculiar things to use as added flavor for his paltry soups. They taste exactly like green apple skins, and upon first discovering this, the man was so enraptured by their sour tang that he shoveled great mouthfuls down his throat, only to learn that when ingested in large quantities, redwood sorrel acts as a natural laxative. Since then he has learned to consume them sparingly.

Forever carnivorous, Arthur sniffs at the man's collection with indifference before trotting off through the brush for a meal possessing a heartbeat. Gathering plants forms an intimate bond with the soil, and soon the man loses his peripheral awareness as he becomes absorbed by the sensation of warm earth on his fingers. He becomes so focused on the peaceful act that for a good few minutes he doesn't recognize Arthur's cries. Not until they grow loud and strained does the man finally look up, and there before him is his little black cat, his tail rigid and ears pinned, emitting a low, grumbling yowl. Arthur stands with his back to the man, for there is something far more important on which to keep his focus.

Not ten feet away stands a mangled, snarling coyote. The man very slowly gets to his feet and returns its piercing eye contact. The creature is terribly malnourished, its ribs visible through a coat of fur that only remains in patches. Its eyes are wild and desperate, its head hung low. A steady, white foam emits from its jaws. Its entire body twitches as if a great colony of worms writhe just beneath the skin. The man glances around the brush, awaiting others to arrive as well, but none come.

The coyote is alone, a pariah banished from its home, far too sick to remain with its kind. All the while, Arthur stands between the man and beast, his cries now heard and so transmuted into a kind of violent growl the man has never heard from him before. As much as he needs the creature to focus on him, its agenda is all too clear. The coyote is dying and is unable to kill a man, but is quite able to kill a cat. To eat a cat. To survive if just for a day longer. He needs Arthur to run, to climb a tree where the disheveled beast can't follow, but Arthur will not. He has made a decision—however stupid, however borne of a protective instinct. The coyote steps closer, the accumulating white foam dripping onto the soil in long, infectious globs. So too does Arthur. A step each, their narrowed postures boiling over with the anticipation of violence. Everything within the man screams for him to freeze, to become a fixture of the Green and blend away, to disappear. But that instinct is now a foreign one, borne of a different place, an altogether different person. And as the coyote takes another step forward and opens its maw, preparing to leap upon the outmatched housecat, the man shoulders his rifle and aims. Arthur screeches, lifting onto his back paws with his claws outstretched, and in one graceful movement betraying its condition, the coyote erupts forward. And there in that split second of frozen time, a great white light expands, and an explosion echoes throughout all the Green. A yelp bursts forth as if simply a continuance of the bullet's ignition, and there, midleap, the rabid creature's body crumples and twists backward, collapsing to the ground in a wheezing heap. Its head sinks into the earth barely an inch from Arthur's adamant position. Even the gunshot didn't frighten the little cat away from his friend. Still he stands between the man and the gasping, dying beast.

The man kneels and turns away to vomit, spitting until the bitter taste no longer coats his tongue, and only now does Arthur turn and approach, rubbing his face against the man's perspiring forehead. The coyote breathes heavily, its body stiff, while its eyes roll around in their sockets as if trying to make sense of the event. Or taking one last good look, trying to see everything left there is to see. The man strokes Arthur again and again until he finally purrs and lifts him up to plop the cat behind his boots. He then ejects the shell casing, reloads his rifle, and stands over the sick coyote. It stares up at him, breathing. There is no malice between the two living things. No anger or hatred. Just separate goals for separate reasons. A victor and victim. He aims the rifle without ceremony and fires a bullet into the animal's head. The shot rings throughout the woods. The coyote is dead. The man and his cat are alive. Nature persists. Mercifully indifferent.

The man drops his rifle and picks up Arthur, squeezing him tight against his chest. He kisses his soft forehead and strokes his fur. The little black cat tucks his face into the man's arm. There are no words shared, but with this act they communicate something as clearly as anything spoken aloud: *You saved my life.*

After this tumultuous experience, the man is more than ready to return home. He swivels around, still standing over the corpse, and finds that he has lost all sense of direction. When first starting off on his treks, the man used to bring along his compass in case he lost his way, but now he has grown so accustomed to his many intertwining paths that the compass remains in the cabin. But from this verdant patch he recognizes no landmarks and can't remember from which direction they arrived. He knows that the sun hangs lower in the sky than it did the last time he checked, and so that way is west. He also knows that when he left this morning it was in a southward direction, for it was the opposite way from the meadow which sits north of the lake. With this in mind—and the only information to go off of—the man glances at the sun and then at the massive swath of greens and turns to head what must be north.

The pair pass by foreign areas lush with flora the man has never yet witnessed, some of which appear edible—but his pockets are full, and after the encounter with the coyote, he feels no inclination towards another kill. So despite the many bounties they come across, he continues on. Arthur is happy either way, entirely at peace with whichever direction they may be going. The man can assume that any place he has not yet been Arthur has already crossed many times. Since the nights have grown shorter and warmer, the little cat has made good use of those dark hours, and it isn't until the earliest morning light that he finally returns home to fall asleep on the man's leg.

The man glances at Arthur quite often as they walk, checking for any signs of effect from the skirmish, but his cat appears unfazed. He is back to his regular self, traipsing through bushes to surprise the man as he always does, stopping once in a while to mew until the man stops so he can climb a tree and bask in the sun. It's as if the event hadn't bothered him at all. This is something about Arthur the man has long known and long desired to emulate: if it is not occurring in this present moment then it no longer exists. The threat is gone, and so any accompanying reaction has no purpose hanging about. He could chalk it up to the poor memory of an animal with a much smaller brain, but that would be reductive and simply untrue. For better or worse, his little black cat is forever existent only within the precise moment he now stands. If in this very second he can draw breath, and there are no signs of an approaching or immediate threat, then there is nothing to worry about. In fact, worrying now would only prove to be its own threat, for that would take him away from the present and thus make him susceptible to things he would otherwise notice right away. It is only the man that still dwells on events that no longer exist, and so he releases this thought into the air where it evaporates with the rest of the summer heat. When that feral thing first pawed at his sliding glass door, the man would never have thought that on that day he had met his greatest teacher. Walking through the Green alongside

Arthur is like having an enlightened child as company. His presence is a blessing like nothing the man has ever experienced.

The trees soon begin to part, and more and more sunlight burns through the thinning canopy. If it weren't for the idling clouds in the sky, the heat may be unbearable. But the man reminds himself that this is only the season's final vibrant gasp before relenting to what's next in the eternal procession. He misses the rain and the crisp coolness of autumn's breeze. He misses the scent of wet leaves and moist earth. And where in the city there were sporadic bursts of colorful trees, here in the woods it must be a sight like nothing else—a whole forest on fire with every warm shade the eye can perceive. The man now looks forward to the changing seasons like a child looks forward to his birthday. There is always something new on the horizon, something gorgeous to look forward to. The Green has carved itself into a timeless pocket of the universe, forever changing and yet perpetually the same.

The man first believes he somehow made a mistake and they've arrived at the familiar meadow past his cabin, but upon entering the clearing, an utterly foreign sight unfurls before him. He had heard stories of the place lifetimes before this one, before it all happened. The memories of voices once a fading echo come to the forefront of his mind as he recognizes exactly what this clearing is, or what it once was, however long ago. The stories had always remained just that, as the man had never visited the place—for what reason would there have been? But now as he stands at the edge of a wide, verdant field in the middle of the Green, the man feels like this is precisely where he is now meant to be.

In his many years alone, with only animals and vaguely humanoid eldritch things for neighbors here on Earth, the man has finally found his kin. He has finally discovered his fellow *Homo sapiens*.

The body farm sits long abandoned, but the fruits of its efforts have come to bloom. Scattered across the meadow are hundreds and hundreds of skeletal remains spread out elegantly like decorative pieces, some having been picked apart by animals looking to harvest the marrow. Others retain their full form: skulls and ribs and arms and legs, hips and shoulders and feet and hands, laid to rest atop the grass exactly how they'd been placed when flesh still covered their now sun-bleached bones. The field runs flat for nearly as far as the man can see, like an ocean of rich emerald, the wind creating waves out of the bristling grass. And all across this green sea, the skeletons float as such peaceful things. There isn't an animal in sight, and no noises carry across the breeze but the gentle coo of the breeze itself. This field is the last bastion of mankind—the last true bastion. For so long, the man wondered where his kin had gone, and all the while they'd been rotting away in the Green, sinking into the earth to feed the grass and the trees and the creatures alike. Their souls have departed, their flesh stripped, but nonetheless, the man has found a certain separation from his lonesomeness that he can't place. Like returning home, perhaps, to a life left behind. There's a shimmering, tangible nostalgia present in the air here—like oil vapors rising from a hot asphalt road.

Arthur trots ahead, finds the massive open area exhilarating, and proceeds to sprint at full speed through the long grass, back and forth, around in circles, entirely indifferent to the death surrounding him. But that's perhaps because this death is a kind barely resembling the dead at all. For as the man sits down cross-legged in the center of the field and stares at the many separated parts of his species, he sees the beautiful end result.

Growing out of each skeleton, intertwining through the ribs, and bursting from out the open jaws and empty eye sockets, are the most vivid bouquets the man has ever seen. As if some great observer had come by to honor the deceased, born from the dead are hundreds of patches of colorful flowers. They dot the clearing like planted flags denoting the position of each fallen man, woman, and child. Foxgloves and poppies, daisies and tulips, roses and lilacs, irises and orchids and sunflowers—all vibrant, eclectic shades of yellows and purples and blues and reds. Concentrated kaleidoscopic arrays, birthed from the very elements broken down by the ancestors of those which now stand so brilliant and full of life. It is the encapsulation of life's infinite cycle a thousand times over. In each bouquet and each collection of bones from which they bloomed is the marriage of two polar opposites, now locked in embrace. It is the ouroboros that pales all others, the physical manifestation of the blurred line between life's end and beginning. And it, the man understands, would never have come to be were it not for humanity and nature's equal cooperation—for a tentative balance to be found.

It comes to the man only after many long moments staring into the vast scene. For perhaps the first time in his life, his brain hasn't emitted a single sound. Not one thought has crossed his mind. For the very first time, the man exists in this field of skeletons and flowers—and nowhere else. He smiles. That is all the recognition he will give of time's passage. There is nothing else to do but be embraced within the glowing nucleus of life and death, nature and mankind. Aware but silent in both mind and body. Present.

When the man is finally willing to return, when the gaps in the far tree line cradle the setting sun like a jewel in a chalice, the man stands and begins walking home with Arthur at his side. The forest hums with life, the heat settles into a gentle, damp warmth, and only now do those oft repeated words come to him in a language at last decoded, the words spoken in dreams, in different tongues and different voices. Different dialects and phrasing. As prayer or threat or plea, but always the same. And the man understands.

He is prepared to face that which is no longer impossible. He is ready to come home.

The man is ready to wake up.

C *ome to me.*

It's still dark out. The man rises from bed and looks around the black walls of the cabin. Arthur sleeps peacefully at the end of the mattress. What an odd dream. He can't remember its events but only the lingering emotion that remains stuck to the inside of his skull, buzzing around like the aftermath of some experimental drug. Something must have shaken him out of unconsciousness—he never wakes in the middle of the night any longer—but as he sits in the darkness, straining his ears to shake off the residual dream-induced hallucinations, he can't hear the voice any longer. He's sure something had spoken, something separate from the overlapping cacophony within his mind—but there's nothing at all.

He stands and pulls away the rabbit furs covering the window, and piercing white moonlight strikes him in the face, flooding the cabin. The man shades his eyes and peers through the glass for any signs of life or movement. There is nothing to perceive beyond the blinding glare. It's a full moon tonight. All the forest's creatures run wild and excited on these nights, exhilarated by the monthly glow that burns away the otherwise unrelenting shadows. A buck or hunting wolf must have scurried past the cabin and bumped into his wood stockpile, causing a commotion that shook him awake. But Arthur remains asleep. That little thing with far keener senses surely would have erupted from the mattress at the slightest noise. And while he can see nothing through the moonlight and hear nothing beyond the walls, the man's skin prickles as if something is breathing down his neck. Though his mind is not yet, his body is very aware of another being's presence somewhere outside. The man has learned to trust this subconscious instinct. The mind takes time to perceive, but like the difference between the speed of light and sound, the body's perception of stimuli is nearly immediate. Choosing to trust his body over his drowsy mind, the man opens the cabin door and steps out towards the lake.

It's cold outside. There are no clouds and no stars. There is only the glowing orb hanging over the lake as if it had risen directly from the water. The sky has never been so desolate. A black sky. The lake's surface is a reflection of the moon and nothing else, its entire surface shimmering white like a portal to some beautiful new place. The man steps closer until his bare feet touch the shore, allowing his eyes to adjust. He can feel it. Something is here. If it were a simpler animal, he could sense a presence in a particular direction, or if it were many he could sense their stares from specific positions around him. But it isn't many—it's a single living thing. He knows that. And yet its presence, its beating heart and expanding lungs, its exhalations, funnel into his ears and eyes from every conceivable avenue. This thing, this living, breathing being, watches him as if it's a part of each blade of grass and each swaying tree. It is everywhere at once.

Something appears on the lake. Not from under its surface but atop the water. This undulating mist condenses into a corporeal entity, like a ghost materializing back into its previous physical form. The man can only stare as it comes into being, first the vague silhouette of a familiar shape, then a skeleton, then the layers of its nervous system and muscles, then organs and fur—its fur...

An elegant black and red coat. Unmistakably unique.

Mable stands atop the lake gazing back at the man with amber eyes, no different than those that looked upon him with affection so many times, so long ago. She doesn't make a sound.

The man wants to dive into the water, swim towards the fox, and embrace her in the way he never could, but something keeps him from doing this. Something is amiss. His description of the lake feels even more apt now. Something beyond his comprehension has occurred. A miracle, maybe. Or a trick. An awful deception. But that's her; that's Mable. There she is. He could never forget her, and he never has. Each detail of her coat is there—even those that he couldn't commit to memory completely, but upon seeing them now, he knows. It was always this way. Either this is the most gorgeous hallucination his subconscious could create, or it is a restoration by the hand of the original artist. A near perfect restoration.

The man goes to speak but can't find the words. Besides, it's written all across his body. Every single thing he could ever wish to say to Mable is being spoken at this very moment, communicated in his welling eyes and broken posture and pained expression. It's all there—and she must know. She has to. Please.

I'm sorry.

As if an answer to his silent pleas, Mable begins walking towards him, gliding across the lake without ever disturbing the surface. Her multi-shaded paws touch the lake's shore, and she looks up at the man, sitting on her haunches, cocking her head.

He can't help it. He needs this new sensation to replace that of her cold, dead body. The man reaches out slowly to touch her, to stroke her face. His hand passes through. It's like a warm mist. He tries again, and Mable still watches, her expression unchanged as his fingers grasp nothing. Tears come, and he makes no effort to stifle them. Mable watches on. And when the man steps away, unable to cope with this grief like a sword, she begins to change. Her silhouette cast by the moon peels away like unthreading silk, and her fur of orange and red and black and silver falls away like water pooling into the soil. From this empty cavity still warm with the presence of a lost friend blooms the ethereal beast, shimmering and translucent, aglow with the full moon's radiance, shifting between creatures. Even in the face of this miracle, the man can only peer into its ever transforming body for any piece of Mable to appear—if even for a moment. For despite this eldritch god standing before him, he wants nothing but her. But as the beast's eyes so briefly become that of a fox's, of a cat's—all just transient layers decorating that permanent human skull—the man understands, because he must, that somewhere within this imponderable creature Mable still lives. As all things live. That is the only solace he can find. The man prays he believes it. Nothing dies. They only sleep.

The beast of the Green transmutes into the form it must at last take, shaping its coat into that of the black stars, and the man watches the communal soul of all beings melt into the lake, sink into its depths, and become the reflection of the new night sky. A velvet cloak unfurls across the black expanse, and the great constellation emerges through the moon's white glow. Its many neurons shift and blink and erupt and live and die and live again in the eternal dream. When all that remains is the beast's dripping silhouette, words never spoken are carried by a sudden and singular gust, and two separate voices, so very different in tone but with the same message, enter the man's mind like telepathy both angelic and demonic:

Come home. Wake up.

The man looks down for the print, the sole evidence of this impossible being, and there it lies impressed into the mud. And rising from its center, blooming before his eyes, is a single white lotus flower. A gift.

He gently cups the flower in his hand and lifts it from the muck and the grime, cradling it close to his chest. He then returns to the cabin, places the lotus atop his table, pulls Arthur into his arms, and falls asleep.

There were only ever two ways this could go, ever since he was first submerged in that starry lake. As long as the man can remember, without precisely knowing until now, every day he has chosen the same path. Tonight, the man has finally chosen the other.

He is ready. Truly ready. It's time he returns to the city to face the inevitable.

The horrific, gorgeous, miraculous inevitable.

A violent thunderstorm approaches from the south. It vomits sheets of rain like the sky is one great aquarium that sprung a leak. Darkness overtakes the land, black storm clouds crowding the air over the forest canopy as far as the eye can perceive. White explosions perforate the constant percussion of falling rain, striking massive trees older than time, felling them with a single blow. All the while, the man and Arthur huddle inside the cabin, crouching beside the fireplace, listening to the rain becoming louder, waiting for the three echoing booms that come in quick succession: the baritone thunder, the sharp whip-crack of the lightning that follows, and finally the inevitable moaning collapse of another tree struck down. The acrid scent of thick smoke carries through the air as fires ignite the woods in pockets though are mercifully doused soon after by the rainfall. This great and cataclysmic war has finally arrived at the Green, as though the city itself is commanding some unseen force to flush the man out, to make him return if he won't on his own accord.

Two weeks pass, and the storm shows no sign of relenting. The morning air grows damp and cold, and the nights colder still, and while the rain stops any fires from spreading, the forest slowly becomes a sea of flames unto itself. The man looks out his window and sees through the veil of mist and unending precipitation that the trees still standing have erupted in new bright colors. As if in response to the storm, they themselves have taken on the many warm hues of the very flames that threatened their survival. Autumn has arrived. The Green is dying. What was once something the man so looked forward to now appears sick and macabre through this chaotic lens thrust over his eyes. He worries the rain will never end, and a genuine thought occurs to him—however ephemeral, however illogical—that if he is to stay in this cabin and never leave, he will have to set about building an ark.

Without a view of the distant city, he has no way to know if the storm threatens that vile metropolis, and so he can only hope that it too is drowning, the waters rising and submerging those twisted beasts, flushing out the sickness and rot. And despite all else, it is this thought that most convinces him to make the trek. He has to see for himself. If these two worlds are equally under siege, perhaps he can accept the invitation given again and again. But what finally urges him to step outside the cabin, to prepare himself for the long march to the city, is the possibility of what remains. The man wants to see if his seedling in the garden still lives. For reasons beyond him, he decides that if the newborn apple tree still stands firmly in the soil surrounded by death and ashes and unspeakable violence, then he too can survive whatever hell is to come upon his arrival. This dim hope will be his torch in the dark.

It is early morning when the man begins. He dons his boots and thick layers, and empties the satchel as a haven for Arthur, leaving behind everything save one item. Tucked deep inside his backpack remains the yellow raincoat. Never touched since the only time it was worn and then folded away, the man unfurls the glittering, beautiful article, slides his arms into its sleeves, and lifts the hood atop his head. He slips the satchel over his shoulders and allows Arthur the time to sniff and accept his fate before he leaps inside, and the man pulls the flap over his little head so only his eyes and nose can poke out through the gap. He then takes the rifle from its place against the wall, loads the weapon, slings it across his opposite shoulder, and stuffs a handful of spare shells into his yellow coat's pocket. Finally, he steps towards the table and picks up the lotus flower, tucking it gently into his breast pocket. It has sat in that spot since he first plucked it from the lake's shore, and in all that time it hasn't received a drop of water—and yet it is still as vibrant and alive as on the night of its miraculous birth. Still as pale white as the full moon under which it arrived in this world. There is no reason to take the flower, but it is the most important item of all. The man knows this without thinking on it. And with that, the man opens the cabin door and steps out into the Green. Toward the city again.

He doesn't once look back at the place he called home. He doesn't glance at the lake, and so does not see its waters have overflown, seeping into the earth like clouded gray tendrils. He doesn't see the leaves' autumnal shades reflected across its surface like flames atop an oil slick. He doesn't see that upon its shores have bloomed a hundred lotus flowers, all moonlight white and alive, as if bred to guard that sacred place from whatever is to come. The man doesn't see anything but the dark path from which he first arrived, for there is only the present and its promise of the future. And it's a wonderful thing that he never once glanced back. For if he did—if the man witnessed all of what he was to leave behind—he would have recognized in the moment that it was the last time he would ever step foot in the great Green again, and in that moment, he would have made the decision to stay. But if the man had then made that decision, the future would have never arrived at all, and he then may never have known how utterly important the future would be.

Without knowing the outcomes, without weighing the options, without the hesitation that may have befallen another, the man has just made the greatest decision of his entire life: to live.

PART THREE

CARCOSA

A great change has occurred. As the man steps through the last layer of trees into the city's outer limits, he no longer sees the towering skyline that once stood like some deific harbinger. The metropolis lies in ruins. What massive buildings do remain on the horizon have been crippled and stripped away, constricted by enormous twisting vines like the Serpent of Ragnarök and its many kin. Not just shrubs and flowers, but adult trees twice the man's size have erupted from the decimated asphalt roads. Any structures not withheld by tons and tons of steel and concrete have toppled to the earth, and from the rubble still more vines have taken hold as if to choke out the life of those dying husks prostrated across the ground. The rain has not let up but instead falls heavier still, feeding the plants and dousing the foundations of a once formidable civilization, and so the streets now glisten, soaked a shade of black that absorbs the sporadic yellow-white bursts of each and every lightning strike until mimicking the alien sky that no longer exists behind an undulating, ash gray ceiling. This storm has no target. It is indiscriminate in its terrible conquest.

Arthur breathes heavily from inside the satchel, daring only to poke out his nose to inhale the scents of a foreign event. He doesn't whimper or whine or meow. Some things are so insurmountable that the mind doesn't yet know how to process the fear it knows is appropriate. The man offers his hand for Arthur to nuzzle and strokes his head until he curls back inside where it's safer. He continues on towards the city center, the rain tapping delicately and constantly atop his yellow hood, unaware of his goal nor where that goal may await. He traverses areas of the city once well-traveled, that once burned with incandescent streetlamps and neon signs, but it soon becomes clear that there is no longer electricity anywhere in this vast swathe of mankind's last surviving artifact. The whole of civilization has plunged into darkness, where the only illumination comes at the whim of the storm overhead.

Deeper still, and any semblance of a city disintegrates block by block, peeled away by shadow and storm and the steady annexation by that vengeful Green. When darkness fully encapsulates his surroundings and the man is blind within this new abyss, they appear at last. As on that final night many months ago, from out of the obsidian walls appear red eyes. A hundred thousand or more, they stare at the man, never daring to approach but following from afar, like an army of demonic familiars, unwilling to show themselves when lightning strikes—or perhaps unable. But they are wary of the man. This much is certain. A sliver of curiosity, to be sure, but it is unmistakable merely by returning their unblinking gaze that fear demands they remain at a distance. He can make no sense of it, just as he couldn't on that past evening, but it matters little. Soon, a far more profound sight emerges through the warbling chasm.

How he arrived couldn't be chance, as if it were the shadowy things themselves that led him here. The man senses a boundary and holds out his arm, and there he connects with a wire fence. Something large looms above him, something that recognizes his presence. It sighs and sways in the violent winds. The man struggles in the dark until finding the latch and he unlocks the gate and steps onto what can only be soft, fertile soil. He then waits for that ephemeral moment—for illumination. The red eyes harbor their own glow, and it's as if he's stepped into a confined box containing the scattered essences of Hell. But through it all there is a peaceful, protective aura, something else alive—far more so even. Something greater than them all. And when that lightning bolt finally appears from the heavens, cracking down on a tall building far away, and the thunder follows like the war drums of Heaven's angels, the man looks up in awe. For within this shimmering chasm, if only for a moment, he beholds. He stands in the garden.

Tombstones lay sundered all around him, the rotted contents beneath now spilled across the earth made ever more fertile by their demise, those remnants of flesh and bone offered up like sacraments. The rain has stopped its pitter-patter atop the man's hood, not because the storm has ceased but because he has been shielded from the elements. When the next lightning strike erupts overhead, the man witnesses the miraculous growth that has occurred in his absence. The apple tree stands tall and wide, not having just survived but thrived. *Thrived*—beyond his wildest imaginings, bearing fruit the size of his head hanging from branches like giants' limbs. His little seedling lives. Out of darkness and ash and rot, this paragon arose. The man reaches out to touch its hardened trunk, half-believing it to be a terrible trick, but no—it is here, its roots engorged, stretching through the boundary and into the graveyard, overtaking everything, sucking heartily from the nutrients all those dead brought about, as if those long-gone pioneers had finally found reincarnation mere feet away from a once eternal prison.

Before the man can inhale the perfume of this accomplishment, the eyes blink. Each red dot, in one single action, disappears. He turns, still sensing their watchful gaze on his back, and sees they have shifted as a fluid amalgam, now drifting away, beckoning. *Come. Come. This way. This way now.* The thousand-eyed beast sinks deeper into the city's heart, deeper into the shadows, into their environment. The man before would never think of doing what he does now, but here is the truth: He is not the same man, and he has come for a purpose. He knows not what will happen next, but only understands that it is inevitable—as it always has been. There is no use putting this off any longer. For time immemorial they have pursued him—those shadowy things and their eyes like smoldering brimstone—and for the man to follow now on his own accord is the only way this could ever be. They could not take him then because they did not have to. It has always been in anticipation for this moment. For the moment he arrives with open arms. Willingly. Ready for the unknown that awaits.

With terror piercing his chest, and the storm raging ever harder with each passing second, the man steps away from the garden. Towards the darkest abyss. The red eyes separate, forming two glowing walls of a certain new corridor, lighting the way down a path taken only once before. No words need be spoken, for the man knows precisely where it leads, and he reaches a hand into his satchel for comfort, for assurance, and there Arthur remains. Purring. Despite the cacophony, and despite the black horizon consuming all hope, the little cat sleeps. Unafraid. Then, so too is the man. This is all he needed. He is not alone. He never was.

Onward.

The path is long. Each step echoes as if in defiance of the tumult from all directions. The farther he walks, the shadowy things too grow louder and louder: a communal hum. A baritone chant only since heard in the earliest morning hours as the pyres were erected across the city. This deathly chorus emerges like locusts spilling out across a soundless valley, chortling, chattering, throaty hymns in an impossible language. Prayer. And still it is naught but their red eyes that reveal themselves—no mouths with which to speak nor sing, yet this horrible noise persists. The man feels as though he is traversing the many steps towards Hell, navigating those nine concentric circles in steep decline. The shadows become a thick veil that blots out all light but the pervading scarlet glow, and though he can hear the lightning erupt somewhere overhead, there is no longer evidence, no white aura to guide his path.

The rain falls now like hurled daggers, the chittering prayer a looming apocalypse, louder and louder, fuller and fuller, until it pierces the man's ears, enters his mind as a parasite, hooking its forked tendrils to the walls of his skull, vibrating, vibrating, vibrating like a drill through concrete. At last, finally at last—the silhouettes of tangible objects appear beyond the black cloak. He recognizes the place before it even arrives, for this place is sacred, and this place was a visited omen that has never left his mind. His vision adjusts, aided by the leering red eyes, and the man beholds this relic of a death-dream. Before him stands the cathedral, withered and crippled, its stained-glass windows shattered, with vines and moss overgrown across its limestone body. The walls of crimson eyes close in, forming a narrow path as if to reaffirm to the man that this is the destination. He has arrived, and there is nowhere else now to go. The hymnal chant builds as he approaches until the very moment his boot touches the first step, and in that moment comes silence. Deafening silence. They only watch, those thousand eyes, awaiting what's to come with tense anticipation. The only thing keeping the man from seizing with terror is the constant purr vibrating against his hip—for despite this all, Arthur still sleeps, dreaming some other, better dream. He dares not lift open the satchel. Better to let his little friend rest in that realm of blissful ignorance. This is something the man must do, and it need not require the participation of another. It almost feels like a great deception, as if he is harboring a fugitive. Smuggling a lay person into a religious rite reserved for an honored few.

He does not know what awaits within the cathedral, but he knows this—it lives. Its beating heart thrums, and its eyes now open upon his arrival, having awoken from its timeless slumber, no longer willing to communicate those distant images from another place the man has done so much to suppress. But that place now fades, for the impossible creature is risen, and as it climbs from out its conjured dream the clocks tick again. Time is running out. A decision must be made.

It's becoming difficult to breathe.

The cathedral doors swing open, and the man climbs its final steps, clutching at his chest, coughing, choking on something that isn't there. But the clock ticks. He can hear it now. Time's march. It's as if he has been reanimated from stasis, forced back into a world he knows nothing about. Something terrific is occurring. Something he cannot understand. Though this entire life—this fantastic, horrible, gorgeous life, the city and its specters of death, the Green and its tribulations and wonder—has been nothing but one grand mystery to be solved. And as the man enters the cathedral and gazes upon what awaits at the altar, he knows that it only presents itself now because only now is he finally ready. The man has seen and lived and survived and learned. Any great king must understand the land over which they reign, or they are no true king at all. And he is. The man is a good and just king.

A good and just king.

The pews are filled with spectators, bodies of liquid shadow without shape or form, dripping and twisting across one another like whirlpools in an ocean of black ink. To make sense of their corporeal existence is to gaze into a static void. Their red eyes follow the man as he crosses the threshold, as he steps down the aisle, towards the living human being. He genuflects upon the sprawling yellow tapestry, shackled by his wrists and held in place by chains nailed to the floor. The man approaches and looks into his eyes. The being's face is pallid and bloated; his flesh peeling away in chunks as though decomposition has begun while the heart still beats, his features are contorted beyond recognition, save the grimace of agony painted across a mangled jaw. But his eyes—familiar eyes, though sunken and bloodshot. Fearful and confused. The being remains silent as if inhabiting some realm between life and death, unable to communicate. He only holds out his open palms, revealing terribly pruned fingers like some poor soul saved at the last second from watery depths.

Upon his head sits a crown. A golden crown.

The man looks around the church. The shadowy things stare. Not a sound is uttered. They are spellbound, as if anticipating a speech. Beyond the chained man, that ancient, yellow tome sits atop the pulpit. He steps around the being and approaches the book. He opens its cover and turns the gnarled pages. They are no longer empty. On each is written the same words:

THE KING IN YELLOW IS WAKING.

HAIL THE KING IN YELLOW.

Before the man can make sense of this gibberish, he lurches forward and chokes. Something sharp is caught in his lungs. He hacks, violently and painfully, as something rises from his insides. Unable to take in breath, he collapses to the floor, coughing, coughing, coughing, until finally a great torrent of black liquid ejects from his body, pooling atop the yellow tapestry laid upon the altar. The man looks at this foreign substance as if he'd swallowed broken glass. Within the black pool swim tiny, glittering fractals. Like stars. Like stars in the night sky. Arthur jolts out of the satchel, shaken awake by the fall, and paws at the man, seemingly unaware of the frenetic scene, but only focused on him. He stumbles to his feet and cradles Arthur against his chest, strokes his head until his cries settle. But as soon as the little cat calms, he immediately leaps from his arms and sprints away, down the aisle, and disappears out the cathedral doors. The doors slam shut.

The man goes to scream at the crowd—precisely what words, he doesn't know—but chokes again, unable to make a sound. The shadowy things only stare with no signs of emotion or recognition of the scene playing out. Indifference incarnate. There is nothing but the red eyes. Unblinking eyes. He collapses to his knees, gags to no avail—though he can feel the substance again filling his lungs—and begins crawling towards the only other living thing. He prostrates himself before the being—the one he's certainly encountered so many times, who ran away but can run no more, and when he looks up to meet those familiar eyes, the man sees only terror. Terror and confusion and anxiety. Beneath it all, he witnesses exactly what makes them so very recognizable. The man sees a desperate wish to die. This is more vivid in a single glance than any sentence could articulate. This poor, familiar thing, wasting away and shackled. Alienated and afraid. The man sees himself. Or what he once was. A lifetime ago.

He struggles onto one knee and places his hand on the being's shoulder. It recoils at the man's touch but can do nothing else. There is only one thing that can be done. This being is not fit to reign any longer, but the man will be a good and just king. He must. For what is this place but the grandest of lessons? The most important that could ever be imparted, so crucial that time itself halted at the very last moment. Through his trials in this new life, the man has learned what this being could not. He pities him for that. And what he does next is only what would have already been.

The man stands up and straightens out as his lungs fill and his breathing shallows, as his consciousness fades into that distant world he's long dreamt in the dark, and he reaches into his breast pocket. He retrieves the moon-white lotus flower, takes the being's enchained hand, and places it on his upturned palm. The man then steps back into the aisle flanked by an audience of those shadowy things, shoulders his rifle, and aims at the shackled, bloated being. And fires.

As the body slumps over and the crown falls atop the yellow tapestry, and the deep-red blood drips across its silken threads like ink on the pages of that eldritch tome, the man thinks of the coyote. He thinks of the doe. The buck. He recalls the disgust and regret and agony that kill had evoked. But this act... so unlike that sordid day in the Green.

No. This was the easiest decision of his life.

The cathedral doors swing open and the man steps down the aisle, out into the black storm. He doesn't once glance back at the body. That is the past, and the past does not exist. The rain falls heavier still, so heavy that each step taken is drenched in swirling, obsidian waters rising higher and higher. Lightning erupts in the sky, only now strong enough to pierce the stygian veil overhead, great white bursts like dying synapses tattooing the night sky in shifting patterns. Still, there is nothing before him but darkness, and the man stops short of continuing forward. He can do nothing but wait for what's next, allowing the water to climb up his legs, to soak through his boots, but beneath the yellow raincoat he remains warm and dry.

He tries to scream out for Arthur, but upon opening his mouth black liquid ejects from his throat, cascading off of his tongue to join the undulating body from which it was born. But at last through the void a muted cry echoes, and two yellow lights like bobbing crescent moons come careening towards the man, and Arthur wades through the flood and leaps into his chest, soaked and shivering and alive. He wraps the black cat into the folds of his raincoat, holding him close until his purrs grow to match the heartbeat pounding against his little body. The waters continue to rise, and the rain pours like the sea has been inverted and sundered, now bleeding across the whole city, the Green, the world and all its denizens.

That horrible prayer, that chittering communal hymn, now arrives at his back, swallowing even the cacophonic violence wrought by the heavens themselves, and the man turns to see the great congregation of red eyes, of living shadows, of formless human beings, approaching through the water, their movements having no effect on the unmarred surface as if they are indeed nothing but nightmarish hallucinations. They halt far shy of the man, but then from the congregation one being glides closer. In its deathly limb, as if being held only by the weight of black matter, is the golden crown. Its red eyes grow large as it approaches, its head of static energy lowered in penitence, and as the guttural chant of a thousand shadowy things pierces even the booming thunder, it holds the crown high, waiting for the man to step forward. To accept.

The flood now reaches up to the man's waist, and he holds Arthur tight, unwilling to let go for anything—be it death or otherwise. The crescent moons have been eclipsed, for Arthur sits curled in his arms, his eyes shut, breathing to the rhythm of his heartbeat. He is not alone.

There isn't thought to the act. It is simply what must be done. It is the inevitable next moment that was foretold by all those previous. The man bows to the creature, and it slowly, gently, hesitantly places the crown upon his head. Almost—lovingly.

The man rises, and the great congregation of living shadows falls. They sink into the water's depths, red eyes averted from the king, still chanting, chanting, chanting. The sound grows louder until it is deafening, painful to withstand, and at the last moment, when finally the man can't bear the painful intonation, the black storm tears wide open. A massive lightning bolt screams down to Earth and erupts upon the ancient cathedral. A brilliant explosion ignites the limestone and shattered windows and writhing vines, and in an instant, like a blink, the whole structure comes toppling down. The congregation doesn't flinch but remains penitent, eyes never leaving the water now consuming their entire being, that emanating red glow seeping into the stagnant rain like phosphorous, acidic blood. From the rubble now comes a terrific lurch of movement. Out of the cathedral's corpse something else rises. It is awake.

Arthur suddenly jolts from the man's arms, alert and afraid, and climbs up his sleeve despite the apocalyptic rains to stand atop his shoulder, his small body rigid as a corpse, eyes wide and aware, staring at that which the man too cannot but witness in awe.

The eldritch being stands larger than any building of the city over which it holds dominion. Larger than every building combined, in width and height. It towers over the groveling congregation, still chanting though even this ear-piercing prayer pales in comparison to the tumult of an entire metropolis coming alive. It has no discernable anatomy but is only a hideous amalgamation of warped steel and concrete and stripped fiberglass and smoking machinery, and despite the inanimate parts of its being, it is undeniably aware. For where there are no eyes through which to see, the man feels its gaze from thousands of feet below. A noxious miasma of pollutants and poisons emits from its every orifice, a labyrinthine system of open drainage pipes hanging like loose gangrenous flesh, dripping brown-yellow liquids into the rising flood like a wounded god's pus and viscera. Its hulking, city-spanning frame creaks with each simple movement like shifting tectonic plates. It is the aborted infant of man's creation given breath, a horrifying golem of an entire species' world-conquering achievements. It is the personification of annihilative progress. Creator, Destroyer of Worlds.

The rain pours and pours. The flood will not stop. Its rancid waters reach the man's chest. He is going to drown here. There is no ark. The eldritch god looks down at the remains of its sunken city with indifference. It wishes not to save what cannot be saved. The crown lies heavy upon the man's head. He thinks for a moment that if he were to take it off, this could allow him a few more moments of buoyancy before the flood swallows him whole with the rest of the city. But it's far too late for such ideas. He will be a good and just king. A good and just king. He will then lead by example. Approach now then, Death. Wash me away with my sovereignty.

The great living metropolis finishes surveying its lands. It gazes at the man and at the little cat standing petrified in the rain. It steps forward with limbs of iron and brass, its gargantuan weight sinking through the submerged asphalt road, and stands between the man and its red-eyed children. They grovel and pray and chortle and sing in baritone, demonic chords, gurgling now beneath the water, allowing the raging current to whisk them to and fro, to take them away to wherever it must.

The man gazes back. The crown fitted atop his brow, he does not flinch, and he does not look away. He is ready. He is finally ready.

The vile golem lurches forward again. It leans over as the flood reaches the man's neck. For a moment, the man believes that he can see its eyes. Beautiful eyes. Shattered stained-glass windows, their many colors bleeding into the water from some light source unknown. This is what the man could never before accept. As hard as he may have once tried, or perhaps never tried at all, for the first time he sees it—the beauty in this awful monster.

The living metropolis then falls. Though it has no legs, no familiar anatomy with which to assume the purpose of this act, still the man understands. The eldritch thing—the city come alive—bows. Its stained-glass eyes surrounded by fractured metal and disused machinery gaze into the water, and it kneels before the man. Bowing.

The sky opens up. The clouds suddenly part, banishing the black cloak that had swallowed all, and the man now sees the light that so tentatively captured this great being's kaleidoscopic eyes. For the man looks overhead, and there, as the waters rise above his chin and Arthur tucks himself inside the yellow hood, pressing up against the man's face, he sees something he imagined would never be seen again: stars. Not those distant celestial things like black neurons, like the scan of a suffocating brain, but the cosmos as it must once have been in a lifetime past. The man looks up as the water finally submerges his entire body and witnesses the very same image as that which remained locked away in the deepest recesses of his fading memory. He feels the weight of his little cat disappear and, terrified, he strains to see around him in the murky depths, but nothing remains. The congregation is gone. The golem of civilization is gone. The sunken city and its rubble are gone. Arthur. Arthur is gone. The man is alone again. Underwater. It is only the black abyss and the glittering night sky above. There is but one thing to do. Something he wouldn't have before. But the past is gone. It no longer exists.

Upward now. Swim.

Live.

PART FOUR

Arise

The cold sensation soaks through to his bones. His lungs burn. He desperately wants to breathe. The man floats upward. He spends a lifetime ascending through the water. Images emerge in the abyss, memories of a life since abandoned. One by one, they are banished again, and still he continues. His muscles ache, his skin pallid and pruned, but he swims. Upward for years. Through a hundred thousand memories, a hundred thousand lives, beautiful and horrific and painful and ecstatic, and he watches as they then sink below, into oblivion, into the past.

Soon the darkness thins, and glimmering specks of light appear, streaming through his fingers as he pushes on. The water becomes like air, his body becomes weightless, and there is for a moment no sensation of up or down but only stasis. And the man, for a moment, floats in a vacuum. The water is no longer cold, barely water at all. And there is only this black expanse, caressing him like an infant in the womb. He gazes through the abyss and sees that he is no longer alone. A million glittering stars encompass him, floating alongside his directionless being, alight and aglow and brilliant and alive or dead, but still, still they exist. For their radiance persists, and together the light of these dead and dying and living stars illuminates the path ahead. They speak without words: *Upward*, they say. *Swim.*

And the man does. He continues by the light of the stars, following the path they've set out for him, and beyond this vibrant, sunken cosmos he can finally see the horizon overhead. He can see the water's surface. It appears like a mirage, but it is true and real. It is there. He can see the refracted image of trees, of a great forest, and the dim red glow of embers by the shore. And just as it feels like his lungs will burst, he emerges. The man breaches the lake.

He climbs onto the silted earth encompassed on all sides by dense woods, dripping wet, and tries to inhale. Instead, a pool of water ejects from his lungs. It spills across the soil, and the man coughs and gasps until it's all out. He then breathes deeply, tasting the night air. A small campfire sits beside him, only the smoldering embers remaining. A calm breeze passes through, frigid against the clothing plastered to his skin. He wears only jeans, boots, and a t-shirt. He reaches up to his naked head and touches wet strands of short hair. He touches his shaved face as if his fingers would pass through like smoke. But he is here. He is alive.

The man labors to his feet and sits down on a nearby log. It is from here that he cranes his neck to witness something beautiful. Stretched across the sky is the purple veil of the Milky Way, decorated with a million little white stars like twinkling ornaments. And there upon the lake's surface is its perfect reflection, as if to sink into its depths would be to drift away into the universe eternal.

Yet something else remains, barely visible at a glance, tucked into the periphery like a meek artist's signature peeking from beneath the frame of a masterful painting. One object that he knows, despite his muddled recollection, cannot be: a tattered, yellow raincoat lies crumpled on the shore, irradiated by the moonlight. The lake's gentle tide laps at its sleeves, urging it to sink into the twin waters of oblivion. But this foreign artifact, this alien relic—refuses. Paralyzed in stasis, isolated in the dark, its gifted radiance is quickly fading. Though the night is cold, and his body numb and shivering, for reasons he cannot explain the man wishes for anything but to wear it. No, he can already feel the coming warmth creeping in from the east, the breeze drying his pruned skin. The blood returning to his chest. He has no use for things content to drown in the shadows.

Far beyond the woods, his city lights beckon, but for now, the man will sit by the lake. Just a while longer. Bathing in the glow of so many mirrored stars, alive and dead and dying, all equally bright. Their ghosts dancing atop the water. And the animals, they yip and howl from the trees, their eyes like sunstones and crescent moons in the dark. Such a lovely, familiar place.

No. The man is not alone. He never was.

He remembers Everything.

ABOUT THE AUTHOR

Jack Moody is a novelist and short story writer whose work includes *Miracle Boy, The Monotony of Everlasting*, and *The Lights That Dim*. He is a former contributor for *Return Magazine, The Bel Esprit Project*, and *Brick Moon Fiction*, and his stories have appeared in various publications including Expat Press, *The NoSleep Podcast*, and *The Saturday Evening Post*. He lives in Portland, Oregon.

IG: https://www.instagram.com/jack_is_moody

A NOTE FROM TIMBER GHOST PRESS

I f you enjoyed *The King of Everything*, please consider leaving a review on Amazon or Goodreads. Reviews help the authors and the press.

If you go to www.timberghostpress.com you can sign up for our newsletter so you can stay up-to-date on all our upcoming titles, plus you'll get informed of new horror flash fiction and poetry featured on our site monthly.

Take care and thanks for reading *The King of Everything!*

-Timber Ghost Press